THE PRICE

OF

JUSTICE

Crime Scene Kosovo Book 2

BY

Tasmin Turner

People and Places

People

Angela Keys, Office Assistant, OIDC

Caitlin (Kit) Chase, lawyer from New Zealand working in the Office of the Chief International Prosecutor in Pristina, Kosovo

Danjel Miceli, a banker from Malta

Dasham Raco, boss of an organized crime group running guns, drugs, and extortion rackets in Kosovo, as well as murder for hire. His gang includes Enver, Musa, and Bledat

Don Edgson, canine-unit leader and general dog handler, US military on secondment to EUFOR

Enver Raco, Dasham Raco's nephew and accomplice

Erwin Pfund, a Swiss investment banker

Eva Refazo, chief international prosecutor, OIDC

Father Peter, Russian Orthodox priest and chess exponent

Frank Stanton, US ambassador to Kosovo

Gregor Petri, a major from the Romanian military on secondment to EUFOR, member of the Khash group

Jacob Mueller, former German ambassador, heading the Organization for International Development and Coordination in Kosovo (the OIDC)

Dr Jyoti Prabhu, International Coroner, Pristina

Leo Varga, Slovenian friend and member of the Khash group, art historian, poet, and tour guide

Maria Montenegro, celebrity psychotherapist

Matthew (Matt) Hackman, Major in the Special Investigations Branch, British Military Police, EUFOR

Michael Burke, Deputy Head of OIDC mission in Pristina, Kosovo

Merita Shala, retired Kosovo police officer, criminal accomplice

Natalia Marin, Romanian friend and member of the Khash group, dream therapist, and tarot card reader

Owen Reese, Sergeant in Special Investigations Branch of the British Military Police with EUFOR

Rosalyn Chase, Kit's mother in New Zealand

Rustem Kupi, chairperson of the Privatization Panel, Kosovo

Sergei Sokolov, Russian Intelligence Officer, also known as Oleg Anton Soroka

Jože Plečnik, celebrated Slovenian architect

Tom Baumgarten, head of the Anti-Corruption Unit, OICD

Vasha Blaku, confidential informant in criminal investigations

Vernon Chase, Kit's estranged father

Viktor Tirol, senior international judge in Pristina

Visar Dreshaj, Pristina politician

Xander Willis, Kit's fiancé in New Zealand

Animals

Bambino, Eva's rescue dog

Max, Belgium Tervuren in a military police canine unit

Places

Archaeological Museum, Durrës, Albania

Belgrade, capital city of the Republic of Serbia

Black and White Café, a café in midtown Pristina

Blue Lagoon Café, Durrës

Café Mignon, a French-inspired café in Ljubljana

Devil's Courtyard, part of a remodelled former monastery, Ljubljana

Dragon Bridge, Ljubljana

Durrës, a seaside resort in Albania

Grand Union Hotel, Ljubljana

Holy Trinity Russian Orthodox Church, Ljubljana

Hunting Lodge Alexander close to Skopje, the former Yugoslav Republic of Northern Macedonia

Ibar River, divides Mitrovica, Kosovo into two parts

Ljubljana, capital city of Slovenia

Ljubljana Castle

Metelkova squat, Ljubljana

Mother Teresa Boulevard, a main pedestrian mall in central Pristina

Mitrovica hospital, Mitrovica, Kosovo

National and University Library of Slovenia, Ljubljana

Obilić power station, Pristina

Pristina, the capital city of Kosovo

Saint Heliers, Auckland, New Zealand, Kit's upmarket home suburb by the sea

Staro Dorbi, the rural community in Kosovo where several Serbian farmers were killed

Task Force Icarus Headquarters, an upmarket apartment rented by Matt Hackman in Pristina

Trepča, the site of a large precious metals mine, spanning Kosovo and Serbia

Vegz Café, Ljubljana

White House, a residence of the US ambassador, close to Pristina

Organizations

European military and police force, EUFOR, engaged in law enforcement in Kosovo during the post-conflict period

Kosovo Liberation Army (KLA), an ethnic Albanian separatist militia that sought the separation of Kosovo from the Federal Republic of Yugoslavia and Serbia

The Organization for International Development and Coordination in Kosovo (OIDC), an international organization assisting with the administration of Kosovo during the post-conflict period. Its European headquarters is in Berlin, and its international headquarters is in New York.

Khash, a philosophical system based on applying lessons from the game of chess to life

Task Force Icarus, an informal crime solving task force

Background

During the 1998–1999 Kosovo conflict, ethnic Albanians opposed the Serbian Government of the former Yugoslavia in Belgrade. Kosovo broke away and sought to set up an independent state, which Serbia did not recognize. Allied forces drove Serbian forces back following a humanitarian crisis. International organizations stepped in to support the government in Kosovo. This story is set in a fictionalized post-conflict Kosovo.

CHAPTER ONE

Pristina, Kosovo

Eva Refazo, Kosovo's chief international prosecutor, pulled a fresh cigarette from the packet on her desk and lit it. Bright sunlight filtered in through the dusty panes of glass, and the smoke pooled around the mounds of legal documents piled high around her. Her office in the Organization for International Development and Coordination in Kosovo, known as the OIDC, was in a state of controlled chaos.

Eva's dark-blonde hair, with silver at the temples, was piled into a bun with tendrils framing her face. She wore oversized reading glasses that magnified her expressive brown eyes. Eva kicked off her black pumps under the desk and flexed her stockinged feet.

She scanned through the telephone call intercepts from Dasham Raco, a dangerous suspect in a mass murder case who had managed to smuggle a phone into prison. He hadn't realized that his phone calls allowed law enforcement to monitor his communications with associates outside. She ran her pencil down the margin until she involuntarily gasped. She pressed so hard on the paper that the lead of the pencil snapped and skittered across the desktop.

The color drained from her face. "*Madre di Dio*, mother of God!" she whispered under her breath. Eva dropped her pencil. Raco had been planning her murder through a clandestine phone call to Berisha, one of his gang members still at large. Since starting her job as chief international prosecutor in Kosovo, she had known something like this could happen, yet it still felt like a personal attack. Also shocking was the discovery that Raco thought that Victor Tirol, a senior international judge in Kosovo, could be bribed to aid his escape from prison. Raco was told that the judge wanted fifty thousand euros in cash for the job. According to the transcript, Raco wanted the hearing for his group's killing Serbian farmers in Staro Dorbi postponed and the four criminals transferred to a hospital with light security.

And Raco clearly wanted Eva permanently gone from the case—which was a kind of compliment. He hadn't even considered bribery as an option for her. Eva was a prosecutor not known for compromise. For her, justice could not be bought. Another part of the transcript sent a chill up her spine as she read how Raco coldly threatened Kit, one of the best lawyers in her office. Eva considered Kit, an auburn haired New Zealander, her protegee. Was she responsible for putting Kit in danger by renewing her contract with the office? Eva had to find a way to keep Raco behind bars to minimize the risk to everyone.

As she searched through the transcripts, she read that Berisha had arranged for a meeting between the judge and Raco's lawyer at Blue Lagoon restaurant at Durrës. Durrës was a fashionable seaside resort in Albania, a few hours' drive south from Kosovo.

"*Maledetto inferno!*" Eva cursed under her breath in Italian. Her train of thought was interrupted by Angel, her twenty-something office assistant, who appeared in the door wearing a black leather jacket, white cotton shirt, and a pair of blue jeans. A Yorkshire rose, her blonde hair framed her face. "Do you need anything, Eva?" she asked. "I'm leaving now."

Eva remained preoccupied by what she had just read. "No thanks, Angel. I've got to get through these telephone transcripts. We're going to need them in court ASAP for the Dasham Raco case."

"The Serbian farmers at Staro Dorbi, right?"

Eva gave a slight nod, keeping her feelings in check. She had learnt to remain composed and unfazed in any situation after all the courtrooms she had been in. Her mind raced ahead of her as two thoughts came to her. During their time together, Kit had proved more agile than most when it came to fieldwork. In addition, Kit's spirit was indomitable; even after she was kidnapped by Raco, she continued to fight on. Despite admiring this aspect of her protégée, Eva knew that Raco was out for revenge and worried about the dangerous actions he would take if he got his chance.

"When's Kit due back?" Eva asked Angel, who managed the office leave roster.

"She's headed back to Pristina at the end of the week and should be back at work on Monday."

"Good. I've got some tasks lined up for her."

"Oh, also, Major Hackman called about the task force meeting soon."

Eva cast her a warning glance. "I told you not to bring that up in the office."

"Sorry," Angel apologized, quickly looking around. "He called me while you were out. It's just the two of us here right now."

"No matter how empty it seems, you never know who might be listening," Eva said, her eyes briefly flitting to the door. She breathed in deeply and dismissed her frustration as she let it out with a sigh. She then managed a smile as she added, "I'll see you tomorrow. I'll take care of Hackman's message myself."

Their last joint case solving the mass killings at Staro Dorbi had suffered from political interference, and they had decided to work the cases between them with a few trusted associates rather than use official channels for everything. But this unauthorized cooperation between the International Prosecution and the EUFOR Criminal Investigation Unit had to be kept under wraps.

Angel nodded before leaving Eva to herself and Bambino, a small black and grey rescue dog on his folded blanket behind her. The dog, apart terrier and part mixed breed, lifted his greying muzzle from between his front paws and whined.

"I know, *Picolo,* little one," Eva said as she typed on the computer. "It's time to go, but I'll just finish this quickly," she said.

Eva rummaged through her bag, pushing aside tissues, lipstick, cigarettes, and lighter until her fingers finally met the cold surface of her phone. Holding it in her shaking right hand, she began to type a message to Major Matt Hackman. "Got your message. Need task force meeting ASAP." Shortly after sending it, a response came back.

"Suggest Monday. Need to talk now?"

"I'll explain in person," Eva replied. She took a long drag from her cigarette.

Eva scribbled some quick notes on her desk pad before putting her phone away. She had suspected for some time that something was amiss with the work of the international judges, but now the phone intercepts provided evidence that Judge Victor Tirol, head of the International Judicial Board, was open to bribery. But she needed to be careful. Any accusations she couldn't prove could end up costing her her job, as well as her reputation internationally and at home in Italy. Her boss, Jacob Mueller, respected her professionally, yet he wouldn't go along with making allegations against these influential judges. That could reflect poorly on the OIDC's own rule of law work. She had noticed him out with Tirol on several occasions, so she had to be careful when she acted.

Eva put the phone down and opened her planner. She quickly jotted down a note to get in touch with Tom Baumgarten, head of their Anti-Corruption Unit. Eva highlighted his name for emphasis. She had to find out if Tirol was the only high-ranking person involved in the corruption. If he was compromised, who else might be? Eva needed Kit back as soon as possible so they could start digging into this mess.

Eva took a deep breath, stood up, and grabbed her keys. She closed her planner, tucked it into her bag, and stepped out into the dimming light. She had a lot of work to do.

CHAPTER TWO

Hunting Lodge Alexander near Skopje,
Northern Macedonia

In the private dining area at the back of the hunting lodge, four men were assembled around a table. Clad in their smart, casual hunting attire, each man subtly communicated his wealth with his accessories: a golden watch, a luxurious designer belt, or a platinum-finished collector's pen.

"I need to be sure I can rely on your support," Jacob Mueller, a senior international official from Germany, said to the others in the otherwise unoccupied dining room. "I need to move a large sum of money to Switzerland soon."

"How much money are we talking about, Jacob?" asked Erwin Pfund, a Swiss banker who toyed with a gleaming gold lighter.

Jacob Mueller gave a small shrug and spread his hands. "At least six hundred million euros. Possibly more."

Pfund nodded, flicking the lighter in his hand so it emitted a small flame. "My bank, the Schweize Bank, can guarantee your deposits remain anonymous and confidential. We accept transfers of up to six hundred million euros or deutsche marks equivalent from Kosovo in one payment or several smaller amounts."

Mueller smiled, and his steely blue eyes lit up as he considered the effects of these generous deposits on his fortune. "That is welcome news indeed, Erwin."

The others at the table nodded in agreement.

"I can also help you with investment opportunities, if you wish," Erwin Pfund added.

"What kind of investments?" Mueller inquired.

"The margins are quite attractive. One of our most profitable sectors is offering discrete organ transplants to high-profile patients in Swiss medical spas away from public scrutiny."

"I think we may mutually benefit," Mueller said. "I have a surefire source of organ donors in the Balkans."

"We won't bore our friends with the details," Pfund said as waiters started serving the meal.

"Will you be joining us, Danjel?" Mueller asked. "I need a Maltese bank to help transfer the funds out of Kosovo and into my private Swiss bank account."

"I'm sure we can work something out," Danjel Miceli replied. The banker from Valletta had a smooth-shaven face and neat eyebrows. The other three men spoke in English to accommodate him rather than German language from their home countries. "But are you sure this won't attract the attention of the regulators or law enforcement?"

"The financial disclosure rules are ludicrous. They shouldn't apply to people like us," Mueller replied. "Besides, I'm in a strategic position. As the head of my organization, the Organization for International Development and Coordination, I don't need to worry. I've got the chief international prosecutor, Eva Refazo and her team, on my admin payroll, so nothing's going to happen."

"But they're still independent, aren't they?" Danjel asked.

Mueller scoffed at Danjel's suggestion. "In theory, yes. But let's be real here. My organization has her on the payroll. And when you have the prosecutor on the inside, you don't need to worry about justice being blind."

"The real question is who pays the price for justice? As a judge, I should know," Victor Tirol, an Austrian judge stationed in Pristina, interjected in his slightly accented speech.

Above them hung wall-mounted heads of deer and other game animals, setting the scene for the other traditional décor—crockery with hunting designs, bone-handled cutlery, and glasses filled with fine Macedonian wine from the lodge's vineyard. The room smelled of cigars, mingled with the aroma of a roast cooking in the adjacent kitchen.

The waiter presented them with their opening course, an immense platter of mixed salads and vegetables, venison, and other meats with baskets of fragrant flat bread and mayonnaise for dipping.

"Gentlemen," Mueller said, raising his glass, "let's toast to our mutually beneficial arrangements."

The Hunting Lodge Alexander was situated a discrete distance from Skopje, the former Yugoslav Republic of Northern Macedonia's capital. Only two hours away from Pristina, it was an ideal meeting spot for them to meet without getting noticed. The atmosphere of Pristina, the capital of Kosovo, was electric. Everyone knew someone, and gossip spread quickly. But here, they didn't expect to be recognized.

The four men at the table, glasses in hand, toasted to their meeting. Danjel Miceli, with his neatly defined eyebrows, spoke up first. "It was a masterstroke to come here. The facilities are top-notch, and the wine is excellent."

Viktor Tirol was a senior international judge . "The borders in Europe are not what they used to be. We should capitalize on this. "

Jacob added that Kosovo was on its way to eventually joining the European Union, as was Serbia. Erwin Pfund observed that Switzerland had shown that neutrality has its advantages and that not every country needed to join the EU.

"If other countries had the benefit of being inside a natural fortress like Switzerland does, I might agree with you," replied Tirol with a shake of his head.

Mueller interrupted them with a broad smile on his face. "But let's change the subject for now. I've arranged for us to use the shooting range nearby. There's an excellent selection of weapons, including some of the best Austrian Glocks you can find on the market." He gave Tirol a knowing nod at the mention of Glocks in acknowledgement of the achievements of Austria in the weapons market. "We have full access to the facilities while we're here. "

Pfund's face lit up at the mention of guns. "Perhaps we could discuss supply contracts with local arms dealers while we're here."

"I've already made arrangements to meet with the local arms manufacturers," Mueller said.

The waiter approached and laid an envelope in front of Mueller, then left. Mueller read the message inside and smiled with approval before tucking it into his jacket pocket. "I should mention that I've arranged for us to be joined by some companions this evening, courtesy of our hosts."

"Did you get my message regarding my preferences?" asked Pfund.

"Yes, my friend, I got your message through our private email account, just as planned. I passed on your preferences to our hosts, and they are more than happy to oblige."

"These Macedonian women are something else," Tirol said.

"Tastes vary," Mueller said.

"How much do I need to pay for these arrangements?" asked Miceli.

"Don't worry, I got this covered. It's a business expense," Mueller assured them. The waiter brought out a suckling pig's head with an apple in its mouth and a side of baked vegetables.

"He looks familiar" Miceli said, glancing at the pig.

"Yes, I think you shot him this afternoon," Tirol quipped, and the men laughed. Mueller grabbed a carving knife and began slicing off pieces of the pigs head and neck.

"I never thought game hunting would be so enjoyable," Miceli said, smiling.

"Tomorrow we'll set you up with even better equipment," Pfund replied.

His words were followed by a large meal accompanied by plenty of alcohol. For dessert, there was an array of rich desserts, served with lashings of whipped cream, as well as a cheese board and port.

The maître d' then stepped forward and addressed Mueller in a low voice before gesturing towards the door.

"Our hosts have asked us to retire to the drawing room for brandy and cigars. I believe our companions will be arriving soon," Mueller announced.

They adjourned to a private lounge on the next floor. The room had soft, dark-hued furnishings and plush carpeting with a scattering of patterned oriental rugs. Heavy curtains hung at the windows for additional privacy. The guests stood around two tables near the bar while a waiter distributed drinks and cigars. Across the room, comfortable chairs and couches were arranged in two seating areas. A fireplace was stacked with wood, and a large antlered stag head served as a centrepiece above the mantlepiece.

A gentle knock came at the heavy, dark-stained door. "*Kommen sie herein!*" Mueller said in German, inviting them in. The maître d' ushered in three women and one young man. Mueller extended his arm towards a petite Asian woman wearing a miniskirt and tight, black top. At just over five feet tall, she reached his shoulder in heels. She glided over to him, carrying a red, designer, leather bag over one shoulder and wearing matching red stilettos. Her glossy, dark hair cascaded down to her waist. She smiled at him brightly and offered him her hand, which he took and raised to his lips. "*Schoen dich wieder zu sehen, mein lieber.* So good to see you again, my dear. I thought you might have returned to Thailand," he said.

"No, I'm waiting to meet you … and to get my passport back," she replied with flirtatious eyes.

The maître d' presented the other visitors. A curvaceous woman wore a form-fitting satin dress that was low cut in the front and back, with sparkling crystals adorning her neck. Her blonde hair was swirled in a style reminiscent of the nineteen fifties. She held out her hand to Tirol and said, "It's such an honour to meet you, sir."

"The pleasure is all mine," he replied.

Erwin Pfund looked down at a young woman wearing a short skirt and white blouse reminiscent of a school uniform unbuttoned to her cleavage. She wore minimal makeup to make her look younger than her years. "How old are you, my dear?" he asked gently.

"I'd rather not say," came the reply.

"Are your parents aware that you're out tonight?"

"No, they don't know," she said with a giggle.

Meanwhile, Miceli had already seated his companion for the evening on one of the leather couches in the bar area and offered him his preferred drink—a German beer. Miceli lit the cigarette of the young man, who then stretched back on the leather couch and inhaled. His long legs stretched out and brushed against Miceli's shins as they started talking about the latest European soccer match.

Mueller spoke to the room. "Our host informs me that there is a private elevator leading to our rooms through the exit just behind me. Enjoy the bar and facilities as long as you wish; they're complimentary. We'll meet for a late breakfast tomorrow before resuming our programme tomorrow. I'll be back in a moment. Excuse me, my dear," Mueller murmured to his companion before following the maître d' out the door leading to the private elevator.

Speaking quietly to the man at his side, Mueller asked, "Can I confirm that the video recording devices are in place in the bedrooms?"

The other man nodded, and Mueller slipped him an envelope bulging with cash. "Something I've learned from my Russian colleagues is that it's important to collect *kompromat*—compromising material—on our enemies, and even more so on our friends."

"I understand, sir," the maître d' said before Mueller returned to the group.

CHAPTER THREE

Pristina, Kosovo

"One, two, three! One, two, three!" Owen shouted, counting as Kit pounded the punching bag with her gloved fists.

They were at the Pristina staff gym of the Organization for International Development and Coordination, the OIDC. Kit wore her black, triple-stripe training pants and a cutaway sports T-shirt that allowed her shoulders unrestricted movement. Her auburn hair was pulled back in a plait. Sergeant Owen Rees assisted Major Matthew Hackman, the head of the international Criminal Investigation Division, European Force (EUFOR). A medium height and a stocky build due to all his years playing rugby in Wales, Owen had short, dark hair and expressive brows that framed an alert face and bright, blue eyes. He had nearly fully recovered from a gunshot wound he'd sustained while attempting to arrest two homicide suspects in their last criminal investigation case, although he continued to favour his left side.

Kit was still recovering from her abduction by Dasham Raco, the prime suspect in a mass murder of Serbian farmers. During the same case, her fight with

Merita Shala, a Kosovo Liberation Army soldier and former female police officer, had made her all too aware of the need to improve her self defense skills. After escaping from Raco and his nephew Enver, who had held her captive for hours, she realized that she had to be more proactive in her physical fitness. While she had received Krav Maga combat training back in Auckland, New Zealand, she had not kept it up since deploying to Kosovo. Her current skills were not enough for the situation she found herself in. Even more important was her need to feel back in control. Owen had offered to help her train at the gym until she could find a local martial arts class.

Her goals were clear, Kit thought, as she slammed her fists into the gym punching bag. She wanted to be physically and mentally fit for her job as assistant international prosecutor in Kosovo so she could meet whatever challenges came her way with confidence. Owen and Kit worked together on an off-book task force under his boss, Major Matt Hackman, with Kit's supervisor, Eva Refazo, Pristina's chief international prosecutor and two other co-workers.

"Keep your arms loose. Strike through, not at, the bag. Raise your fists!" Owen shouted.

Kit wiped away the sweat glistening on her face and glanced up at Owen.

"Look at the target, not me!" he said. "Now, move around. Swing left when the bag moves right!"

Her eyes blurred with perspiration, and the image of Raco's harsh face flashed in her mind from when he had pulled off her blindfold. She struck hard and felt the force of the punch jar through her shoulder and elbow. She threw another swing with her other arm, but it suddenly felt weak.

Kit paused and gulped in some air. "I don't know if I'll ever get this," she sighed, steadying the bag.

"You're doing great," Owen comforted her. He checked his watch. "You've been training for almost thirty minutes now. Shall we cool down?"

They proceeded to the treadmills standing side by side, facing the gym's window.

"So, how have you been? What was your vacation like?" he asked.

"I went to Croatia for a few weeks, sailing with my fiancé Xander, my mom, and a few friends; it was such an amazing experience! But they weren't ecstatic when I reported that my contract had been extended for another year."

"That's too bad," Owen said as he tucked a towel around his neck while on the treadmill.

"I wanted Xander to stay here for a bit but he had to go back to work and study."

Owen nodded in agreement. "It can be difficult away from home."

"Here I am discussing my troubles while you're in deployment too. Do you have family back home in the UK waiting for you?"

"Yeah, it's what I signed up for—a chance to see the world. I got a girlfriend back home. My family and friends all look forward to when I get back."

"You're lucky there are regular flights from England. New Zealand is too far for me to get a military flight from Kosovo."

Owen shrugged. "It's a bummer, but I hope it's worth it in the end. So, I wanted to let you know Matt called a meeting for our task force this week to give us an update."

Kit smiled. "Awesome! Can't wait to see my buddies again. Any special projects happening?"

"I guess we'll find out soon enough. He said he wants us to meet at least once every two weeks even if nothing urgent is going on."

"My boss told me she needs me to help her with a case. Something about corruption in high places," Kit said.

"If you need any help, let me know," Owen said as he switched off the treadmill and hopped off it. "Same day next Wednesday?"

"Yes, please. Till I can find a karate class here, I have to keep training to stay in shape," she said and rubbed her arms with a chuckle. "I think my muscles are going to be sore tomorrow."

"Do you have anything planned now?" Owen asked. "We could grab something to eat."

Kit hesitated before she answered. "I do have some errands to run, and I'm meeting a friend soon."

"Alright then, maybe next time," he said and made his way towards the men's changing room.

***

A short time later, Kit exited the OIDC building with her gym bag and handbag over her shoulders. As she walked through Pristina, the bells from the Catholic cathedral mingled with the call to prayer from the mosque, and rap music blared from a curbside store. Cars of all shapes and sizes drove past, from old, beat-up cars to fancy sports cars belonding to those returning from work abroad. Agricultural vehicles went by, boys sitting atop piles of wood or straw. Girls linked arms and giggled as they shopped, while young men hung out at outdoor cafes puffing smoke and sipping coffee. The aroma of freshly ground coffee beans and warm pastry filled the air. Kit spotted a bakery and bought a croissant, which she stuffed into her gym bag.

Kit came to a quieter area of town with an apartment block standing opposite a primary school—the place of her appointment. She had lain awake many nights from harrowing dreams since her abduction during the previous criminal investigation. Eventually she sought support from a psychotherapist that Angel, her discrete and reliable office assistant, suggested.

As she considered the impact of not further sharing her plans to visit a therapist, her stomach knotted with anxiety. Rather than involving her employer's in-house counsellor, she chose to find a local clinical psychologist and trauma therapist. The prices in Pristina were economical when compared to elsewhere in Europe, so she decided that this was the ideal opportunity to discuss her issues.

Kit approached the back of the building and pressed the button to be let in. When the outside door clicked open, she made her way along the hall to the psychotherapists studio. A woman in her mid-forties opened the door. Her blonde hair was styled in a sleek bob, and she wore a comfortable cashmere twinset and blue trousers. Around her neck hung a dramatic ceramic pendant with a gleaming crystal in the centre. Dr Maria Montenegro's lips curved into an inviting smile, but her eyes remained sharp, scrutinizing Kit from head to toe.

Kit left her jacket and belongings at the coat stand and glanced around the room. Sunlight poured through a large east-facing window. Cream-colored walls were lined with a desk with a swivel-chair, and a bookshelf was filled with psychology books and memorabilia. One photograph on the bookshelf caught Kit's eye. It showed Maria standing on a beach with a man who had his arm around her, with a second man who seemed familiar.

"Is that your husband?" Kit asked, looking more closely at the photo.

Maria came to stand beside her.

"Yes, that's Richard, looking rather possessive." Maria smiled at the recollection. "Some therapists prefer to keep their space more neutral, but I think it's fine for people to know a bit more about me. It fosters a reciprocal conversation."

"It looks as though that was a nice day at the beach. And the other man, a friend …" Kit trailed off as she looked more closely.

"That was a long weekend at the beach in Durrës. It's known as the Riviera of Albania."

Kit finally remembered where she had seen the other man. "Isn't that US Ambassador Stanton?"

"You have a keen eye," Maria said. "My husband knows him through work connections. Richard works as a lobbyist for a US aid organization in Kosovo. That's why we moved to Pristina."

"Where are you from originally?"

"Slovenia, but I was educated in the UK before marrying and moving here. But that's enough about me," Maria moved on briskly. She indicated that Kit should take her seat on the couch while she settled into armchair and placed a clipboard on the table.

"Of course," Kit said, settling onto the couch. "I'm just wondering, do you have ambassadors and international officials among your clientele?"

"I have a policy of not talking about my clients," Maria replied. But then a small, satisfied smile played on her lips. "But I can say that I have a number of high-profile clients without breaking confidentiality."

"I am international, but not high profile," Kit said.

Maria smiled again, and tapping her pen on her clipboard, she guided the conversation back to Kit's session.

"One day you may become high profile yourself. But we're getting diverted from the purpose of our meeting today. The last time we talked was an introduction, a chance to get to know each other a little. Have you had any thoughts about what you would like to get out of therapy? What are your therapeutic objectives?"

Kit had run out of distractions, her hands fidgeting with her clothes. She shifted in her seat before she spoke.

"I wanted to talk about my nightmares after I was kidnapped, but I'm open to discussing other topics as well. My career is going well—I love being an assistant prosecutor in Pristina—but I don't see myself doing this forever." She paused, waiting for Maria to comment. When she didn't, Kit continued. "Something has changed in my relationship. I recently spent a month sailing around Croatia with my fiancé, but I don't feel the same connection with him anymore. I don't know which direction our relationship should go from here."

"Last week, you mentioned that your boss had put you on medical leave from work, but you came back early. How did you feel about that?"

"When I saw the crime scene from a multiple homicide case, I was so shaken up that I fainted. My boss thought I should take some time off to recover, but I felt like it was important for me to get back to work to prove myself. I had to show them that their faith in me was justified. If I took more time off, it would be admitting I'm not strong enough to deal with the case."

"Did you get any support at that time?"

"I thought I had. I opened up to a friend I thought was trustworthy, but…" Kit stopped talking and wrung her hands, tears threatening to spill from her eyes. "This conversation remains confidential, right?"

Maria nodded in assurance. "Yes, of course. Anything you say to me here is strictly confidential. This is a safe space."

"It turns out the person I trusted had ties to the case I was working on. It devastated me. How could I have known that? Everything about meeting him and being with him felt so easy, so natural. Maybe that should have made me suspicious. Nothing good can be that easy— and that flattering. He worked at the Russian Liaison Office. I loved the way he gave me advice on life philosophy. It never occurred to me that he might have been a criminal. Unfortunately, his office used diplomatic immunity so he could get away. He lied to me about being single when he was married the whole time. That cut to the core."

"Russian liaison officer you say," Maria said and jotted down a note. "Surprisingly, it happens more than you think. When people are away from home on international missions, they might lie about their marital status or simply play the field."

"Your explanation does make sense, Dr Montenegro—Maria—but at the time I was devastated. He told me his wife had died, but later he admitted that due to injuries, she had undergone a personality change. In his eyes, the woman he married was gone. But I felt manipulated."

Maria nodded. "Had you been intimate with him?"

"We were heading in that direction." Kit downplayed the level of their closeness. "Thank goodness I uncovered the truth before things went too far. I believe he used me as an informant." While she felt comforted by Maria's assurance of discretion, Kit felt too exposed to be totally honest with her.

"What makes you think that?"

"He acted like he really liked me and encouraged me to discuss the investigation I was part of. He must have known I was looking into crimes he was connected to."

Maria nodded in understanding.

"So, you were under immense strain during your first assignment and didn't take enough time to process it. What are you working on at the moment, if I may ask? Is it also a high pressure case?"

"I'm not sure yet. I still have to be properly read in on the file. But I think it might be something about high-level corruption and bribery."

"Interesting. What do you mean by high-level?"

"I'm not sure yet. Senior officials, maybe."

"I see," Maria said, making a note. "I want you to know that whatever passes between us in these sessions remains strictly confidential. Feel free to talk about anything. It can be surprising how much better we can feel if we share a burden with someone else."

"Thank you, Maria. I'll keep that in mind. Everything I say about work has to be treated in strict confidence."

"Of course. Now, from what you said, you may be sensing a shift in your relationship with your partner from New Zealand. We can go back to that later if you want. For now, can we talk about your childhood and parents? Is that okay?"

Kit forced a smile. "I guess it's expected. Psychiatrists always need to hear about people's pasts and their parents' relationships."

"We can be predictable," Maria said, smiling.

Kit briefly described her family life. Her father Vernon had left when she and her sister were still young and had gone to Australia to work as a defence contractor. Her mother, Rosalyn, had raised them both alone until Kit's sister died from cancer at an early age.

Before she knew it, the fifty-minute session was over and Maria was wrapping up. She marked down some more notes on her pad.

"If you want to continue our weekly meetings, I suggest you start making a log of your dreams and sleep disturbances. We can go over them during our next session. It's important that we keep up momentum now that we've started."

"Thank you, Dr Montenegro—Maria. I'd like to keep going with our sessions. I'll start jotting down my dreams and lack of sleep if you think it will help."

Kit left the therapist's studio feeling lighter than when she'd entered it. She was getting closer to her goal of becoming stronger physically and mentally to prepare for whatever life had in store for her. She just might even begin to get a better understanding of herself. The photo of Maria and her husband with Ambassador Stanton on the Albanian beach made her reflect that Kosovo was such a small place. Everyone and everything was connected.

Chapter Four

Monday morning was Kit's first day back at work after her vacation. She quickened her pace as she strolled down Mother Teresa Boulevard in the center of Pristina. A place of cultural and religious importance, the boulevard was named after the beloved Catholic saint who was born to Albanian parents in Skopje, which was a part of the Turkish Ottoman Empire. The saint had felt a calling to her vocation as a nun at eighteen while in a small village in Kosovo.

Kit's long, auburn braid draped over her left shoulder and her backpack was slung over her right. She'd chosen to wear a neat navy jacket and pants she had purchased from the Hillary Store on Bill Clinton Boulevard, which sold pantsuits inspired by Hillary Clinton. The shop was close to a statue of Bill Clinton, built to commemorate his support for Kosovo against Serbia during the conflict. To finish off her look, she wore her signature black, high-heeled shoes. The striking and witty style of the shop appealed to Kit. She wanted to look professional and serious for work.

Her extended trip with Xander and her mother to the Croatian coast had ended, and Vasha Blaku, their confidential witness, had travelled back to New Zealand with a family friend as part of a witness protection program until she could give evidence against their prime suspect in numerous murders and other serious offences. Kit had expected to enjoy the vacation more than she did. There were still lingering questions about her relationship with Xander that she hadn't sorted out yet.

She couldn't shake the suspicion that her fiancé was seeing someone else, although he denied it. She, on the other hand, felt emotionally involved with Sergei Sokolov, the Russian liaison officer. She had felt taken advantage of and deceived when she realized he was still married—not to mention his involvement in a massacre of Serbian farmers to create unrest in Kosovo. Worst of all, she wanted to see him again. She recalled their last rendezvous at the Boom Boom Room nightclub. She had confronted him, slapping him several times, yet he still offered for her to come with him. How could Xander, a part-time accounting student, compare to Sergei Sokolov, a criminal mastermind and philosopher? She already knew the answer. Sergei was like a forbidden fruit that she knew was bad for her health, but she still desired more. Her heart skipped a beat when she received his text in Croatia saying he hadn't forgotten about inviting her to Ljubljana with his group.

Kit quickened her pace, extracting her earbuds from her bag as she went. She plugged them into her ears and cranked up the music until she was slightly out of breath. All she wanted was to forget about Sergei and those awkward feelings and focus on getting to work. Christina Aguilera's song "What a Girl Wants" was at risk of being drowned out by the Turkish pipe music played by an old man wearing a white, Albanian, felted hat.

Amidst the chaos of the crowded marketplace, she searched for a vendor who could satiate her craving for something unique. Her eyes landed on a collection of quartz crystals sparkling with fool's gold and garnets, which reminded her of her mother's shop at Auckland International Airport. She approached the vendor and pointed at the specimens before inquiring how much they cost. After paying in cash, she left, feeling contented by the weight of her backpack that now held the crystals wrapped in newspaper.

Kit took a deep breath, feeling more optimistic about life. She was soon to be back at the office on another criminal case, and her apartment cost only a small fraction of what she'd be paying in New Zealand. Her boss was now appreciative of her work, though they had gotten off to a clumsy start when she spoke out of turn at a meeting. Maybe talking to Dr Montenegro would help her sort out the emotions related to the men in her life.

Her heart began to pound when she arrived at the apartment building where Major Matt Hackman had set up base. This was the nerve centre of their covert operations, yet they lived in constant fear of interference from high-ranking officials. They were a small group tasked with gathering incriminating evidence and making arrests without political disruptions. They had to toe the line with their superiors and keep them informed without revealing everything. The last major case had been a success, but nobody knew how close they'd come to failure and serious repercussions.

The apartment block was clean and modern, with a white, rectangular design surrounding a lush, green courtyard. This particular building had been built in Pristina after the conflict, when international organizations flocked to Kosovo. Kit arrived at the lobby, where Granit stood. His signature camo T-shirt and khaki pants revealed his impressive frame—evidence of his days as a bouncer and bodyguard. Thanks to Granit's connections, Matt had found an affordable and comfortable apartment. Plus, he said he could always depend on Granit for backup.

"Hello, Kit," Granit said with a smile that made the scar on his left cheek wrinkle up. "I haven't seen you in weeks. I heard you went on vacation with your family."

"Hi, Granit," Kit replied. "I'm here to see Matt."

"Sure," Granit said. "The others are already there." He took Kit to the elevator, swiping the card that granted access to the penthouse duplex apartment before pressing the up button.

Kit's mood brightened as the elevator took her up to the eighth floor. As the doors opened, she was met with a sophisticated, modern penthouse suite. The walls displayed bold abstract paintings from local artists, while potted plants made the space feel like a tranquil sanctuary where the team could discuss their plans in secret. Adjacent to the main suite was an operations room with a computer linked to various encrypted networks, as well as a large display screen and several chairs for the group to view any ongoing investigations.

Angel had set up a coffee station with pastries and baked goods from the local bakery, while Eva sat on the edge of the couch, smoking and petting her rescue dog Bambino. Owen was taking notes as Matt dictated a list of discussion points. Don Edgson's tall frame lounged in the chair, Texan boots crossed under the table and hands laced behind his head. His partner Max, a Belgium Tervuren canine with mahogany and black fur, was pressed against Don's side, at the ready for their next mission as part of the

US Army's canine unit deployed to Kosovo. Max was the first to notice Kit as she stepped into the room. His ears pricked up and his tail pounded excitedly on the floor in greeting. Don saw Max's reaction and glanced at the elevator. "Hey there, Kit. Glad you came back," Don said with a smile. "Come on in and have a seat."

Eva tore her gaze away from her thoughts and started when she saw Kit. She rose from her chair and greeted Kit with a handshake and two kisses on the cheeks, as was customary in Italy.

"*Ciao, bella*," Eva said. "So glad you're here; we're really short-handed in the office." Kit smiled happily in response and gave her two kisses back on the cheek. "It's great to be back," she said.

"We're thankful your fiancé didn't take you back to New Zealand," Matt said, grinning. "Eva's just getting ready to tell us about a new case."

Kit walked over to Owen and planted a kiss on his cheek. They didn't need to say more than a greeting since they had already trained together.

Angel beamed brightly when she saw Kit enter the room. Her blonde hair was newly cut and styled into layers that framed her face with bangs. She brought over a tray of coffee made the way each of them liked it best— black, black with two sugars, macchiato, and tea—and put it down on the table before turning to give Kit a hug. She pulled back and looked at Kit from head to toe.

"Looks like you've lost some weight. Darn! We'll have to fix that soon enough. You're just in time for coffee and pastries!"

"Actually, I think I gained weight while I was away," Kit replied with a laugh.

Everyone settled around the table, helping themselves to sweet pastries and coffee. Max caught a piece of pastry that Don tossed to him in midair. Matt thanked them for coming and commented on how the food from the international prosecutor's office was much better than at police headquarters. He reached for a slice of Burek, laying it on a napkin in front of him.

"After the last case, we decided to keep our group going behind-the-scenes," he said, "in parallel to whatever our organizations might be doing."

"In case we get bumped off the case, you mean," Owen said with a wry grin.

"I like to think that won't happen again," Matt said. "But we can put together our own prosecution case if we need to.

"We can just say that the evidence miraculously appeared and then all we needed to do was draw up the court filings. *Ecco*! There it is!" Eva joked. But then a moment later, she looked tense again. "Do you mind if I smoke? I need to steady my nerves."

Matt shrugged and looked around.

"Actually, OIDC has a strict no smoking policy," Kit said. "But I think we could make an exception in this case—and you're the boss."

"We're not on OIDC premises, so the rules don't apply," Eva said. "Another advantage in running our own task force."

"Don't try to argue with the chief prosecutor," said Don, laughing.

Eva sighed and pushed away the cigarette packet and lighter.

"All right, you win," she said. "Let me get right to it. I think one of our senior international judges is crooked.

I was going through some telephone intercepts the other night, and there was a clear arrangement to offer him a bribe to fix a case."

"What did they say?" Matt asked.

"They mentioned meeting in Albania to negotiate a deal and make the payment, because Pristina was too public."

"How much money are we talking about?" Max asked.

"Fifty thousand euros or the Kosovo equivalent. We're still using German marks as currency here. But I think that's the tip of the iceberg. I've had the feeling for a while that something isn't right with some of the judges' rulings. It's as if they're being threatened or bribed."

Kit's joy at reuniting with her friends faded as Eva spoke. She pushed her pastry and coffee aside. "What case were they referring to?" she asked. Even as she posed the question, she had a feeling the answer would be unwelcome.

Eva's dog, Bambino, whined and pawed at her leg as if he could sense Kit's discomfort. "I'm so sorry, *bella*. It was about Dasham Raco and his co-defendants. He wants to be transferred to a medical facility—and also coincidentally push us both off the case."

Kit shook her head and asked incredulously, "But why?"

"What exactly did they say?" Matt interjected.

"They said that Judge Tirol was known among prison inmates for his openness to influence—for a price. They made arrangements to meet in Durrës, Albania, to make the payment."

"They didn't want to be spotted in Pristina, so they're going to Albania to meet," Matt said.

"Too many prying eyes," Owen said.

"Exactly. But I think that's just the tip of the iceberg," Eva said. "For a while, I've had the feeling that something's wrong. Some of the international judges' decisions just don't make sense. I started to wonder if perhaps they might be subject to undue influence—either threats or bribery."

Kit swore softly under her breath.

"I have a bad feeling about this," Eva continued. "Firstly, it points to Judge Tirol's willingness to accept bribes; it also indicates that Raco is up to something. Probably planning to escape from the medical center."

Matt slammed the table in frustration. "That son of a bitch! We had to go through a lot of trouble to catch him."

"I can go!" Owen volunteered. "Do you have the date and place of their meeting in Durrës? I can go and keep an eye on them. Maybe I can even plant a listening device…"

Eva looked at Kit, not responding to Owen directly. "What do you think, Kit?"

Kit replied without hesitation. "I'm going too, no question. But don't we need a warrant for any kind of surveillance? So we can use the evidence in court?"

Eva paused for a moment and frowned. "You are right, we should have a warrant. But in this case?" She left the question hanging in the air.

"We don't know how many international judges Tirol could have influenced," Kit pointed out. "So even if we asked for a warrant, he might find out about it from them."

Eva nodded her agreement.

"We can still monitor them if they display suspicious behavior, right?" Matt said.

Owen smiled. "So Kit and I can just hang out at the beach in Durrës… and if we notice any criminals acting fishy, then we follow them and see what happens!"

Kit returned Owen's smile and added, "Exactly!"

"Let's not worry if we're wrong," Matt suggested. "And if we're right, then we can pursue it further. It's safer to keep this information to ourselves for now." No one spoke further about applying for a surveillance warrant from the court.

"Does anyone have a decent picture of Tirol?" Kit asked. "Do you think he would go there in person or send someone to represent him?"

"It's hard to tell," Eva replied. "Maybe he'll go himself, or he may decide it's too dangerous to show up himself and send someone else."

"I found a great photo online," Owen said as he handed an open tablet over to Kit. The photograph showed a tall, thin, balding man wearing a dark suit with a bright yellow tie. He had thin eyebrows above thick, blue-gray glasses, and his lips were pursed, as if he was about to deliver a reprimand to a defendant in court. Kit picked up the device to take a closer look at the man.

"My concern is that this might not be an isolated event," Eva said. "I suspect something bigger is going on here."

"If you're correct, this is very serious," Matt said gravely. "It could weaken the entire judicial system in Kosovo. We don't know how far this corruption might reach."

Eva nodded emphatically. "That's exactly why we have to stay tight-lipped about our suspicions. If any news of our activities gets out, we won't be able to keep ourselves safe and secure. I don't think I need to spell out what happens then."

Matt shook his head grimly in agreement. "Suicide —either personal or professional!"

Eva nodded again. "You mean the kind of suicide that often follows confidential witnesses in major criminal cases? That's what I'm worried about here. We need to approach this with extreme caution!"

"Exactly," Matt said. "Murders dressed up as suicides or unfortunate accidents. From now on, let's call this this mission Operation Icarus. You know—the mythical Greek inventor who flew too close to the sun and crashed? People trying to fly too high for their own good?"

"Right," Kit said, nodding in agreement. "So what kind of in-house expertise do we have to trace illegal transactions?"

"Tom Baumgarten might be able to help," Eva suggested. "He's the OIDC anticorruption guy. I can just tell him we have some organized crime cases that need financial analysis. He doesn't need to know what we're really up to. We need to monitor the international judges to check on them."

"Good idea, but if you don't mind me asking, how did the hospital transfer come up?" Kit said. "I thought Raco was locked up."

"He probably wants more lenient prison conditions," Eva hypothesized.

"Let's make sure he doesn't get away then," Don warned. "It's probably easier to break out from a hospital than a prison."

"I can recommend increasing security on Raco and his gang," Matt said. "But I don't know if Corrections will follow my suggestion. Plus, he hasn't even filed the necessary paperwork for a transfer with the court yet."

"I suppose his wanting us off the case is a sign of professional respect," Eva observed.

"Do you need to have a security detail put on you and Kit?" Matt asked.

"No, not for me. I don't want people constantly trailing me. Kit should have a security detail if she wants, though. She's seen more of Raco."

"Yeah, I was face-to-face with him," Kit said. "But I'd rather not have someone watching my every move either." She thought of close protection officers accompanying her to therapy or her workouts with Owen and checking up on her conversations with Sergei. That wouldn't do at all. "Let's just keep monitoring his communications and see what turns up."

Eva walked over to the window and looked out at the courtyard between the apartment buildings. "There might be a connection between what we've seen in Operation Icarus and some of the judges' decisions that I've noticed lately. They were ruling in favor of defendants more often than expected. Like saying a suspect had behaved well enough in prison to be released, even though they had previously threatened witnesses."

"This sounds like a big job. What do you need me to do?" Kit asked.

"I'd like you to go through transcripts of judicial decisions with a fine-tooth comb. Look for patterns that could point to foul play. I'm primarily talking about criminal cases, but if you have time, also investigate privatizations of state assets that have been a hot topic lately. Local reporters are worried that some of these properties have been sold undervalued and assets stripped away." Eva paused before continuing with a tone of authority, "If you detect something suspicious, do your best to get to the bottom of it."

Kit nodded in agreement. "I can start by exploring court decisions on criminal prosecutions and follow that up by looking for red flags in other areas. I'll be sure to draw up a concept paper for you with my research plan so we can get started on this as soon as possible."

Angel then inquired, "Boss, I tried to collect some of the records from the courts and the state enterprises panel this week. But they told me that many of the documents had been sent off to the archives and aren't accessible now. It seems the boxes were couriered to the archives in Berlin. For safekeeping, they said."

"Kit, can you put together a list of all of the records we need? If they aren't available, we'll have to hunt them down," Eva said. "According to the rules, the paperwork must stay here in Pristina for at least a year or two prior to being archived."

"One day we're chasing suspects, the next day we're researching archives," Kit said with a chuckle.

"We'll have to stay in touch about this. But it's too easy for someone to track our conversations, so don't go into detail over the phone," Matt said.

"It's too easy to think they can't catch us out," mused Don.

"We could use closed-circuit radios or encrypted internet messaging services that are hard to intercept," Owen said.

"Since you're our communication specialist, investigate all of our possibilities, Sergeant. Remember that we're on our own; I don't want to alert official sources yet," Matt said. "Although I'm going to have to keep London in the loop."

"Same here," Don said. "I have to let my contact at the American embassy know or else they'll send me back home when they eventually find out."

Matt agreed. "All right. We may need some help from your US counterparts. But I'd rather not end up with a repeat of what happened when Raco evaded arrest—not that we were the ones at fault. The Romanian police unit should have done their job and we would have gotten him in jail earlier."

Kit scribbled down question marks on her pad as she sat in deep thought. Matt had been fuming ever since he was taken off the investigation but then put back in charge. Raco had managed to kidnap her due to the mismanagement of the event, and the danger that posed to her career was too great for her risk any more mistakes. They were all uncertain about their safety and reputations, so they ought to keep the mission limited only to people they could trust.

Chapter Five

Kit unlocked her office, musty from being closed for a month. She opened the window, switched on the lights, and surveyed her room; she hadn't accumulated much since she wasn't expecting to stay in Pristina for long. Now, she had a contract for a year. She pinned a photo of herself, Xander, her mother Rosalyn, and family friend, Charles, on the yacht close to the Croatian coast to her noticeboard along with a mug from Dubrovnik announcing "Winter is coming." All she needed was a kettle and some plants to feel at home. There was a tentative knock on the door, and Kit looked up. Angel struggled to carry a tall pile of files. "Can I put these down somewhere?"

"Sure," Kit said. "Right there on the table."

"That's the first pile," Angel said, brushing away a stray lock of blonde hair with the back of her hand. "The boss said that she wants you to research these judges' decisions. I got a list of files from the archives service." She put down a thick document.

"Thanks, I think," Kit said, looking at the thick stack of files and wondering how long it would take her to read them.

"The problem is a lot of the files are missing. Felix in the archives unit said that he'd received a request from headquarters in Berlin to send several boxes of binders there for storage. No one questioned it at the time, so he just shipped them off."

"Do you have a copy of that request?" Kit asked.

"I can get it."

"Great, thanks. Can you ask Felix to send me an Excel spreadsheet listing of all the files?"

"No sooner said than done."

"You're an angel," Kit said.

"Angel by name, angel by nature," Angel responded in a broad Yorkshire accent.

"Something tells me that this is not the first time you said that. Very witty," Kit laughed.

Another knock on the door made Kit look behind Angel to see Eva with a fit-looking man in his mid-forties. He had silver hair, brown eyes, and a direct gaze.

"Kit, I'd like you to meet our colleague Tom Baumgarten. He's in charge of the OIDC anticorruption unit. He can help with any bank records we need. Tom, this is Caitlin Chase. She's our new assistant prosecutor. I thought it would be good if you two met."

They shook hands.

Eva continued directly to Kit. " Tom needs to brief us on a case of his own. I don't have time right now. I have to get into court for a hearing. Would you mind taking his brief, and we can discuss later?"

"Sure, " Kit said.

"Sorry, I've got to run," Eva said.

"I'll be off as well," Angel said. "I'll get that info you need ASAP."

When they were alone, Kit invited Tom into the office and pulled up a chair for him.

"It looks like you got your work cut out for you," Tom said, indicating the large stack of files on the table.

Kit laughed. "I just got back from vacation, and look how they welcome me back."

"Are you new in the mission? I haven't seen you here before."

"I was here for three months, mainly working on a couple of cases, then I had a month off, and now I'm back again. How long have you been with the organisation?"

"A long time—over twenty years—but not in Pristina for the whole time."

"Impressive," Kit said. "I can't imagine being with an organisation for that long. Has it been interesting?"

"Never as interesting as it is now," he replied. "My office has no executive powers. We can only make recommendations through management. We monitor the privatization processes and observe board meetings in the newly privatized companies."

"That would provide insights," Kit observed.

"Yes, you could say that. I report to the deputy head of mission, Michael Burke."

"I haven't met him yet," Kit said. "Where's he from?"

"The US, like me," Tom replied. "He asked me to pick a priority focus for this year. I chose improving corporate governance at the public-owned enterprises and I wrote him a paper about it."

Angel returned with coffee and left them alone, closing the door softly behind her.

"How can we help?"

Tom sat down across from Kit at the desk. He drew the coffee cup towards him and started absentmindedly, stirring it with a plastic spoon.

"I'm pretty short-staffed at the moment. I welcome all the help I can get." He smiled at her as if in appeal.

"Anything we can do," Kit responded. She pulled over her legal notepad and poised her pen above it.

"Actually, I'd prefer it if you didn't take notes," Tom said.

She put down her pen and look at him expectantly. "All right, we're off the record."

"This is hard to me to say after having spent so many years dedicated to the OIDC and its humanitarian objectives," he said. He was not looking at her directly but rather out through the window. "I've got the responsibility to oversee the way our organisation works in utilities and infrastructure. I've been approached privately by a several staff members on a confidential basis. They all had the same story in different words. They told me that a number of managers have been accepting kickbacks and directing business to favored companies."

"Those are serious allegations. Did they provide any supporting evidence?"

"Not really," he said. "Apart from what they said. Three staff members made similar allegations."

"Could they have a grudge against their managers, so they agreed to make false accusations?"

"I don't think so. They seem to be coming to the issue all from their own perspectives in different words. When co-conspirators agree on a plan, they usually come with a similar story. These staff are all afraid to lose their jobs and are adamant that they don't want to be quoted in any investigations."

"What kind of business arrangements did they allege?"

"The most dramatic is a proposed power plant for Kosovo worth the equivalent of US five billion dollars. The allegation I heard was that two senior managers are going to receive a ten percent kickback for directing the business towards a particular company."

Kit got out her mobile phone, opened the calculator program, and tapped in the figures. "That's five hundred million!"

"There's more. Another allegation is that pressure has been applied to the special panel that oversees the privatisation. Similar story—business is directed towards certain companies, and the individuals concerned receive a percentage, or a finder's fee. Because the enterprises are not going to the best qualified bidder, several major enterprises have been stripped of their assets and gone into liquidation."

"What kind of sums are we talking about?"

"Not as much, more like hundreds of thousands of dollars, not millions of dollars, but the effect is cumulative. Collectively, we could be talking millions."

"We'd need to investigate and find evidence of this."

"As you know, as an international organisation, OIDC staff enjoy functional immunity. For real accountability, it has to be proven that they were acting outside of their authority."

"Innocent until proven guilty," Kit said. Tom nodded.

"Also because of these immunities, I can't call in local Kosovo police to investigate. I'm going to have to find some evidence myself and prepare a case. Then maybe the OICD regional HQ in Berlin or the global HQ in New York might take action." Tom sagged in his chair. He looked dejected, but Kit saw embers of anger smouldering in his eyes.

"I think the head of the organisation would have to waive the privileges and immunities if there's enough evidence to make the case."

"That's what I hope," Tom said.

"You don't seem very sure."

"The more senior the official suspected, the more likely it is that the organisation will turn a blind eye, or even lose evidence to avoid taking action. All this would be really bad for our reputation. There's supposed to be an official policy of protecting whistleblowers, but it's more honoured in breach than in the observance."

"The organisation does seem very concerned about its public profile. On my first day here, I spoke out of turn at an international conference in town and was hauled across the coals for it. Apparently, I embarrassed the head of mission. Not intentionally, of course." Kit blushed at the recollection. Eva had told her to observe and say nothing, but she spoke out about the conflict related sexual violence issue that everyone had been brushing under the carpet.

"You seem to be in the good graces of your boss now, and I heard good things about you from management."

"That's good to hear. I hope it stays that way," Kit said. "What can we do for you?"

"I need your help to assess the evidence to see if it supports a complaint. Any case needs to be watertight so that the organisation can't avoid taking action. I think the gravitas of your office would really help."

"We'd be pleased to assist in whatever way we can. These economic crimes may not be as dramatic in their effects as war crimes, but long-term, they can be just as corrosive."

"I think so too. Some of these reports are really heartbreaking. Major industries are closing down and people are losing their jobs because of mismanagement and asset stripping."

"Where have the assets been diverted to?"

"I'm not sure. I did see reference to a connection with Romania. But we shouldn't assume that it's all going to Eastern Europe."

Kit frowned. "Which managers may be implicated?"

"This is where I need to be very careful. I can't afford to bandy around serious accusations without solid evidence. I'm going to have to inform senior managers of the allegations."

"Have you shared your concerns with anyone else?"

"Not so far, only the staff members who came to talk with me."

"Better keep it that way. I'll brief Eva. I'm just thinking aloud here, but I wonder if we could put some of these people under surveillance to gather evidence."

"I appreciate your support, Caitlin. But probably the best thing for now is for me to discreetly gather what information I can, like from auditors reports and official records. Then we can speak again, assess the evidence, and discuss possible next steps."

"I agree," Kit said. "Do you think this high-level conspiracy might go beyond this organisation?"

"Anything's possible. In fact, it's quite likely that senior politicians in the utilities ministry could be involved in the kickback scheme. The chairman of the privatization panel called me to arrange a private briefing.

This has never happened before, and I wonder if he has some information to share with me."

"What's his name?"

"He's a local business person, Rustem Kupi."

"Why would he want to talk to you?"

"Our organisation has some responsibilities for overseeing the privatization process. Our head of mission signs off on a lot of major transactions, like the sale of state-owned enterprises to private owners. But I don't know what he's going to say."

"I hope he's not going to try to bribe you as well," Kit said dryly.

"I've been working against corruption for most of my working life. For me, it's unthinkable to consider taking a bribe. He doesn't know that though." Tom looked troubled.

"Please keep us in the loop."

"There's one other thing. The preliminary evaluation report on the impact of the power plant indicates that over seven thousand Kosovars will be forcibly displaced to make way for an open pit lignite mine. This doesn't comply with the international standards for international financing. But the World Bank is still backing the proposal."

"Where can I get more information on that?" Kit asked.

"I'll get you a copy."

"If that gets out, it could affect the reputation of the organization," Kit observed.

"And the lives of seven thousand people. The people that we're supposed to be here to help."

"No doubt about it. This is all very disturbing." Kit jotted down some notes. When Tom frowned at the paper, Kit added, "Just a few key words. Sorry, I know you want this off the record."

"I know," he responded. "How do you think I got this grey hair so young?"

"You're young?" she asked.

Tom smiled. "I was young and idealistic once, but now I feel old before my time. It's the kind of thing you think about lying awake at three a.m. But I won't take up any more of your time for now."

Kit got up and walked around her desk to Tom. She extended her hand and shook his warmly. "Thanks for reaching out, Tom," she said. "We'll be in touch."

"Thanks, Caitlin."

"You can call me Kit."

Tom Baumgarten reached the door before Kit called him back.

"One more thing. Would you also consider the money laundering angle? If the allegations are true, they must be funnelling the money out of Kosovo somehow. Actually, we were going to ask for your support for a case we're investigating."

"Like they say, follow the money. I have some experience in forensic accounting if we can get access to the banking records." Tom smiled. Kit noticed that he was standing straighter and seemed more upbeat than when he arrived. "By the way, I'm going brief senior management on this next week. I'd appreciate it if you or Eva could be there."

Kit nodded and made a note in her work planner. "Sure, no problem," she said.

After he left the room, Kit dug out her mobile phone and texted Eva and Matt: "Operation Icarus might have just got bigger." She wanted to see if there was evidence of a connection between the suspicious behavior of the international judge and the allegations of corruption.

She knew she had to record the information from that conversation, but Tom was right that they needed to be discreet. If any of the suspects got their hands on her notes, it could compromise the investigation before it even began. She decided to take a few handwritten notes and store them in her home safe for extra security.

CHAPTER SIX

Kit tingled with excitement and a touch of nerves at the prospect of staking out Judge Tirol at Durrës, a wealthy seaside resort in Albania. Early Saturday morning, she and Owen picked up an SUV from a car rental agency in town. They expected a three and a half hour drive and wanted to ensure there was plenty of time before the supposed meeting at noon in case of a long wait to cross the border into Albania. Eva and Matt wanted them to find out who was there at noon at the Blue Lagoon Café restaurant, and whether they could see any money exchanged.

Kit wore camouflage sweatpants, white sneakers, and a cutaway T-shirt. She was carrying her go-to trail bag slung across her chest, but she took off her khaki hat before she got in the car. Owen had on jeans, a blue polo shirt, and some sunglasses Kit had never seen him in before—ready for the beach. They were embarking on their mission to uncover if this could be an intricate scheme to tamper with justice and misuse power. If not, it would just be a day of relaxation at the shore. Both prospects were exciting.

They decided it would be better not to take an obvious official car but rather pose as tourists in a regular vehicle. Owen had rented the car with Kit as the co-driver, and they pretended to be colleagues taking a vacation together. They planned to reach Durrës—one of the closest beach resorts close to Pristina—but the car rental agent gave Owen an enigmatic smile that made Kit feel like he thought they were two lovers out on a jaunt.

"It looks like our cover is blown," she muttered.

"What do you mean?" Owen asked, settling into his seat. The SUV was new and unfussy, comfortable but unlikely to draw too much attention. Kit breathed in deeply, inhaling the leather interior's fresh aroma.

She shrugged. "I think he believes we're an item." Feeling embarrassed, she busied herself checking the map again. "We should make it through the border without much traffic if we leave now. At this hour, there shouldn't be too much traffic at the border crossings."

"Did Eva give you instructions what to do once we get there?" Owen asked.

"Not really," Kit said. "She just said to go to the Blue Lagoon at noon and see if anything suspicious is going on. What did Matt say?"

"More or less the same. He suggested we take photographs if we can get close enough without being too obvious."

"We don't have a surveillance warrant, so photos aren't useful as evidence in court."

"But they could help us identify people."

"I could pose as a tourist, and then you could photograph me with the suspects in the background," she laughed.

"It's just possible I'll do that," Owen said. He put the car into reverse, then eased out of the car park and onto the road. It was a warm, late autumn day, but the air-conditioning kept them comfortable as they made their way through the light, early morning traffic.

"I could even enjoy this assignment," Kit said. She slipped on her sunglasses, stretched her legs out comfortably, and turned on an international radio station that played a mixture of popular music and nostalgic themes from the eighties. "Just getting into the role," she said. "As a tourist."

"I wouldn't mind if no one turns up at the Blue Lagoon. Then we can just have lunch and come back again. Or go to the beach." Owen grinned.

***

Kit and Owen chatted easily until they got to the border crossing at Albania, discussing their training schedule at the gym, the task force, colleagues, and what they expected the next year to bring. Kit pulled her bag onto her lap and got out her passport. She briefly checked to see how long the queues were waiting to get through immigration controls. After looking through the window on her left and her right, Kit did a double take. Opposite her was a balding, bespectacled man wearing a dark suit sitting in the rear of a dark limousine. Beside the driver in the front passenger seat sat another man.

"Owen," Kit said breathlessly. "Look, is that Tirol?"

"Where?" Owen said, looking around.

"Right next to us on the right. Look!" Kit faced straight ahead and leaned backwards so that Owen could look across her into the next car. He looked for as long as he dared and then sat back behind the steering wheel.

"I'm not sure, but you might be right. I recognize those glasses from the press photo."

"I think we should follow him," Kit said. Owen checked his watch.

"The timing's right. Like us, they could be heading to the Blue Lagoon."

"I should message Angel. Let her know what's going on. She can tell the others in case we need backup."

"Right," Owen said. "When he pulls away, photograph the number plate."

Kit got out her mobile phone and on the pretext of speaking into it, she opened the camera and clicked a photo of the side of the car. She opened the messaging app and sent a message to Angel. "At Albanian border. Might have eyes on target." She sent the photograph of the number plate. Within a few minutes, Angel messaged that the plate numbers were confirmed as registered to Victor Tirol.

"Attempting to follow," Kit responded.

"Keep us informed."

Kit put down her mobile phone and turned to Owen. "Have you done surveillance training?"

"Yep, they teach that sort of thing at cop school in Wales."

"Here's your chance to put it into action," Kit said.

Owen's phone beeped. "It's Matt," he said, reading from the text. "He says, 'Keep eyes on target, do not approach.'"

"It surprises me that Tirol doesn't even bother to take another car," Kit observed, frowning in the bright sunlight.

"The arrogance of the man. He doesn't even consider getting caught."

"He thinks he's above the law."

"He has been. Until now."

She wound down the window and casually let her elbow rest there. She glanced over again at Tirol. A small smile played around the edge of her lips. She smelled the hot tarmac and the exhausts of nearby cars mixing with the resinous scent of the nearby stand of pines. They had him in their sights already.

"We have the advantage that we know what he's doing, but he doesn't know what we're doing," Owen said. "Game on."

Owen stayed as close to the limousine as he could without raising suspicion. The sun shone brightly on the long, winding roads that led between sharp mountains that looked like ogres from fairy tales. At other times, there were vast reservoirs, small farmers with their vineyards, and other crops scattered around the rugged terrain. As they came close to a bend in the road, Owen allowed the limo to accelerate out of sight.

"I have to let them go ahead," Owen said. "We can't risk arriving at the Blue Lagoon restaurant and them recognizing us."

Kit nodded in agreement. "Sticking to Plan A is our best bet. We should get there sooner rather than later instead of worrying about following them."

"We should leave the vehicle several blocks away. In case anyone notices it," he said.

"I guess our plan to see Tirana is off. I've never visited there before," Kit noted sadly. The idea of going for a sightseeing adventure had disappeared with the appearance of their target.

"Maybe we can try it next time," he replied.

Traffic built up as they got closer to Durrës. Kit consulted the map as they approached a major intersection and directed Owen to take a left.

"It's well sign-posted," she observed.

"We might need your navigation skills more once we reach Durrës to find the restaurant."

"I'm on it," she said.

"For next time, I'll see about activating a data roaming package so we can use satnav."

"You're such a geek," Kit laughed.

"That's partly why Matt likes to keep me on the team."

"And why else?"

"I know when to keep my mouth shut," Owen said.

"A useful skill," she observed. "One that I should learn."

They both laughed. "You don't need to be quiet around me," Owen said. "I like your New Zealand accent."

"Thanks for that," she said with a smile and turned her attention back to the road.

CHAPTER SEVEN

Durrës, Albania

The sun was high in the sky as they drove along the busy street that ran parallel to the seashore. Along the beach, umbrellas of red, blue, and yellow shimmered in the sunlight, and people soaked up the last of the warm weather. The road beside them was lined with apartment buildings, their windows reflecting the bright day. As they passed a bakery, a small shop that sold fishing equipment, and a few cafes, normalcy seemed to prevail. But underneath it all, Kit had a feeling that something extraordinary was about to happen.

"The Blue Lagoon is close to the Archaeological Museum. If you find a park near that, we can walk down to the beach and find it," Kit said, tracing the streets on her map.

They parked the car and then strolled down an alley lined with summer speciality shops selling children's toys and beach accessories. Kit stopped at one stand and bought a couple of postcards.

"To send to New Zealand. Part of our cover," she explained and handed over some coins to the vendor.

Owen glanced back up the street while she made the purchase.

"I think I just saw their car drive past," he said.

She quickly tucked the cards in her bag. "Let's keep going," she whispered urgently.

"Let's find a spot where we can watch the restaurant," Owen suggested as they carried on walking.

"Now I wish we'd come earlier so we could scope out the area," she said. Kit started to be concerned that they hadn't taken this assignment seriously enough and were having too much fun pretending to be tourists.

"I thought we had plenty of time." He glanced at his watch. "But they're here early."

"This is my first experience with surveillance," Kit said.

"I've done it a couple of times back in Wales, usually for drug exchanges."

He took her arm, and they walked together. She looked up at him curiously.

"It's for our cover," he said, responding to her unspoken question, looking straight ahead.

As Kit felt Owen's arm wrap around hers a little too tight for the situation, she couldn't help but notice that he had moved closer to her than was necessary. She knew they had to keep up their cover as a tourist couple, so she bit down on her lip, hoping he wouldn't notice her confusion and apprehension. While Owen had suggested they go out for dinner before and seemed keen to be friends, Kit had shut down any suggestion of romance; after all, her love life was already complicated enough.

"I think an ice cream will help our cover," she said with a half smile, subtly attempting to distance herself from him. She chose vanilla and hazelnut while he opted for chocolate and raspberry ripple—a strange combination, she thought.

As they walked along the promenade, their hands were occupied by the dripping cones, providing her with the opportunity to subtly edge away without creating tension.

They approached the Blue Lagoon café restaurant. While Kit didn't enjoy getting too close to Owen, she enjoyed his easy companionship. In some ways, it was easier to be with him than with Xander, who seemed to always find something to complain about. She liked working with Owen on the task force. He didn't put her under pressure.

"So, there's the Blue Lagoon," Owen said, indicating where the restaurant lay a few meters up the road. "Let's try to find somewhere we can watch it from."

They sat down on the low wall between the boulevard and where the beach began. They could see the entrance to the café restaurant. A large outdoor seating area catered to a smattering of guests sitting under large, white sun umbrellas.

"It's not noon yet," Kit said. "I suppose that's early for lunch here." Kit took a last bite of her ice cream cone and wiped her fingers clean with a napkin.

"I'll send another message to HQ to update them," Owen said and pulled out his mobile phone. Kit also extracted hers, ready to take photographs.

Kit and Owen were so preoccupied with keeping an eye on the restaurant that they didn't notice the trio of men approaching from the left. Judge Victor Tirol had on beige cotton slacks and a white polo with boater shoes. He was flanked by two men in jackets, despite the sweltering heat, who seemed hyperalert as they strolled along the beach. It was clear they were there to provide protection.

Kit's eyes widened in astonishment and she gasped when she finally noticed them. One of the figures stopped and seemed turned to look at the source of the sound. Kit jolted, now fully alert. The man slowed in front of them and seem to be about to say something. Suddenly Owen wrapped his arms around her and kissed her. If it had surprised her to see their target right in front of them, she was even more astonished to find herself suddenly embraced by Owen, the sun cap partially obscuring their faces. His arm was around her shoulders, and his hand rested on her knee. Time felt like it was both extending and intensifying simultaneously. The danger, the unplanned intimacy—it was too much. Now she could feel his muscle-bound body against hers, and she was too shocked to do anything but freeze. Their kiss was sweet and salty, flavored with chocolate and vanilla. Miraculously, the figures had moved past them without further incident.

She stayed still for a moment longer, feeling an urge to look for more of that kiss. He slowly moved away from her, his face still close and a bit flushed. His eyes sparkled as he gazed into hers.

"Sorry about that. I needed to distract those men," he said.

Kit took a deep breath and tried to settle herself. "I think it worked. I mean, it distracted them and me," she replied. Kit stood and adjusted her clothing, straightening her bag. He rose up next to her. She looked up at Owen and remembered how she would have been able to rest her head on Xander's shoulder when they were standing next to each other. Despite being shorter than Xander, Owen was stronger, more muscular.

"Let's get closer to see what they're doing," he said. Now he was all business, and she tried to shake herself clear of what had just happened.

"Okay," she muttered while they began walking distractedly towards the Blue Lagoon. The three men had taken shelter under an umbrella in the back garden of the café. A waiter had just served coffee on a tray, and Tirol paid for it.

Owen elbowed Kit and pointed. "Look who's coming."

A man was approaching the group wearing dress pants and a white linen shirt with a gold chain glistening at his neck. He carefully placed a briefcase beside him as he pulled up a chair at the table. Tirol stood up to shake his hand and then pulled over an extra chair for the bag.

"The funds must be in the briefcase," whispered Owen.

"Cash or an automatic transfer device," Kit whispered back. "Let's get closer to them. I need to get a photo of these guys so we can identify them."

They moved towards the café. Kit had her phone out and opened the camera app. They approached the low border made of concrete planters, getting even nearer to the men they were surveilling. She cautiously pointed the device at the men and snapped pictures of them. Suddenly, one of the bodyguards stood up. His dark glasses could not hide the piercing gaze directed towards them. The other men also stood, their eyes firmly on the pair.

"We've been spotted. Let's get away, fast!" Owen shouted, gripping her arm and propelling her away. Kit twisted around to see the security personnel chasing after them. They bolted in the direction they had come from.

Tirol grabbed the briefcase and departed in a steady walk in the opposite direction with the man who had just joined them. Panic shot through Kit, and any contentment she may have felt from their beach cover was erased by the fear of being pursued by vicious criminals.

"Shall we go to the car?" Kit panted.

The idea of heading toward their vehicle was tempting, but if they did that, it'd be easy for the men pursuing them to catch up.

"Let's try our luck somewhere else first," Owen suggested.

Nearby stood the Archaeological Museum and its nearby park with ragged grass and weathered rocks. They hurriedly raced across the street, bounded up the entrance steps, barely noticing an old sign on the door in Albanian and English declaring "Museum closed for repairs."

Owen yanked open the door and beckoned Kit inside. He glanced back one last time and spotted two men sprinting down the street, one of them tightly clutching a firearm.

"Do you think we should call the police for help?" Kit proposed.

"There's no way they could make it in time," Owen said. "Besides, even if they got here, joining forces with the Albanian police could put us in more danger."

Kit nodded. There was no way to know who had connections with the criminal underworld in Albania.

Owen closed and bolted the door from the inside. "But this won't keep them out for long," he said. "Let's try to find an alternate exit! Hurry!"

They ran to the right and through an arched doorway. The museum was undergoing repairs and filled with crates of artifacts, and worker's tools were scattered about. Some display cases were broken with missing or shattered glass. Dust and debris covered the floor, and several larger statues stood in their path. Kit almost tripped over a wooden plank blocking their way before they heard loud blows, as if someone was trying to break open the entrance. An exit sign pointed left, so they quickly ran in that direction, only to find the door bolted shut.

Kit then felt drawn towards a dark room beside the hallway with blinds covering the windows and a heavy velvet drape further reducing visibility. When she glanced around the room, she noticed a pile of faded curtains strewn on the floor and just enough light to make out a gigantic sculpture standing on a plinth close to the wall. The statue had a jackal-shaped head with a human body wearing a golden robes. A gold earring dangled from one of its ears, and its eyes were rimmed with black paint. A label underneath it read "Anubis, Egyptian God of the Dead" in Albanian and English, sending shivers down Kit's spine.

Kit could hear the heavy footsteps of the men drawing closer. She tugged on Owen's arm, motioning frantically towards the statue's plinth. He gave her a confused look, but they had no other option. They had to hide somewhere, and quickly. They scrambled behind the statue, which was large enough to hide them both. Kit grabbed the velvet curtain, despite it being dusty, and covered both of them with it. They flattened themselves close to the ground.

Kit's heart was in her throat as she felt Owens body pressed against hers. Though all she could think about was the bodyguards, she was hyperaware of his breath and their earlier kiss. Both of them attempted to take deep, even breaths and lie as still as possible. The men came into the end of the corridor and spoke Albanian among themselves. Then footsteps crunched their way into the room. One of them had a pocket flashlight that he was sweeping around. Kit held her breath as the flashlight drew closer, her pulse thumping loudly in her ears. She was aware of Owen's body lying still beside her.

She heard the other man speak to his companion from the adjoining room. The footsteps came closer to the statue, and the flashlight swept even closer to them, passing over the curtains and again down to the floor. He walked over to the windows and checked behind one of them, determining that it was bolted shut. His companion called again and he slowly, almost reluctantly, walked away from the statue and out through the doorway. By then Kit was desperate for breath, and she permitted herself as quiet an intake as possible. The flashlight probed the darkness one last time, encountering the even deeper darkness of the Anubis statue, which proved to be impenetrable. As the men's voices in the next room faded away, neither of them dared to move. It sounded as if the men had gone through the museum lobby and closed the main door behind them.

"I think we should stay here for a while in case they come back," Kit whispered.

"Agreed," Owen said.

"Do you think they've both gone? Or could one still be here?"

"It sounded like they both left, but we can't be sure. Have you got your mobile phone?"

"Yes." Kit moved slightly to reach into her handbag and pulled out her phone, which shone brightly in the darkness. "I guess I should send a message to HQ and let them know what happened?"

"Yes. Let them know we're fine but Tirol's guards chased us."

"Okay," Kit said, and composed a message to Angel, who quickly replied with a loud beep. "Dang," she said softly. "I forgot to mute my phone. Thank goodness it didn't ring while we were hiding."

"It just has," Owen joked dryly before Kit gave him a nudge with her elbow. The immediate risk seemed to have passed, and Kit felt lightheaded, laughing at the absurdity of their situation, stuck beneath the heavy curtain.

"ETA at Durrës one hour. What is your location?" Angel messaged.

"Archaeological Museum."

"Are the men still there?"

"Not as far as we know. Sending the photo of targets." Kit opened her camera and sent the clearest image of the four men at the restaurant table.

"Got it. Matt says keep your position."

"Roger that. Out," Kit texted and put her phone away.

"We've got some time to wait before they get here," Kit said. "Matt says to stay where we are. I hope those guys don't come back."

"Me too, but I doubt it. I suspect they want to get Tirol away as quickly as possible, just in case we call for help. I wonder if they identified us from the border crossing."

"Maybe so, but the snapshot came in handy," Kit replied.

"I think I was too confident in our own cover story," Owen said.

Kit sighed. "I understand where you're coming from," she said, thinking of how often she had felt out of her depth since arriving in Kosovo. "Let's save some details of this assignment for ourselves."

"Good idea," he said, turning a shade pinker in the dim light. "Sorry about that kiss; totally unprofessional of me. I was afraid they would recognize us staking them out."

"Don't worry about it," she replied. "You know what they say: what happens in the field stays in the field. Anyway, it allowed us to get a closer look at our target."

"Yes, sorry," he said. "It won't happen again."

Kit was taken aback by her own response to his apology; a sensation of regret, and even emptiness filled her heart. That couldn't be right. She didn't even find Owen attractive.

She brushed off her clothes and spoke. "Let's take a look inside this building to see where the exits are."

"We can take photos of the guys' footprints or maybe even fingerprints," Owen suggested.

"Now you're starting to sound professional again," Kit laughed. When she pulled the thick curtain away from wall, a small, metal object clinked on the hardwood floor. "What was that?" she said and switched on her phone flashlight. In its beam, a small, golden ring glinted. The delicate, metal ring was decorated with a detailed engraving. It had an aged yet unfinished look to it, as if it had been handcrafted and then dropped from one of the broken display cases. The design resembled an ankh, a symbol often found in ancient Egyptian art.

"What's that?" Owen asked, peering over her shoulder.

Kit switched the light off. "It's nothing important. Just something on the ground," she said, pocketing the ring. If it were truly valuable, it wouldn't have been there in the first place, she reasoned. Adrenaline spiked through her as she realized she was pushing the boundaries by taking it, yet there was no way she would leave the ring where she found it. Owen studied her carefully for a moment before shrugging and turning to check the street for any further activity.

The museum had proven to be an inspired place to take refuge from their attackers in its current state of disrepair. Room after room was in disarray, filled with renovation equipment, furniture covers, crates, and boxes. hey took a seat beside the front windows to watch for movement at the front of the building. After about an hour, an OIDC vehicle pulled up. Matt was driving, and Angel was sitting in the front passenger seat. In the back of the jeep sat Don Edgson with the other half of the canine unit, Max.

"They're here sooner than I expected. Let's go meet them," Owen said. He pushed open the lobby door, now damaged from their pursuers efforts to break in. Kit hurried towards the vehicle. They needed to leave Durrës as soon as possible to avoid further attention. Even though four men meeting at a Durrës seaside café was hardly evidence of criminal wrongdoing, it confirmed the intel gleamed from Raco's call transcript. Judge Tirol was likely willing to accept a bribe, and he had taken direction from the prime suspect in the Staro Dorbi massacre case to receive a payment.

Matt drove them to where Owen had parked the rental car. Matt and Don inspected the car closely. Don let Max circle and sniff under the car, but there were no signs that someone had tampered with the vehicle or any traces of explosive residue.

"Thanks for coming so quickly," Kit said to Angel, who had stayed in the vehicle and was texting Eva to update her.

"No problem," Angel responded. "I asked Eva if she was sure you and Owen could manage on your own, and she was certain." Angel grinned. "But she told me to make sure Matt and Don were ready to come if needed."

"Not exactly a flattering assessment of us," Kit said, stiffening slightly at the implication that Angel thought they couldn't manage the stakeout alone.

"I wouldn't say that," Angel assured her. "We all know you can handle yourself against the bad guys. But sometimes you need a little help, and we'd rather be safe than sorry."

Kit smiled in relief, feeling some of her tension dissipate. She was still trying to prove that she could handle herself in the field. "I know you're right. I was glad to hear you guys were on your way when we sent out the call for help."

"When we got your message about Tirol and his group being close, Matt said that we needed to get to Durrës ourselves," Angel explained.

"You didn't think to tell us that?"

Angel shrugged. "It might not have been a problem, but it could have been. As it was, you did successfully escape, but it might have been otherwise."

"I was concerned about getting out of Durrës without meeting them again. Plus, the guy who bought the briefcase—we don't know his contacts. It's possible they might have called for more support. I appreciate you checking our rental car. It didn't cross my mind that they might have messed with it."

"Those photos you took will help us identify the people involved."

"It was the photos that got us chased," Kit said. "If I hadn't tried to get those, they wouldn't have noticed us."

"Still, they could be useful."

"But now they would recognize us."

"Maybe. It's your auburn hair that makes you so recognizable."

"I should have worn a wig like I did at a Pristina nightclub for that last operation."

Kit's hand went to the ring in her pocket, and she lightly touched it. She had considered saying something to Angel about it, but then changed her mind. While she enjoyed sharing confidences, she was getting used to keeping secrets. Sergei's messages triggered a fresh wave of adrenaline when she thought of them. Kit was now faced with some important decisions in the coming days. She hadn't told Angel about Owen's kiss as she had agreed with him what happens in the field stays in the field, making the situation even more complicated. While Kit hadn't found Owen attractive before, they had been working out together at the gym, and maybe he'd developed feelings for her. The kiss could have been a way to hide their presence at the stakeout, but the way she responded had taken her by surprise. The combination of thrill and peril had taken them somewhere unforeseen.

Maybe she could discuss it with her psychotherapist. Maria might see this as a sign that Kit was progressing into a more independent person rather than fulfilling everyone else's wishes. She considered switching the Egyptian ring for the Irish Claddagh ring that she wore to signal her commitment to Xander. The Egyptian ring felt like a mission trophy. She'd managed to get the photos and outrun the pursuers. Quietly, she removed the Irish ring and slipped on the Egyptian one instead.

They travelled back to Pristina together and agreed to meet up at their task force headquarters for a full discussion with Eva present. Only Kit was aware of the ring she had found in the Durrës Archaeological Museum.

Chapter Eight

Pristina, Kosovo

The next day at the office, Kit started the day by checking emails and news bulletins. She still wore the ring with the ankh symbol, a cross with a loop on top, which was the ancient Egyptian symbol known as the key of life. It could mean either a long and prosperous life or a soul's passage into the afterlife. These connections between life and death made Kit think of her upcoming meeting with Maria Montenegro and possibly Sergei. She experienced a mix of anticipation and uncertainty at the thought.

Back at her computer, on impulse Kit did an internet search on Maria Montenegro. She was surprised to find a British women's magazine edition from about a year ago had an article about her. Originally from Slovenia, Maria had been educated in London and had gone on to become something of a celebrity therapist. She and her husband had been spotted at fashionable parties at European capitals. While Maria would neither confirm nor deny clients' identities, several high-profile businessmen and politicians, or their partners, had spoken in glowing terms about Maria's skills as an inspirational life coach. Kit leaned forward to examine a photograph of Maria at a birthday party for Victor Tirol's wife, Sabine Tirol, in Vienna, Austria.

Before she could read more, Kit was startled by a knock on the door. She minimised the internet window on her computer and got up to find Tom Baumgarten standing in the doorway, looking agitated.

"Do you have time to talk now? I have to discuss that matter with the boss in a few minutes," he said.

Reluctantly, since he had disturbed her plans for the morning, Kit grabbed her notebook and pen and followed him out. Angel was on the phone when they arrived at the front office.

"Is Eva here?" Kit asked.

"No, she had to go to court this morning. There was a last minute request to transfer some prisoners."

Kit's stomach sank. She hoped that Raco's plan to get a court to transfer his gang to a medical facility wasn't going ahead. The timing worked.

"Okay, just let Eva know when she gets back that Tom asked me to go with him to a meeting upstairs," she said.

Angel grabbed a pen. "Will do."

Kit and Tom took the stairs up to the senior staff meeting room. "Do you want me to say anything?" Kit asked.

"No need," Tom said. "I just need someone to back me up later if needed."

"Do you expect a fight?"

"It's a possibility."

Tom had his paperwork, and Kit carried a small shoulder bag with her notebook and pen. Her feet dragged, and she felt reluctant to go to the meeting. The topic was a sensitive one, and she felt that senior management was unlikely to be sympathetic to Tom's views. The meeting was to take place in a functional room with glass walls and a long table with chairs around it. A telephone sat in the middle of the table, and at one end of the room was a large video screen for videoconferencing sessions. Tom checked his watch. They were on time, but the senior managers were running late. Finally, about twenty minutes later, the head of the OIDC mission, Jacob Mueller, and Michael Burke, his deputy, showed up with an executive secretary and assistant in tow.

Kit hadn't seen Mueller since she had returned to the office. He nodded to her with a curt smile. He sported a formal three-piece suit from Germany that fit him perfectly. Despite his age, he emanated an understated vigor. But his icy eyes lacked empathy. "Welcome back, Ms Chase. I take it you had a pleasant vacation."

"Yes, sir. Thank you," Kit answered politely. "I had an amazing time with my family, and now I'm excited to get back to work." He had agreed to extend her contract for a year after her success in the last high-profile criminal case.

In stark contrast to Jacob Mueller, his deputy, Michael Burke, took up more space both physically and in the way he spoke. It was no secret that Burke often enjoyed fast food and was a big fan of fried chicken restaurants. While Mueller was known for his manners, Burke was not known for his diplomacy. He had a penchant for profanity and a reputation for speaking his mind. He liked to wear Western-style neckties, and his large statement belt could barely contain his belly as he sat.

Mueller's executive assistant sat behind them with his pen poised over his notepad, looking earnestly at his boss. Burke's secretary busied herself around the table, bringing water into the room and presenting Burke with a pad and pencil. With teased, big hair, full makeup, and a tight-fitting blouse, she scribbled down a note for her boss before he scrawled a comment on it. She took it away with a sense of urgency that seemed exaggerated.

Mueller signalled to Burke to start the meeting before settling into his chair to observe.

"What is this nonsense?" Burke's voice held a note of indignation.

Tom stiffened and inhaled sharply. "Sir?"

"I thought I warned you that no one likes your office and to watch your step. But you still wrote this paper on something that is none of your business."

Kit quickly glanced at Mueller to gauge his reaction to Burke's critique of the anti-corruption chief. Despite his impassive expression, his eyes darted between the two men, watching them keenly.

"Sir," Tom said, his jaw firmly set. "We went through this during our last meeting, and you were in full agreement with what I had outlined."

"I was not," Burke disagreed. "Not like this anyway." He waved his hand dismissively. "You say officials, civil servants, should not be involved in holding any assets. Come on now. That's ridiculous."

"But Mr. Burke, it's plain to see that this could lead to political manipulation in their decision-making process."

Burke snorted contemptuously. "This is such a pile of crap," Burke mocked him. "These people are all businessmen. They know how to run a business and make sound decisions without any conflict of interest."

Tom was undeterred by Burke's remarks. "I'm sorry, sir, but I can't agree with you. Businessmen should not control publicly owned enterprises," Tom persisted.

Mueller coughed softly as he leaned in closer, his voice low, but the steeliness in it unmistakable. "Tom, I understand your eagerness to do what is right, but sometimes we need to be flexible for the benefit of everyone. Mr Dreshaj is acquiring a majority stake in the power station, and we need to support him as this venture would benefit Kosovo greatly."

"You bet," Burke said in agreement with his boss.

Mueller then shifted his focus to Kit. "What do you think, Ms Chase? What's the legal perspective on this topic?"

Kit felt the eyes of everyone in the room as they watched her with an expectant expression. She cleared her throat, trying to ignore the fact that she had not had time to prepare properly before coming to this meeting. "I need to study it more before giving an opinion. I haven't read Tom's paper yet."

Mueller's lip curled into a sneer. Without lifting his gaze from his documents, he spoke in a low voice. "I'm not sure Mr Baumgarten has read it either. You should both go back and get acquainted with the details of this before we discuss it any further."

Kit paused for a moment to process what had just been said, then asked hesitantly, "Sir, did you say that Visar Dreshaj is about to gain a controlling interest in the new power station?"

Mueller nodded and rose from his chair. His aide rushed to keep up as he made his way out of the office. "That's what I said," he called over his shoulder. "Haven't you been keeping up with your local news? They appointed Dreshaj Minister of Energy while you were having your family time."

Tom spoke quickly before Burke could leave. "Sir, can I prepare another issues paper for review in a few days? We should then be able to talk more."

Burke gave a noncommittal shrug at Tom's suggestion and followed after Mueller, mumbling something about needing coffee for the morning.

After the others had gone, Kit turned towards Tom with wide eyes and asked tentatively, "Is he always like this?"

"He's been like this more often lately," Tom said. "You know I mentioned rumors about payments for the new power plant, a multibillion euro project?" Kit nodded, and he continued. "The steering committee for that project is chaired by the Minister of Energy and Mining, soon to be Mr Visar Dreshaj. Burke's also on that committee. The rumours I heard concerned the payment of what we call a 'facilitation fee' in millions to a local partner, should that bidder win the tender. Part of that payoff is rumored to be going to Burke, and maybe others. I also wonder about our head of mission. He seems to be involved in everything."

"It's taking me a while to wrap my head around all of this," Kit said, rubbing her forehead. "You told me there was talk about possible kickbacks but not the details. We would need an investigation to determine whether any fraud has occurred."

"I don't have solid proof, but I think it's possible."

"How much money are we talking about, again?"

"We're talking millions . . . hundreds of millions of euros."

"Both Mueller and Burke seem hostile towards your work," Kit noted. "And there doesn't appear to be any good reason for that."

"I'll include these allegations in my revised paper and we'll see how they respond. If I don't like their responses, I'll complain to the OIDC headquarters in New York and Berlin," Tom said.

"So, do you mean you'll inform the internal investigation department of OIDC?" she asked.

"That's right."

"I need to discuss this with Eva. Burke and Mueller have diplomatic immunity through the organization, but that could be lifted if we find enough evidence of a criminal conspiracy."

"But how can we get the proof?"

"And what do we do with it then? OIDC won't want the embarrassment of charges against senior officials for serious financial crimes. Plus, even if we did prosecute, I have doubts about some of the judges here."

Tom frowned. "What do you mean? Have you heard something about the judges?"

"It's too early to tell." Kit shrugged. "Maybe."

"Keep me in the loop if you find out more. Thanks for coming to the meeting today, Kit. You saw what I'm up against. Mueller seems to like you; that could be useful."

"I don't think he likes anyone," Kit said. "He finds me convenient to have around, for now at least. But the two of them seem to get along very well given their opposing personalities."

"Like two peas in a pod," Tom commented as they slowly made their way down the stairs and went their separate ways.

Kit went back to Eva's office, where Angel signalled that Eva had returned from the court hearing. Angel whispered to Kit as she went Eva's office, "She seems upset."

As Kit entered, she found Eva with her back turned to the door and facing the window, cigarette in hand. As she turned towards Kit, a cloud of smoke filled the air between them.

"Good morning, Eva. How'd it go in court?"

Eva regarded Kit through thin slits of her eyes and motioned towards a chair with a flick of her wrist. "Not good," Eva said in a strained voice. "Guess who Judge Tirol transferred from detention to a medical facility today." She took a deep drag from her cigarette and let out a puff of smoke before continuing. "Come in and I'll explain more."

Kit felt her stomach drop as she realized what had happened. Tirol had accepted the bribe and moved Raco and his gang to the medical center.

"Just as we suspected," Kit said. "Tirol took the payoff?"

"Seems that way," Eva replied.

"Raco's still in captivity in the hospital for now, but for how much longer? I think I need one of these," Kit said, reaching for one of Eva's cigarettes and lighting it up.

CHAPTER NINE

Mitrovica, Kosovo

Mitrovica Hospital was located in the Albanian area of the city, located south of the Ibar River. The Ibar divided Mitrovica into two parts. The northern part was predominantly inhabited by Kosovo Serbs, and the southern part was mainly inhabited by Kosovo Albanians. Tensions frequently flared between them.

The hospital complex was comprised of multiple buildings connected by corridors and a nearby parking lot full of dilapidated cars. A staircase made of crumbling cement rose up to the road paralleling the entrance, where white-clad nurses and attendants were congregating and smoking. Trees circled the perimeter of the hospital, tucked behind a high fence for added security. Supply warehouses were scattered throughout the property. Past them lay the Sitnice River, a tributary of the Ibar, that served as a boundary between the hospital grounds and the massive Trepča mine that spanned Serbia and Kosovo. While the medical center's facilities were basic, they were spotlessly clean due to its popularity as a regional institution; police vans, ambulances, and military vehicles regularly transported sick or wounded people from nearby areas.

On this particular day, five new patients were admitted to the hospital, escorted by several orderlies and uniformed police officers. The head doctor, wearing a lab coat and stethoscope, led the group into the building. The tallest patient was a powerfully built, bald man with a scowl on his face. Behind him was a much younger and shyer-looking man glancing around nervously. The other three men in the group trailed behind them, quietly conversing among themselves. They were taken to the back of the facility and ushered into a large room that contained five slim, metal beds against the wall. Each bed had a thin mattress, some sheets, and a blanket.

The doctor took a position in the center of the room, surrounded by police escorts, orderlies, nurses. He consulted the documents on a clipboard, which contained a description of each man's medical condition and the court order signed by Judge Tirol transferring them from the detention center to the medical facility. Obediently, Dasham Raco nodded when the doctor mentioned his hypertension. The doctor listed off each of the prisoners' ailments from migraines to back pain, anaemia, and bladder infections. "The chief orderly will show you where the hospital's facilities are located and tell you about the meal and treatment program."

"Where is the gym?" asked Raco. As someone whose livelihood was dependent on his physical capabilities, Raco himself was eager to stay in optimum shape. Plus, he had plans that required them all to stay fit.

The doctor nodded. "I'll get the orderlies to escort your group to the gym for physical therapy three times a week. And I should mention that police officers will be watching the ward's exits at all times."

Raco and his group scanned the room with calculating gazes, taking note of every exit. They had to remember where each one was; it was only a matter of time before they needed to make a move.

CHAPTER TEN

Pristina, Kosovo

When Tom Baumgarten arrived at Kit's office, his usually healthy complexion was ashen. His hands shook slightly as he placed the revised report on her desk. She could tell he had been nervous since their conversation about corruption in the new power plant contract.

"We have a problem," he said, gesturing to the document as he placed it on Kit's desk. "I sent Burke my revised report, and he called me into his office this morning."

"What happened?" Kit asked, picking up the report.

"I told him about my suspicions about the new power plant deal. The new Minister of Energy has the power to control who serves on the panel overseeing the contract. That's a conflict of interest if he's involved with the company that will build the power plant. It seems that most of the people on the panel are unqualified; one is even listed on a terrorism watch list. The only person who appears to be impartial and well qualified is the chairman."

"You mean Rustem Kupi?" asked Kit.

Tom nodded. "The same. I told Burke about the rumor I'd heard about a hefty 'facilitation fee' amounting to hundreds of millions of euros going to local partners should a certain bidder win the contract. I'd heard a chunk of that payment could go to Minister Dreshaj and unnamed individuals at OIDC. I added that the World Bank would be hesitant to allow a speedy, negotiated settlement to be given to just one bidder, and it could even pull its funding for the project."

Kit scribbled down some notes on her legal pad. "I guess he wasn't pleased."

"Burke tore into me and shouted orders to his secretary to call his contact at the World Bank. He then said that my office was being downsized. He said the head of mission, Mueller, was incensed at my refusal to cooperate and that he was going to sack me."

"Well, you wanted to find out how he'd react to the claims. Now you know. If anything, this overreaction tends to confirm your suspicious. He might even be involved himself."

"I have an awful feeling about this. Burke said he'd heard from people he trusts that I'd been bad-mouthing him. I denied it."

"Is he concerned about his image?" Kit asked.

"I told him I didn't agree with his lack of backing for my office. Our oversight is essential for the credibility of the organization."

"Then what did he say?"

"That's when he said that my office should be shut down, and I should look for another job. Our confrontation only made matters worse. In the end, I left the meeting."

"What will you do now?"

He shrugged. "I'll try to find another job, but in my area of expertise, nothing happens quickly. But first, I'm writing a report to headquarters about this illegal deal that could go against all integrity rules. Could either you or Eva review it for me?"

"Review what?" said a voice from the entranceway. Eva had arrived, carrying Bambino underneath her left arm and holding a cigarette in her right hand.

"Tom showed Burke his report that outlines his suspicions regarding the kickbacks for the new power station contract," Kit explained. "Burke flew into a rage and threatened to sack Tom and disestablish his office."

Eva grimaced. "That's horrid. Tom isn't the only one in danger here. I also explained to Mueller and Burke my questions regarding a possible investigation into judicial corruption."

Kit gasped. "You spoke of it?" She felt panicky at the mention of their botched stakeout in Durrës.

"I told them that phone taps of criminal suspects showed cause to suspect that a certain judge is happy to accept bribes." Eva glanced at Kit and shook her head. "I didn't supply any further information."

Kit relaxed. Eva hadn't mentioned their unauthorized surveillance of Judge Tirol in Durrës.

"And then what happened?"

"They said that an investigation into the judiciary was out of the question and that we don't have the resources to go on this kind of witch hunt. His term. We should rather focus on prosecuting burglaries and family feuds."

"That's insane," Kit said fiercely. "If the judiciary isn't following the law, no one is."

"Do you think they all could be in this together?" Tom asked.

Eva thought for a moment, skimming through the report from Kit's desk and its conclusions. "It's hard to make a direct link between kickbacks for an energy project and a biased judge," she said. "But I wouldn't rule it out."

"Kosovo can be a lawless place; if there are no consequences for wrongdoing, people end up enriching themselves. We need more proof though," Kit said.

"We can only get solid proof through a full investigation," Eva said.

"Our organization has protections for whistle-blowers," Tom noted. "But do they work in practice?"

Eva frowned. "The rules haven't been fully tested yet, so I can't say with any confidence." Bambino took that moment to wriggle out of Eva's arms and sniff around Kit's shoes with a happy wag of his tail.

"At least someone is in a good mood," Kit laughed, scratching the dog behind his ears. "So, what do we do?"

"I'll draft letters to Berlin and New York requesting their help," Tom said.

"I need to think," Eva said. "Maybe I should also contact Berlin and New York about investigating the judge situation. But they're going to ask why we're not going through the chain of command here. Kit, could you check rules on protecting whistleblowers. Are there any procedures we can use to protect Tom? We might need them ourselves. Did you find anything suspicious in the court cases you reviewed?"

"I didn't have a chance to complete a full review. But many of the organized crime or war crimes cases—anything linked with high-profile political figures—seemed to consistently favour the suspects," Kit answered. "Also judges seem to rule very quickly on property transfers without a full hearing to consider the evidence. But the files with the detailed evidence, like financial statements, have already been shipped for archiving or destroyed, so I can't examine them."

"That's convenient that the files were shipped out early. It going to take time to sort through this tangled web," mused Eva.

Tom was getting more agitated as they spoke. "Listen, I'm uncomfortable about what's happening. I'm going to grab some things and then head to Greece using my leave from the office. I need space to review my situation and prepare those messages to Berlin and New York. The office owes me some days off for all my overtime."

"Sounds like a plan," Kit said. "Thessaloniki isn't too far away."

"It's only a six-hour drive," Eva said.

"I'd better make myself scarce. Let's exchange our personal phone numbers. I might need to call you. Let's keep in touch," Tom said. They exchanged phone numbers, and he exited Kit's room.

Eva requested a copy of the report, and Kit began operating the copying machine outside her office while they talked.

"What should we do now?" Kit asked.

"We need to look for more proof of wrongdoing by the judge. I'll continue reviewing the phone intercepts, and we can ask Matt to increase the amount of monitoring done on Raco's associates and build up a file on Judge Tirol and any other suspicious people. If worse comes to worse and Mueller and Burke still won't take action, we can either appeal to HQ in Berlin or New

York. If things really go bad, I could consider going public, but I'd probably lose my job if it came to that. You should keep reviewing the judge's decisions and try to get those files back from the archives."

Kit handed a copy of Tom's report to Eva and returned to the files on her desk. Only ten minutes later, Kit received a message from Tom telling her to come quickly since security had arrived. She scooped up her bag and phone before sprinting towards his office. She was just in time to see Tom being escorted out by three uniformed OIDC security guards, one on each side and one behind speaking on his mobile radio phone. The two men in front of Tom's office were local security contractors, while the security officer behind them was an international.

"They've declared me *persona non grata*, an undesirable. I've been told to leave the building. They've taken my computer and work phone!" Tom said. He clutched his briefcase tightly in case they decided to snatch that too. He seemed determined to stand his ground.

Kit stepped forward and demanded to know why Tom was being removed. "We have to do as we're told," one of the guards said, shrugging apologetically.

"Senior management ordered us not to share any information about the situation," the other security guard said. Kit followed his gaze up towards the top floor, from where Burke watched them down the stairwell.

The guard presented her with a notice. It showed Tom's photo beside the words "*Persona non grata*" and "Do Not Admit" splashed across it in big letters, by order of the deputy head.

Kit pulled out her mobile phone and snapped a photograph of the notice and Tom being escorted from the compound to show Eva.

"This is serious! It seems like Tom was right! Burke and Mueller really want to get rid of him." Eva lit a cigarette and tried to see what was happening out the window.

"We ought to set up another task force meeting. Maybe Matt will have some ideas," Kit suggested.

"Yes, we should. But we must remember: *Quis custodiet ipsos custodes?*" Eva replied.

"What?" Kit gave her a perplexed look.

"Oh, sorry. Latin again. It means 'Who watches the watchers?' It's an old phrase from a Roman satirist," Eva said. She extinguished her cigarette. "We can't prosecute the top officials in our own organization without approval from elsewhere."

"Are we stuck unless either Berlin or New York get rid of their immunity from prosecution? They might have to put in new senior management."

Eva nodded in agreement. "We need to consider all our options. And time is of the essence. When is the power station contract due to be finalized?"

"Tom's report said that the privatization panel will meet soon to decide it," Kit said.

"We're dealing with millions in kickbacks that need to be laundered out of Kosovo," Eva said as she started sketching on a pad of paper.

"This level of money laundering makes Tirol's kickbacks look like small change," Kit added.

Eva paused and looked up from her doodling on her legal pad. "Not necessarily," she said thoughtfully. "Judge

Tirol's bribe might part of the bigger picture."

"Judge Tirol took the bribe to move Raco and his accomplices to a medical facility," Kit said, still shuddering at the memory of being manhandled by Raco. He was brutal and intimidating. She tried to shake off the fear and continue. "I can't believe Raco and his gang need urgent medical care."

"Of course not. Not all five of them at once. It's probably because they want to make it easier to escape custody. Maybe to commit another crime." Eva tapped her pencil on her notes, her gaze falling on Judge Tirol's name. "Tirol is the presiding international judge in Kosovo. If anyone could waive immunities for OICD officials, it would be him. But we can't rely on his support if he's part of a bigger conspiracy. Especially not now."

Kit groaned with frustration. "It seems like they have everything planned out, and we have no way to stop it."

"We need more evidence before we can make any moves," Eva said. "Mueller and Burke won't help us, so I think Berlin regional headquarters might be the best bet."

"Maybe," Kit said. "But Mueller was a German ambassador once. What if Berlin won't go against one of their own?"

"I hope they will," Eva said firmly. "We need them to take urgent action. New York is too far away care much about what happens here."

Eva drew a rectangle on the notepad representing the privatization panel and circled it, with an arrow going up to JM, Jacob Mueller. "The panel includes twelve people and its chair, Rustem Kupi. Mueller signs off on the Panel's decisions."

"Do you think the Minister of Energy might be involved too?" Kit asked.

"Visar Dreshaj? He helped us solve the Staro Dorbi massacre case," Eva replied.

Kit swallowed hard at the mention of Staro Dorbi, the village where a contract team had taken out a group of Serbian farmers. Sergei had ordered the hit, and against her better judgement, Kit had kept in contact with him. "What about Dreshaj?" Kit asked.

"Maybe he could help us again," Eva said thoughtfully. "Could you contact him for a chat and see what he says? At least hear his side of the story." Kit noted "Visar" down on her notepad.

"He offered to take me to a casino," she said.

"That casino is off-limits for OIDC staff," Eva replied briskly. "It's a high-risk area."

"Right. I didn't mean to go there," Kit said. "Necessarily."

"We don't always pay much attention to the rules," Eva teased with a laugh. "I need a drink," she announced suddenly. Eva seemed to slip out of her role as supervisor and into the role of a co-worker and friend.

"Me too," Kit agreed eagerly. "Do you have something here?" She reached for one of Eva's cigarettes and asked with a grin, "Do you mind?"

"Please, be my guest," Eva replied.

"Thanks." Kit lit the cigarette and looked out the window while Bambino slept in his basket, occasionally whimpering and twitching.

"G&T?" Eva asked as she opened up the high wooden cabinet in her office filled with case files and office supplies. Eva grabbed a bottle of turquoise Bombay Sapphire Gin and two glasses from a round, silver tray, along with a bottle of tonic and ice cubes from a small fridge. She mixed the drinks, offering one to Kit, before they both turned to gaze out the window. The dusk cast shadows in the park below, while occasional sirens of police cars or ambulances broke up the steady hum of rush hour traffic.

"So, are you still glad you came to Kosovo?" Eva asked.

"Yes," Kit replied without hesitation. "It's been . . . perhaps interesting is the best word. Nothing in my life in New Zealand prepared me for being kidnapped or chased by gangsters." She paused.

Eva added, "And maybe working with some of the most corrupt men on the planet?"

Kit raised her glass. "Here's to justice. The kind that can't be bought."

"*Cin cin*," Eva said, raising her glass. "This might get difficult. But I won't stand by and watch a corrupt judge jeopardize everything we've done here."

"Do you reckon it could come back on us?" Kit asked.

"Especially me," Eva replied sadly. "I hope it won't touch you though."

Kit shrugged nonchalantly. "I can go back to Auckland if it does."

"Our reputations could be in tatters."

Kit laughed. "You might have noticed that I don't always play by the book."

Eva joined in with her laughter before the fluorescent lights dimmed and flickered around them before returning to their normal brightness. "That's the emergency generator kicking in. There's a power cut," Eva said.

Kit's phone buzzed. It was Tom.

"I'm at the Macedonian border, on my way to Greece, but the Kosovo Police took my passport and arrested me. Can you help?"

Kit passed the message to Eva.

"They can't do that! We've got to go down there and remind them that Tom is still a staff member with the OIDC. We better call Matt to help us out. They're playing hardball," Eva said.

Chapter Eleven

Mitrovica Hospital, Kosovo

The detainees known as the Podujevo Five, named after the area they hailed from north of Pristina, went through their daily exercise routine. Officers from the international unit on duty accompanied them during the day, with extra personnel at night. These guards became comfortable with their visits to the hospital fitness studio and developed a rapport with the detainees, occasionally sharing a cigarette. The older guard would sometimes doze off in a chair while the younger officers sent texts to family and friends.

Raco spotted for his nephew Enver, who struggled to lift weights, as Raco thought he needed to build more muscle. As for himself, Raco generally preferred his workouts to focus on functional fitness. He did press-ups, then one-handed push-ups and chin-ups on a high bar, while the other three men lifted free weights. Driton chose to ride a stationary cycle so he could read the newspaper. As the guards settled into their own routines, the men talked in Albanian about their plan to escape.

Raco watched Enver's workout and kept an eye on the guards. "I called my friend Berisha and confirmed what we discussed."

He had smuggled in a phone and charger so he could contact his friends outside the hospital and arrange for Berisha to arrange payment of a bribe to Judge Tirol in order to secure their transfer to the medical facility. That had worked brilliantly, and the judge had transferred them to hospital with no problems. But Berisha had later told him that during the handover of cash to the judge, a redheaded woman and a solidly built man, who looked like law enforcement, had observed them. They had given chase, but the two had disappeared in the Durrës Archaeological Museum. Raco guessed it must have been Caitlin Chase and Owen Rees, whom he had encountered before. Both had been involved in his arrest.

Raco cursed under his breath. "I'll kill their mothers!" He was still furious with Kit for escaping from him and wounding Enver. The humiliation of his nephew being bested by a mere woman provided him with additional motivation to train the young man. Although if he were honest, he would have to admit that Enver did not have the temperament for more serious, and therefore more lucrative, crime. Still, he had proven himself to be a reliable getaway driver, which they needed. Once Raco got out, he would see to that redhead bitch and put the Welshman away permanently. And that time was coming nearer, Raco told himself. That they had known enough to tail Judge Tirol was troubling. Perhaps Chief Prosecutor Refazo had been listening in on their telephone conversations and put two and two together. That Italian witch was also on his hit list.

Raco had to take the weights from his nephew's hands when Enver's strength faltered. Subsequently, he picked up two heavy dumbbells himself and began to work them vigorously. Raco's body ached with the pleasure of pushing himself past the limits of pain. He was a man who could always depend on his physical capabilities.

He mulled over their current situation in his head. The judge had followed through on his promise to move them to the medical facility, and he had heard that a big deal was going through regarding the sale of a big power station. Perhaps the current Minister of Energy, Visar Dreshaj, a client for whom he had supplied trafficked weapons, needed his help, or one of the other crime bosses he contracted for. Raco and his group were available for hire. It didn't matter which side of the Ibar River their clients were on, whether Albanian or Serbian, or in the case of the last hit on Staro Dorbi village, Russian. He had heard that the lucky bastard Sergei Sokolov had escaped Kosovo without being charged, thanks to his status as a Russian diplomat. Either way, Raco would be out soon and have more options. He could lay low outside until Judge Tirol took another bribe and dismissed all charges against them.

"We'll take a break from training tomorrow to prepare for what we have to do tomorrow night. I got ahold of some people who can help us. Just be ready."

That evening, Raco and the men lounged in the room as the guards watched over them. Two of officers chatted about family news while a third worked on a crossword puzzle. A nurse and a doctor arrived to check on the patients before bed. The nurse, a woman in her thirties with light-colored hair, carried a tray of hot beverages and medicine. She went from man to man, taking blood pressure and pulse readings, checking their eyes, and asking about their general well-being. When the nurse and doctor were checking the men on the other side of the room, Raco snatched two teacups and tablets from the tray and put them under the nightstand with a small towel covering them. By the time they got to him, he was sitting on his bed with his sleeve rolled up, ready for his examination.

"How do you feel today, Mr. Raco?" asked the doctor.

"I still can't sleep; my war injury bothers my leg."

"I'm prescribing sleeping tablets and anti-inflammatories: take two of each tonight and we'll see how you feel tomorrow," the doctor, a young man with dark hair swept to one side wearing thick glasses, said. "Do you feel better after coming to hospital?"

"I feel the same," grunted Raco. The nurse made a few notes on a clipboard when the doctor turned away. She exchanged a knowing glance with Raco before they left the room. She drew the curtains closed as if to block out the light, and when her hands were hidden behind the fabric, she used a key from her pocket to unlock the door.

Raco took out the two untouched cups of sweet tea and added sleeping pills to both cups. He gave them to Enver, who offered them to the duty guards. "Chai? Would you like tea?" he said with his friendliest smile.

The guards looked at each other and shrugged. "Why not?" one of them said, accepting the drink. The other followed his example, and after about ten minutes, they began to feel drowsy. One guard settled down on a bed in an adjoining room while the other reclined on a nearby chair and sighed with relaxation. Suddenly, their supervising officer appeared in the entrance of the room.

"What's going on here?" he asked, holding his radio telephone in hand.

"Nothing," Enver replied. "We are expecting a guest. I know it's late, but she's very friendly. I think you may enjoy her company. She should be here soon."

"Visiting hours are over," the guard said. The other men said nothing but watched carefully.

"Yes, yes," Enver responded with a nervous smile. "We'll tell her that when she arrives." He glanced up to see two figures approaching down the hall. "Here she is now."

The two figures entered the room. The blonde nurse stepped in first, followed by a young woman with an olive complexion. Her long, dark hair cascaded down her back, and she wore golden hoop earrings. A shawl adorned with embroidered flowers draped around her shoulders, and she wore black stockings with ankle boots under her miniskirt. Her face was meticulously made-up. The nurse nodded to Raco, acknowledging that her work was done, before leaving them together in the room.

"Hi, Tina," Enver said hesitantly. "Here's the man I told you about. He needs someone to talk to."

Tina smiled confidently, her hand resting on her hip. "How are you doing this evening, sir?" she asked in a friendly tone. He put down his radio and glanced at her with a curious expression. She moved closer, and the smell of roses filled the space around them. "How long have you been in Kosovo?"

"Er . . . three months," he stammered.

"You look very important with that badge! I hope you're not lonely here."

Raco motioned for his comrades to take up their own tasks in order to not add any pressure on the senior office that might make him feel uncomfortable. Tina was fully aware of how to handle this dilemma, and as time passed, the guards seemed less suspicious of her being there. Before long, snores could be heard from the next room; the sedated guard sprawling out on the armchair within seemed oblivious to what was taking place.

"Bring them to the other room as we discussed," Raco said in a low voice in Albanian to Enver. Enver seemed better-suited for this job since his appearance was less intimidating than Raco's. He nodded and went back to the couple. Tina held tightly onto the officer's arm, her khol-rimmed eyes glittering under dark lashes.

"You two might like some privacy for a chat. Allow me to show you somewhere nearby," Enver said, pointing towards a hallway lined with empty rooms at the end of which lay a sleeping guard.

"That'll be fine," the officer replied. Tina directed him into one of them and closed the door behind them.

When Enver returned, Raco was trying to open the exit door leading to the fire escape behind the curtains. His associate, Berisha's contact, the nurse, had accepted cash in order to facilitate their escape. The fire exit creaked opened.

"Let's go," Raco said to the men. His orders were met with a flurry of activity as the men scrambled to gather their belongings. With a heavy hand, he shoved the exit further open and held back the curtain as they made their way out into the darkness.

Enver hesitated for a moment at the top of the fire escape, peering out into the darkness. No moonlight pierced the cloudy skies, and only a damp wind moved the trees at the back of the hospital.

"Are you sure about this, Uncle?" he asked.

"Just move it," Raco commanded him sternly. "Wait for me at the bottom."

The rest of the group descended the fire escape while Raco stayed to double-check the room. The security guard was asleep, snoring softly in his chair. The other guards were safely out of sight. Taking out his cell phone, Raco punched in a numerical code to signal his contact that they were good to go. With a satisfied smirk, he said, "*Naten e mire*, good night," to the unconscious guard and slowly shut the door behind him as he followed the others onto the fire escape.

He descended the metal stairs of the fire escape and spotted the four figures of his crew waiting at the bottom. In a hoarse whisper, he commanded them to follow him and to remain silent. After inspecting the hospital grounds for several days, Raco was familiar with the thick line of trees and fence along the back. He jumped over the fence and motioned for everyone else to do the same. Although Enver was lagging behind, Raco thought to himself how much worse it would have been if he hadn't spent the last days preparing his nephew for this mission in the gym.

He was still seething that Enver had let the red-haired woman lawyer escape, which had led to their arrest. But Enver had got himself seriously injured with stab wounds from her, so he supposed the boy had had his punishment. He shook his head to clear it. He couldn't afford to be distracted by thoughts of Caitlin Chase. Not yet, anyway.

Raco jogged along a dirt track that ran behind the hospital, close to the Sitnice River. He had to slow down occasionally when one of his associates tripped in the darkness.

"We need to get away from here before someone sounds the alarm," Raco warned in a growl.

"Yeah, but how can you even see where we're going?" one man asked.

"Shut it, Razor," another man spoke up. "Move your ass already."

"I'll move your ass when we get out of here," Razor muttered. Raco gave a low hiss for quietness, and the men obeyed. They continued in silence except for the occasion sound of someone missing their footing in the dark. They had made a smooth getaway, but they had to move quickly. As they neared the end of the hospital buildings, Raco saw a light on in the switchboard room that hadn't been there before; perhaps the third guard had woken up and was calling for assistance. Tina's distraction hadn't lasted as long as Raco had hoped. It was best that they kept going; he had no idea how fast reinforcements would arrive.

Soon enough they passed more buildings and arrived at a road intersection where a van waited with its lights off. Raco knocked on the driver's window, and it rolled down, revealing a woman with short, dark hair and delicate features.

"Ciao, Merita," Raco said softly. "Thanks for coming."

"Just like old times," she remarked.

One of the men approached the van window. "I thought you were in Munich," he said. "And married." It was Razor, her erstwhile lover and the subject of her incriminating private diary that fell into the hands of the police in the course of their investigation into the Staro Dorbi killings.

"I was married. For a while," she said. "But it meant nothing to me. I just had to get a German passport. I came back through Serbia to attend a wedding," Merita said. "And help you lot out."

"Enough of the catch-up, you two," Raco interjected. "We gotta get out of here before someone finds us. You think your brother's farmhouse is still available?"

Merita nodded. "Plenty of food, too, and there's an old car without plates that you can use."

Raco grunted his appreciation as they all piled into the van. Before Merita could shut the back door behind the men, Razor grasped her arms and kissed her hard on the lips. "I missed you," he murmured against her face.

Raco scowled. "If you two can't keep it together for five minutes, we're all going right back in prison!"

Merita tucked her dark hair back behind her ear, and with a quick glance at Razor, she slammed the back door. She got into the driver's seat, started the engine, and headed back onto the main road with the van's lights off. A few moments later, Merita's phone vibrated with a message from Tina, the sex worker they had left behind to keep the senior guard distracted while the men made their escape. Finally, the officer had realized they had escaped about fifteen minutes prior and reported it to HQ.

Raco sighed in resignation. "It won't be long before we see flashing lights," he said.

"Maybe not. It's funny," she mused. "Apparently the officer called HQ several times, but there wasn't anyone to take his message."

Raco chuckled. "Classic incompetence. I love the way they make my job easier."

Chapter Twelve

Pristina, Kosovo

Kit sprawled out on the couch of her Pristina apartment, which overlooked a tree-lined avenue. Fehmi Agani Street was renowned for its nightlife. Cafes, bars, restaurants, and music emerged from the streets, which glistened from recent rain. The chilly autumn air caused her to get up and close the double-glazed windows.

After reaching for a mug of aromatic herbal tea, she settled by the coffee table in her pajamas with a bowl of nuts at hand. As expected, she heard an incoming video call ring and accepted it on her laptop. The image of her mother, Rosalyn Chase, materialized on the screen, her hair still beach-blonde from their recent cruise around the Croatian coast.

"Hi, Mum. How's it going?" Kit asked cheerfully.

"All's well here. What about you?"

"Also good. I wish we were still together on the yacht. I've been back at work for over a week now."

"Any interesting cases? Oh, I forgot you're not allowed to say, are you?"

"Well, plenty going on as usual..," Kit replied before taking a sip of her tea. "How was your trip back? And how's Vasha getting on?"

"The journey back was okay. Although at my age I should travel business class. The airline spaces are so much smaller these days."

"I noticed the same thing," Kit replied with a smile.

"Actually, Vasha, or I should say rather Susanna, is settling in very well, and her cousin too."

Vasha was the confidential informant providing evidence against Raco for organized crime and sexual assault. For her safety, she went into witness protection with her cousin, and they both moved to New Zealand with the help of the EUFOR military police. She had changed her name from Vasha to Susanna.

"So, what's the news?" Kit queried.

"They both have jobs. Susanna is a receptionist, and her cousin is working at a supermarket on the checkout. It helps them make some money and learn English. They're staying with me in my B&B room. It's got twin beds and a kitchenette, so they're quite comfortable."

"That's great, Mum," Kit said, feeling a sense of relief wash over her. She had been concerned about how the two women would adjust to life in New Zealand.

"They're doing my housekeeping in exchange for their rent. It's a win-win, really." Rosalyn shifted in her seat and smiled. "So when will Susanna be due to testify?"

"I don't know," Kit replied. "I heard that Raco and his gang were transferred to a medical facility."

Rosalyn frowned. "He doesn't sound like the kind of person who needs medical attention very often," she commented. "Maybe somewhere with better security would be more suitable."

"I agree," Kit responded. She chose not to mention her worries that Raco could take advantage of the lack of security at the hospital and attempt an escape. She hadn't shared with her mother the full gravity of the danger she'd been in and how Raco had kidnapped her.

"I am sure Susanna will love living in New Zealand," Kit said. "We could help her apply for residency there."

"Our friend Charles is helping with some visa submissions, helping with background checks and managing the paperwork," Rosalyn said. "Susanna is so thankful to you and to your team for arresting that criminal and putting him on trial."

"That's wonderful," Kit said, but underneath her words she felt a twinge of doubt. While it was true they had apprehended Raco, the news that a corrupt judge was handling his case left a bitter taste in her mouth. She pushed aside her concerns for the moment and asked, "Anything else?"

Rosalyn took a deep breath before speaking, her hand reaching for a piece of paper that lay on the table in front of her. She paused for a moment longer, gathering her thoughts before beginning to read from the letter in her hand. "I received this when I returned home from vacation. It's from your father, Kit. He wants to meet us."

Kit's heart jolted as she heard the words. She had grown accustomed to startling headlines from her work as a prosecutor, but this was something that had never crossed her mind. They hadn't heard from her father in twenty years and had long ago given up hope of ever seeing him again. After the bitter divorce and acrimonious custody hearing, he had gone to Australia to work as a defense contractor, leaving them behind without a word.

"When I received the surprising letter from Vernon after so many years, my initial urge was to rip it up. After I calmed down, I asked Charles to investigate where he's been and what he wants. Charles believes we should be cautious. The letter says: 'Dear Rosalyn, I apologize for not being in contact with you before now. I often think of you and the children. I regret my past behavior. I would like for us to meet if you are open to it.' He gives a post office box address in Canberra, Australia, and signed off 'Respectfully, Vernon.'"

"Oh my God!" exclaimed Kit, her mind racing with a mixture of emotions. She couldn't believe her father would have the nerve to try and return to their lives after all this time.

"Vernon has no clue that your sister died of a rare form of bone marrow cancer," Rosalyn added, her voice heavy with sadness. "He just wasn't there when we needed him."

"Listen, could you please scan a copy of his message and both sides of the envelope so I can search for any further clues? How do you know it's really from him?" Kit asked.

"It's his handwriting and signature. That much I know. But I don't know where he got my address from. I have an unlisted number. The B&B room is advertised publicly, but my name isn't on the internet page."

"Don't meet him until we find out more about the situation," Kit said, her mind already starting to work through the various angles and possibilities.

"Don't worry, I won't."

"He has a lot of nerve trying to get back into our lives after all this time," Kit said. "I hope he's not after money."

"I'm afraid I spent all my funds on the trip to Croatia!" Rosalyn chuckled.

"This is a job for a psychiatrist!" Kit blurted out then winced, hoping her mother hadn't heard the slip. She knew Dr Montenegro would ask her to spend many sessions going over her emotions regarding her father and her dread of being abandoned.

"The man definitely needs therapy," Rosalyn said. "I'm not doing anything until Charles comes back with his report. We can keep him busy with private investigations."

"Are we paying Charles?" Kit asked.

"I had to cover some of his charges, even though he's a friend of the family," Rosalyn answered. "His fees may increase if he begins investigating what your father has been up to for the past two decades! It could be anything."

Kit checked her watch as she stood from the couch, her mother's image still frozen on the screen. "Xander should be calling soon. I should go," she said, trying to shake off thoughts of the past and focus on the present.

"Of course," Rosalyn said. "I haven't seen much of Xander since we returned from Croatia. He used to come by for coffee at least once a week, but that hasn't happened in a while now."

Kit nodded, frowning. "He hasn't been in contact with me recently either. Maybe his accounting firm is undergoing a big audit or something. How did you think he seemed during vacation?"

"He seemed to enjoy it. You can't blame him, the scenery was gorgeous as was the weather," Rosalyn said, a hint of hesitation in her voice. "But he was disappointed you weren't coming back with us. He made some comment about how you weren't sharing your plans lately."

"That's not true," Kit said, a twinge of guilt pulsing through her. Xander didn't have any idea of her true situation in Kosovo, and she couldn't shake off the thoughts of Sergei and Owen that kept seeping unbidden into her mind. She had wondered, more than once, if it came down to a choice between Xander and Sergei, which of them she would choose. And then there was Owen, with his unexpected kiss during the Durrës stakeout. She tried to push the thought aside, knowing that Owen wasn't her type.

"Don't you think?" Her mother's voice pulled her back into the present.

"Oh, sorry. Got distracted thinking about Xander," Kit admitted.

"I was just telling you that all will become clear with time," Rosalyn said, her tone of voice understanding.

"Mum, definitely. Look, I need to go now. Glad you're doing alright. Can't believe Dad made contact after twenty years of no news. Please send me a copy of the letter, and let me know what Charles finds out about him." Kits thoughts were already shifting to her estranged father and the revelation of his attempted contact.

"Charles has ties to Australia through his private investigation business, so we'll see what he discovers."

"Thank you, Mum. Keep safe. Love you." Kit blew two kisses towards the screen, then turned it off.

She settled back on the couch, her thoughts taking her places she hadn't visited in years; her father's memory had only come up recently in therapy sessions with Dr Montenegro. The doctor believed Kit was attracted to men similar to her father, and that since she expected rejection, she made herself emotionally unavailable. Her gaze shifted to the computer, and she noticed Xander's status was inactive. She quickly typed out a message, "Waiting for your call." But the expected call never came.

With a sigh, Kit stepped into the kitchen and downed two sleeping pills with some water. She was going to need help to drift off, even if just for a couple of weeks. As she lay in bed, thoughts of Xander, Sergei, and Owen swirled in her mind, interspersed with vague memories of her father from childhood. They left her feeling uncertain of her feelings and her future.

CHAPTER THIRTEEN

As the off-the-books task force gathered around the conference table in Matt's penthouse, the tension in the room was palpable. Everyone was focused on the task at hand—discussing the investigation into suspected corruption of senior OIDC and judicial officials.

"*Buon giorno,*" Eva greeted the group. Angel had set out coffee and pastries in the center of the table, but no one was hungry.

"We are here to discuss Operation Icarus," Eva said. Everyone waited with anticipation. Kit picked up Bambino from beside Eva and placed the dog in her lap. "Kit, you know some of this already, but not all. I told you at our last meeting that our colleague at work had suspicions about some senior OIDC officials and kickback schemes from the sale of a power plant."

"I went back to Tom's office later to check on him," Kit added. "But it was blocked off like a crime scene with yellow tape. He had already been removed from the building."

"Tom seems like such a nice guy," Angel murmured. "There's no way he would undermine the mission without cause."

But the situation was more dire than they had initially thought. "Things got worse for him," Eva continued. "He was on his way to Greece for rest and recuperation when the police arrested him and took his passport. We got a phone call from him at the border, and I had to argue for his release."

"Why did they do that? You'd think they would want him gone," Owen asked.

"His theory is that they just wanted to make sure he knew they could take him whenever they wanted. Later on, when he returned to his apartment in Pristina, he found that it had been broken into and searched."

Matt queried, "So where is he now?"

"He's laying low in a safe house. I've contacted a lawyer who specializes in international law to help him get his passport back with the help of the US embassy," Eva explained.

Owen responded indignantly, "It's outrageous! Management wants to silence him!"

"I agree," Eva said. "He's already filed a complaint with the regional headquarters in Berlin and the global headquarters in New York, but there's been no response."

"What will he do next?" Matt asked.

"I advised him to leave Kosovo as soon as possible, once we get his passport back," Eva answered. "He might be able to fly out on a US military aircraft, which would make it difficult for anyone to stop him leaving."

"Tom gave us some documents which could be used as evidence in a prosecution case. Angel has been scanning them over the past few days," Kit said. "We're going to store electronic copies of all his reports and files in a standalone, encrypted, password protected database, so it can't be accessed via the internet. We have a backup in a safe place."

"If you need help with that, let me know," Matt offered. "I've got a secure safe in this apartment."

"Thanks, Matt. I think it would be best to move the hard drive out of the OIDC office. May be this would be a good place to bring it," Eva said. She turned to Angel. "Can you arrange for that as soon as possible?"

Angel gave a curt nod and jotted something down.

"I'm worried about the funds for the power plant contract," Kit said. "The deal is going before the privatization panel soon. It could be worth up to five hundred or six hundred million euros. Once that's through, it's going to be hard to get hold of the funds. I don't know how they're going to transfer it out of Kosovo."

"We've dealt with money laundering cases before, but not one on this scale," Eva said, frowning. "I know how some smaller amounts were sent out, but without solid proof, we wouldn't stand a chance at getting an intercept warrant or seizure order from court."

Don whistled and leaned forward. "It's bad," he said. "Maybe I can get help from the US mission?"

"It might work, but I'm not sure," Eva mused. "Tom's lawyer has asked the US for a new passport but he hasn't received one yet. Mueller's German and Burke's American. Neither country may want to admit to one of their senior officials being involved."

Matt cleared his throat and sat back in his chair. "Let's review all the facts and come up with some ideas," he suggested.

Eva nodded her agreement, her eyes squinting in thought. "I asked Kit to contact the new Minister of Energy, Visar Dreshaj," she said slowly. "It's a long shot, but he helped us once before. If we don't threaten his interests directly, he might share something useful with us. Assuming he isn't benefiting himself."

Kit inclined her head in agreement. "As long as we protect him. Maybe he could qualify for immunity in exchange for giving evidence, if it comes to that."

"I have more news." Eva's voice was deadly serious. "The Podujevo Five, including Dasham Raco, have managed to break out of custody. They were transferred from a detention centre to a medical centre with less security, and they got clean away."

The table erupted in anger and disbelief at this news. The group had been counting on law enforcement to bring the gang to justice.

"This is related to those phone calls we intercepted," Matt said with conviction, his eyes burning with intensity. "And that bribe paid to Judge Tirol!"

"You're right on the money," confirmed Eva. "Judge Tirol ordered the gang be transferred to a medical facility for treatment. It seemed shady even then, like it was all part of a plan to help them escape more easily."

"I haven't seen anything about this in the news," Owen interjected while scrolling through online articles.

"It hasn't gone public yet as it doesn't look good for our organizations," Eva replied. "Not only were the guards drugged, but there was also a prostitute involved in their scheme. And get this: they managed to leave the door unlocked."

Don groaned audibly at these revelations.

"And it gets worse." Eva delivered the final blow. "There was no one manning the switchboard to take calls when the escape was reported; then, a team went out searching for them, but they found nothing."

Matt slammed his fist down onto the table with a furious curse, while Owen tensed up and gripped the edge of the table until his knuckles turned white.

"Bloody hell," Matt exclaimed before turning to Owen with an expression of determination. "We'd better get out there and look around."

Owen agreed, and they both stood up at once, ready for action.

"They saw a van driving away from the hospital at around that time, but there was no number plate or way to identify it," Eva continued. "This looks really bad for both OIDC and EUFOR."

"That's an understatement," Owen muttered under his breath.

"After all we've been through to get those arrests, now we're back to square one," Kit said, her shoulders sagging. Her mother had been so relieved to learn they'd arrested Raco, and Vasha was ready to testify against him. Bambino whimpered and nuzzled her in an attempt to console her, but she kept her face away from the dog and put him down on the floor.

"It all leads back to Judge Tirol," Eva said, her words clipped. "If he hadn't allowed them to be transferred to the hospital, they would still be in detention. I found some more conversations on phone intercepts that confirm my suspicions about him obstructing justice and taking bribes."

Eva lit a cigarette and held it shakily with trembling fingers as the others waited for her to continue. Inhaling sharply, she went on. "I talked about it with management yesterday; they were dismissive and told me to focus on other crimes in Kosovo. But I can't just stay idle while the entire fabric of justice unravels."

"From what happened to Tom, it's clear that rule of law is not their priority," Matt said.

"Finally, after I argued with them, they agreed to a short three-day investigation into the judge. I pulled immigration records that show who left and entered Kosovo over the time concerned. I looked into phone records, credit/debit cards, and car registration plates but none of them yielded any proof that Tirol was in Albania at all this year, let alone that he accepted a bribe there."

"But we did observe him in Durrës. We even took photos, so we know he was there," Owen argued.

"Unfortunately, since the surveillance was not authorized, any evidence we gathered won't be admissible in court," Kit said.

"And since Tirol is the senior judge in Pristina, I don't think we'll get a sympathetic hearing," Eva added.

"What can we possibly accomplish in three days?" Owen questioned.

"It appears that someone has been meticulous in erasing any incriminating evidence. This is why I have decided to go public with my story. I have a meeting scheduled with a journalist from the *Pristina Daily Times* this afternoon," Eva announced.

"You can't do that. It could endanger your position!" Kit exclaimed in alarm.

"I will have done it before anyone can stop me. And there might be more interviews next week. I know that I'll probably be suspended at best. I must make sure that my replacement can be trusted. Kit, you are the only person I can rely on. I'll give you a detailed handover note and Angel will help with the files. You will do just fine.

"Me?" Kit's voice was shaky. "I'm new here; I don't

know what to do as chief prosecutor. I've never appeared in court here, for example."

"You'll get detailed instructions," Eva said reassuringly. "Everyone else in the office will help you out. You'll be okay."

"When are you doing this interview?" Matt asked.

"In two hours," she replied.

"Alright," Matt said. "Let's decide what to do. Owen and I still have to go to Mitrovica to try to trace Raco. Don, you can stay close to Eva and guard her during and after the interview. Angel, maybe you could go with him. The situation's volatile, and we don't know who else we can trust at the moment. We have to cover for each other. Kit, are you able to move in with someone you know? You shouldn't be alone with the Podujevo Five at large."

"There's no need for a bodyguard," Kit said.

"I'm overruling you this time," Matt said firmly. "Raco has already targeted you. Who knows when he'll come back? Eva, surely you'll agree with me on this one." With his tone of authority, Matt made it clear there was no room for disagreement or discussion.

"She can stay at my place if she wants to," Owen suggested. "My apartment has two bedrooms. I could drive her to and from work until this situation is over. I'm sure we'll capture Raco and his gang soon."

Matt looked at Kit. "Will that work for you?"

Kit gave a small shrug in response, acquiescing to the suggestion before she recalled the day they had shared at Durrës eating ice cream and exchanging a passionate kiss. Her life had just gotten a lot more complex. She wondered if Mueller would approve of her taking charge as the chief prosecutor for the case. That made her feel just as nervous.

Matt nodded in agreement. "That's settled then," he said. "You will stay in Owen's apartment until this business is sorted out and Raco and his gang are off the streets. Eva, are you still certain about speaking to the reporters?"

" Yes," she answered, stubbing out her cigarette. "My choice is final."

***

That night, Owen drove Kit home in a military jeep, where she gathered together a few personal items and threw them into a suitcase.

"Do you have coffee at your place?" Kit asked.

"No, only Welsh breakfast tea," he said. Seeing the look of dismay on her face, he added, "Are you joking? Of course I have coffee. I even have one of those Italian coffee makers."

"That's a relief." Kit laughed. "I'm going to bring some snacks just to be on the safe side," she said and began searching through her cupboards for chocolate and nuts.

"You don't need to worry about that," Owen said. "I was a chef before I joined the police. Not many people know that I used to run a bistro in Cardiff. It had quite a good reputation."

Turning around to face him, she looked at him with a newfound enthusiasm. "Oh yeah? Impressive! What kind of restaurant was it?"

"Nothing fancy, but we had an excellent reputation among the locals," he said.

Kit stood with her hands on her hips, grinning at Owen for a minute before returning to her cupboards. "I think I'll still bring my nuts and chocolate just in case," she said with a smile. "How do you get the ingredients you need in Kosovo?"

"They've got everything you need, plus you can get really fresh produce at the farmer's market, and sometimes I go to Skopje for frozen meat from the supermarkets. It's been better since the conflict ended."

She grabbed her snacks and stuffed them into her bag before suggesting jokingly, "Looks like we got something in common. You like to cook, and I like to eat! Maybe this won't be so bad after all!"

Owen chuckled nervously and replied, "Sorry if I jumped in too quickly with the offer to stay at my place. I know you usually prefer to be independent."

Kit shook her head and smiled reassuringly. "No worries. I'm grateful for your offer. I learned my lesson last time when Raco kidnapped me, but let's not dwell on that. I know I should have told you about Merita Shala, the woman who broke into my apartment, but I didn't want to make a big deal of it."

"What do you mean?"

"I didn't want people making a big fuss about it. One night I got home and found that she'd broken into my apartment. But that's water under the bridge. I'll tell you about it some other time."

"I remember something about how we lost one translation of the diary."

"She came to get the translation of her diary and left me with bruises."

He looked at her with concern, but finally said, "I think I heard Shala had left Kosovo and gone to Germany. Let's discuss it over a glass of good Merlot tonight. If the experience helped you to be more cautious, then it can't be altogether a bad thing."

Kit grabbed some clothes and her laptop and threw a bottle of sleeping pills into her cosmetics bag. She was keeping that one a secret for now.

"So, what do you like to do in the evening?" Owen asked once they got into the jeep. "Do you want to go to the gym?"

"Usually I like to chill," Kit said. "I may have a video call to the folks at home and watch some television unless there's extra work to do. Sometimes I bring work home from the office, but as often as not, I don't do it."

"Same," he said with a grin. "I'm sure everything will be alright. I have enough lamb cawl soup in the fridge for both of us. I can pick up some bread from the bakery near my apartment when I get home."

Kit relaxed a little in the passenger seat of his jeep. She couldn't remember the last time someone else had cooked her a homemade meal; usually, she and Xander were too busy to slow down and sit down to eat a meal made from scratch.

When they arrived at Owen's apartment, he set the table for two and started prepping dinner. "The soup will be even better having been left in the fridge overnight," he said as she checked out the photos he had displayed in his living room.

"Is that your old rugby team?" she asked, pointing to an image on the wall.

"Yep, that's my old university rugby team," he replied from the kitchen. "I still keep in touch with them. But I just play socially for a local Pristina team these days."

Kit moved on to the family photos and asked if it was his parents. He looked back at her from the kitchen. "Yes, but don't look at the other photos. They're all out of date."

In one image she saw him with a blond-haired woman on a deserted beach; he had previously mentioned having a girlfriend, and she chose not to comment. Was the photo out of date? Did it mean the relationship was over too? If so, why was her photo still on display? Not that it mattered—he wasn't her type and she was already engaged, kind of.

The apartment was part of a house split into four two-bedroom dwellings. Clean, modern, and functional, it was nonetheless a bachelor pad with minimal décor. Furniture was limited to a couch, TV, table, and chairs.

"Sorry for looking at your private photos," she said.

"No trouble at all. Make yourself comfortable. Dinner is served. It's basic Welsh-Kosovo fare," Owen replied.

Kit savored the flavors of the dinner before her. Owen provided a tasty lamb and vegetable stew called cawl, which was served with local flatbread and specially sourced red wine from EUFOR's duty-free shop. He generously ground black pepper onto the meal and added a slice of aged cheese for an extra kick of flavor. For dessert, there was an aromatic apple crumble accompanied by a local yoghurt.

"This is delicious! Much better than what I usually eat—beans on toast or cheese with fruit," Kit enthused as she dabbed her mouth with the napkin.

"Let's try some Macedonian grilled chicken tomorrow—the former Yugoslav Republic of Macedonia that is!" He was referring to the country bordering Kosovo to the south. Greece objected to the use of the name Macedonia as they had a province by the same name. They had agreed to tolerate a somewhat more lengthy version of the name that both could tolerate.

"They've been debating that name forever!" Kit noted, shaking her head. "It's hard to understand as an outside observer, but there is a lot of regional feuding here."

Just then, a sound came from the hall. Owen glanced at his watch and startled. "I forgot someone was supposed to bring something to me. Would you excuse me for a minute?"

Owen got up from the table, walked down the hallway, and opened the door. Kit heard a woman's voice and Owen replying, "Thanks for bringing this. I'm in the middle of something right now, but let's catch up later this week."

Kit got up and peeked around the corner to see a young, blonde woman handing Owen a package. She didn't recognize the woman, but she seemed to be an international because of her accent. Owen closed the door and turned back, while Kit returned to her seat at the table. Owen gave a brief explanation: "That was just a friend dropping something off for me. She had picked up some craft beer on duty-free coming back from Greece the other day."

"Great," Kit responded before they settled on the couch. She sipped her wine while Owen cracked open a beer as they watched some Welsh TV show that Owen had downloaded off the internet. She savored every bite of her homemade apple crumble, feeling comforted by its familiarity—it reminded her of home in New Zealand. Just as she started to forget about the woman at the door, her phone buzzed with a message from Xander.

"Sorry I wasn't able to make our Skype call the other night. Can I call now?" Xander texted.

It wasn't the right time to mention that she was staying with Owen for her safety; it wouldn't sound good to her fiancé if she said she was sleeping over with an male colleague and eating home-cooked food with him. So she sent a message back.

"I have to work late tonight. Let's try again later in the week." That was true, she told herself. She was at Owen's because of a work-related matter. Owen was looking at her. If Xander called when he had said he would, this wouldn't have happened, so it was his fault.

"Ah, it's just a message from my mum. We'll have to chat later," Kit said. She thought it would be a good idea to arrange an appointment with Dr Montenegro soon; she had some issues to talk about, such as her new habit of covering up what she was really doing. She sat back down on the couch and reached for a second helping of dessert from the coffee table. Just then, her phone vibrated once again. This time it was from an unknown number. The most likely caller was Sergei, although Silver was also a possibility. Her stomach turned into a knot and she put the treat back on the table. Of all three men, Sergei was the one she felt most affected by.

She quickly read his text. "Your ticket's all booked for the weekend. You just need to go see Vista Travel agents and collect it. Need help with a hotel?"

Without looking up she texted back: "Nope, I can handle it myself."

"Your mother again?" Owen asked.

"Nothing major," Kit remarked, stuffing her phone back into her pocket. After a moment of thought, she said, "I'll stay in your guest room tonight, but afterwards I'm headed back to my own place. I don't want to be a problem." She was still feeling uneasy about the woman who had showed up earlier—clearly part of Owen's social circle. She also felt uncomfortable having to explain every new text she received to Owen. Kit was grateful for Matt's concerns for her safety, but she couldn't always live in fear of Raco. Despite this, she had genuinely enjoyed Owen's hospitality.

"It's no imposition. Really," Owen responded. "I was hoping…" He trailed off uncertainly.

Kit got out her mobile phone again and started browsing email. She didn't understand why she felt this tension with Owen. He was just a stocky, rugby-playing policeman from Cardiff, even if he made a delicious apple crumble.

"What was that you said?" she asked.

"I said you can stay longer…" he mumbled softly.

She chose not to respond to that comment. "By the way, I'm taking a weekend break in Ljubljana."

"I was thinking of visiting there too," he commented.

Kit frowned; it wasn't like they were dating, but it seemed that Owen wanted to be around her all the time. Maybe he was concerned about her safety.

"I'll be alright," she said confidently. "The Podujevo Five won't make it past the border."

"I meant it sounds like Slovenia is a nice place to visit," Owen said.

"Maybe some other time," Kit answered as she continued scrolling through her messages.

After that, she retired to the guest room and spent about half an hour texting with her mother and Xander before finally snuggling up for bed. The sleeping pill ensured she had an uninterrupted night of sleep, and by the morning, she was back to her typical routine.

CHAPTER FOURTEEN

The next morning, after returning to her own apartment, Kit methodically unpacked the overnight bag that she had taken to Owen's place. Matt had been insistent, a sentiment that Eva echoed, that she stay put at Owen's. But the arrangement had chaffed against her independent spirit. Kit was someone who lived by the rule that it was easier to ask for forgiveness than permission, and this was a textbook case. She tended to live by the principle that it was easier to get forgiveness than consent, and this was a prime example. She made herself a potent double espresso, then dropped a slice of bread in the toaster for a simple breakfast. She dedicated time to freshening up after — unbinding her hair from its braid and giving it a good brush, indulging in a rejuvenating shower, and applying just a touch of makeup to her face.

By the time she was finished with her morning routine, she had received a message from Matt telling her to meet him at the international village on the outskirts of Pristina. Eva also sent her a message mentioning that Angel was coming to pick her up in an OIDC vehicle. Apparently, there had been some kind of incident and Kit was going to be taken to the crime scene to help collect evidence. She responded with a simple "Roger that" and finished her toast before heading out the door to wait for Angel.

Her stomach fluttered as she made her way down the stairs. The new case, whatever it was, provided a welcome distraction from worrying about Sergei and her relationship issues. When she opened the door out of the apartment block leading to the tree-lined avenue outside, Angel was already there waiting for her in the office vehicle.

Kit climbed into the raised, four-wheel drive, sliding onto the passenger seat. Angel had placed two paper coffee cups in the holder along with a brown paper bag containing fruit pastries.

"Did you eat breakfast already?" Angel asked.

"Not much, just some toast," Kit answered before biting into the flaky pastry with a tart red-berry filling. "What type of incident is it?"

"We've had a death; the head of the privatization panel. It looks suspicious."

"Isn't that Rustem Kupi?"

Angel looked over at Kit and remarked, "How do you know his name?"

"He was scheduled to see Tom this week."

"Well, he won't be doing that now. He won't be seeing anyone."

Kit grabbed her phone and started to send a text to Eva, but she then thought it best to assess the situation firsthand before hitting send. Eva would have already had her first interview with the news media, and who knows what kind of reaction Eva was getting from her managers about breaking rank.

"Do you know if there's anything unusual about the crime scene?" Kit asked.

Angel replied, "I heard something about the manner of death."

The thought of the crime scene dampened Kit's appetite and she closed up the paper bag, tucking it into one of the side pockets of the vehicle. She swallowed a few sips of hot coffee and regained some energy, despite not being a morning person.

"Sorry for getting you up so early," Angel said, grinning. "Eva requested it. She seemed to think it might be linked to Operation Icarus."

"What's Eva doing this morning?" Kit inquired.

"Eva's done her share of crime scenes. She told me to go with you this morning. I think she's bracing for any fallout from the interview."

"How did it go?"

"It was alright. They tried to pin Eva down on details but she kept things quite general. Eva is incredibly brave to share her suspicions with the public."

"Suspicions that are based on sound evidence," Kit added.

"We'll know how OIDC management reacts when the story hits the headlines."

"I'm sure they won't be pleased," Kit said, then added, "By the way, I'm heading to Ljubljana for the weekend."

Angel looked at her. "I'm surprised you're going on vacation with so much going on here right now."

"It's only for a couple of days," Kit replied. "I booked the trip weeks ago."

"We can still reach you by phone though, right? You may have to be in charge of the office if Mueller goes berserk after Eva's revelations."

"Yes, of course. I'm just a phone call away.

She shifted uncomfortably and changed the subject. "I'm still embarrassed when I think back to my first experience of a crime scene at Staro Dorbi," Kit confessed, placing her cup down.

"A lot has happened since then. You're more experienced now. And it probably won't be as bad this time. As far as I can tell there aren't multiple killings, but who knows," Angel said.

"Did we ever find out anything more about that guy, Sergei Sokolov?" Kit tried to sound casual, but her voice wavered slightly.

"From what Eva said, he flew to Moscow on a Russian military aircraft out of Serbia. His ministry is still protecting him using diplomatic immunity. There wasn't much we could do about that. We're currently applying for a red notice from Interpol, although Russia will probably object and have it cancelled."

"It's too bad when diplomatic immunity is abused to avoid justice. He admitted his guilt to me, and it's written in Shala's diary. But without Raco's testimony, it won't be enough to convict him," Kit said.

Angel quickly glanced over at Kit. "Did you find him attractive?"

"Who, Raco?" Kit said.

"No, of course not! Sergei."

"It was hard to see past his personality," she replied carefully. She recalled gazing into his eyes—a warm golden-amber—and she felt her face flush as she shifted her gaze away. "I suppose some might find him attractive."

Angel continued to press the topic. "If you'd had the chance, would you have gone out with him. I mean, before we found out about his involvement with the mass murder?"

"I have a fiancé back home," Kit said. "So even if I'd wanted to, it wouldn't have been easy." She couldn't help but wonder if Angel knew about her relationship with Sergei. This was an awkward topic indeed.

The discussion trailed off as they drove through the crowded morning streets of Pristina. At the edge of the city was the Marigold complex: high-end homes, fancy boutique shopping, and upscale restaurants surrounded by a security fence with a checkpoint at the entrance. People of influence and diplomats lived there. It was better maintained than many of the other residential areas in Pristina.

As they approached the gate, they noticed police vehicles blocking their way in. More cruisers were located near one of the residences past the checkpoint—the wrought iron arch spelling out "Marigold Residences."

Angel drove up to the entrance and presented their IDs to the guard, who waved them through. They left their car behind Matt's police jeep and got out. Owen hurried over to greet them.

"Kit, Matt needs you at the scene now," he said.

Angel stayed behind to wait at the vehicle while Kit grabbed her bag to follow Owen. They went towards the yellow-taped house surrounded by a small garden fence.

"It's Rustem Kupi, who was the head of the privatization panel," he informed her. "He didn't appear at a meeting, so they sent somebody to locate him. They found his body, with multiple stab wounds."

Kit paused in shock when she heard this news. Kupi had had an appointment to discuss something important with Tom about privatization panel concerns—the panel that was due to approve the energy plant contract. That meeting would now never take place. Tom was now declared unwanted at work, persona non grata, and

Chairman Kupi was deceased. She forced herself to take a deep breath and nodded slowly. Even though she had never met Rustem Kupi, a single tear fell from her eyes. He was another victim of an awful business: money taking precedence over all else, including life itself.

A movement in Kit's peripheral vision as they entered the garden made her look up. A woman with loose, blonde hair and green eyes strode towards them. Owen introduced her as Zena Lace Letalova, a criminal profiler from EUFOR. She was more petite than Kit. She seemed familiar, but Kit couldn't place where she had seen her before.

"You've got an interesting job," Kit said as she shook Zena's hand.

"I like it," Zena replied with a smile.

"I thought profilers might get in the way at fresh crime scenes. So why are you here so early in the investigation?"

"Collecting evidence is best done soon after the crime has been committed," Zena explained. "New to this sort of thing?"

Kit bristled at the suggestion that she was inexperienced with crime scenes, but before she could respond, Owen jumped in. "Zena, this is Caitlin Chase with the Chief Prosecutor's office. Major Hackman asked her to assist with gathering evidence."

As Owen spoke, she suddenly remembered where she had glimpsed Zena before. She was the woman who had arrived at the door of Owen's apartment and presented him with a souvenir from her travels. Annoyance sluiced over her but she kept a polite expression on her face and tried to maintain a businesslike attitude.

The uniformed officer handed Kit a clipboard with a sign-in sheet. She jotted down her initials and affiliation: OCP, Office of the Chief Prosecutor, at 9:35 a.m. She glanced at Zena Lace Letalova's initials and saw that she had been there ten minutes before her. Owen and Matt had arrived ten minutes before that.

Zena picked up the topic again. "If you had more experience, you would have seen profilers at work before."

Kit tried to think of a retort, but the sight of the crime scene inside the house caught her attention and she walked towards it. Even with the chaos of the scene, the hardwood floors and beige carpet in the entrance looked normal enough. But the sound of clicking and recharging cameras echoed through the room. Crime scene investigators moved around in white coverall suits, dusting for prints and cataloguing every inch of space— looking for whatever evidence could be found. A cold cup of coffee sat on the table beside magazines and a mobile phone.

"Better have that bagged and tagged," Kit said to Owen, gesturing towards the phone. Owen nodded and signalled one of the CSI members. The officer took it with a gloved hand, slipping it into a labelled plastic bag.

The scent of fresh paint and varnish hung in the air, mixed with the bitter smell of blood. Kit inhaled slowly, holding her hand near her nose, letting the floral aroma of her perfume mask the other odors. Her pace slowed as she remembered the conversation with Sergei weeks earlier. He had given her advice on how to focus her mind when facing a difficult situation, helping her to avoid a repeat of what happened at Staro Dorbi when she had fainted at the sight of a murdered child. She knew Sergei was a criminal, yet she was still grateful for his advice: stay focused on what she wanted to get out of this situation; identify any adversaries; and above all, remain calm and in control. Her endgame was to prove her worth as a professional and to secure enough evidence for a successful prosecution.

"Is everything okay?" Zena's Czech accent snapped Kit out of her thoughts. She shook her head to clear it.

"Yes, I was just thinking."

Kit noticed Zena's features appeared even more delicate as she looked up at Kit from close quarters. But she felt uneasy with Zena watching her every move, and so to take the attention away from herself, Kit gestured to the corner of the room that held a home office. She had an odd suspicion that Zena was profiling her in her head, although there was no way to know for sure.

A figure lay slumped over the desk, crimson spots staining the surface. Dr Prabhu, attired in her white medical examiner's outfit and wearing surgical gloves, spoke to Matt, who stood a couple of steps away. Kit stepped forward, focusing on maintaining her composure. Zena's eyes met hers, and Kit felt uneasy again. She wasn't here to be studied by a psychological profiler—or romantic rival for Owen's attention. The thought came unbidden into her mind. She was here to do the job of a legal professional among law enforcement officers. Gathering courage, she grabbed her notepad and pen before she stepped closer. Matt motioned her to approach them.

The metallic odor intensified as Kit advanced towards the corpse. She made a note that she should dab eau de toilette beneath her nose the next time she visited such a crime scene. Kit took a few more steps before she heard Dr Prabhu speak again. "He was killed about twenty-two hundred to midnight last night. Cause of death appears to be multiple stab wounds. We'll know more once we do the postmortem."

"What can you tell us about the wounds?" Matt asked.

"As far as I can tell, there are around eleven stab wounds, and no defensive wounds are apparent."

He indicated a bloodied A-4 page on the desk. "We've got this 'suicide note' here."

Kit leaned in to examine the note, which was written in Albanian.

"Can you make out what it says?" Kit asked.

"We need to get it translated," Matt said.

"Kupi blames his suicide on business rivals and bad press," Zena said.

"Wow, you know Albanian?" Kit asked, surprised.

"I've been taking classes," she said with a shrug.

Matt gestured to a CSI officer, who bagged the note as evidence.

"Why would someone stab themselves eleven times?" Kit pondered aloud. "Isn't it usually enough to slash your wrists if you're intent on suicide?"

Dr Prabhu shifted the victim's collar to reveal a gash across his throat. "It seems this was the cause of death."

"Once we have all the forensic evidence, I'm sure Ms Letalova can help us determine whether it was a suicide or not," Matt suggested. He pointed to a blood-soaked hunting knife still in the victim's left hand on the desk. "I don't think we'll have to look far for the murder weapon—or suicide instrument."

"We need to check which was the victim's dominant hand. If he was right-handed, we can assume this scene is staged."

Zena studied some handwritten notes still lying on the desk beside the body. "He was right-handed," she said.

Dr Prabhu nodded and then motioned for two CSI officers to come over with a gurney. "I'll check which direction the wounds were inflicted from. It doesn't seem likely that a right-handed person would have attempted self-harm with their left hand." They placed the body onto the stretcher, and Dr Prabhu accompanied them to the waiting ambulance.

"I'm not buying this suicide story. I want every inch of this premises examined for signs of an intruder," Matt said to Owen. Owen nodded and began giving directions to the officers. When Zena left to scour the house for details about its occupant, Kit spoke quietly to Matt. "It might be a coincidence, but Mr Kupi was coming to discuss something with Tom Baumgarten this week."

"Any idea what the meeting was about?"

"Tom told us about allegations of irregularities with the privatization panel, which Kupi chaired. If Kupi knew something, perhaps someone wanted to stop him from whistleblowing."

"Can you check the panel's minutes and any court cases they're involved in?" Matt said.

Kit nodded, already envisioning the stacks of papers on her desk climbing higher and higher.

"I'd love to get my hands on any files you find here, either in hard copy or from his laptop," she said.

"We can set you up a space at the police station so

you can examine them," Matt offered.

Kit glanced over at Zena, who was flicking through the magazines on the coffee table. "What's with the profiler?"

"She comes highly recommended."

With a smirk she asked, "Does that mean she's a good worker or that she's a nuisance and they're trying to get rid of her?"

Surprised at Kit's scepticism, Matt answered, "I think she's good at her job. People call her 'the Black Cat of Prague.'"

"What did she do to get that nickname?"

"Zena's the youngest police captain in the Czech Republic, and probably soon a major. She gets the job done," Matt said. "As for the nickname, I can't say how she got that."

"Perhaps because it's bad luck if she crosses your path. I wonder if she could make up profiles on our colleagues? They're interesting psychological types." Kit smirked. She wasn't sure why she was making unfriendly comments about Zena. She wondered if it might be some kind of territorial instinct and decided to drop the subject.

"Perhaps," Matt said. "We need to look at all possibilities. We don't know how high this thing goes." He then moved on to look at more items on the desk.

"I'd like to look through his files, and some of our own accounting files have already been sent to archives," Kit said.

"Sergeant, make sure the files are recovered, secured, and available to Kit later on," Matt told Owen.

"We'll take his laptop in too," Owen said.

"Make sure you're there when they examine it. I don't want it going missing," Matt said.

Kit didn't need to ask why Matt was concerned about evidence going missing. He was thinking about their last case, where a key piece of evidence in a diary had gone missing from the chain of custody.

"Does the deceased have any family?" Kit asked.

Matt sighed heavily and nodded his head in confirmation. "Yes, he's married with three children. His wife and children are in Prizren right now visiting her parents. We'll break the news to them after we're finished here."

"You'll need to interview them, I suppose."

"Sergeant Reese can take a preliminary statement from his wife. Try to find out from her if he had any enemies she knew of," Matt said as Owen made a note.

Kit examined the other rooms of the house and checked the progress of the Crime Scene Unit. She read through their evidence log entries to make sure all items were accounted for, then said her goodbyes to Owen and Matt. Angel was waiting by the vehicle, talking with a couple of security guards. She drove them back to the office. Once there, Kit completed most of her paperwork. The rest could wait until next week. With that taken care of, it was time to begin preparations for her trip to Ljubljana, Slovenia. It had been an exhausting week so far, and what she needed now was a change of scenery. She could forget about Raco, Tirol, and Zena Lace Letalova for a while and enjoy the company of her favorite adversary—Sergei Sokolov.

CHAPTER FIFTEEN

Ljubljana, Slovenia

Kit's heart raced as she stepped off the Adria Airplane and set her sights on Ljubljana. In a dizzying blur, she collected her ragged suitcase from baggage claim and made it through customs. Then, as she scanned the bustling airport waiting area for her ride, her eyes locked onto a familiar figure standing beside a pillar: Sergei. There he stood, dressed in black jeans and a leather jacket, his hair much shorter than before and a light beard shading his face, but it was him alright. Aviator sunglasses hid his deep amber gaze and Kit froze, rooted to the spot. After all this time, there he was.

He stalked towards her, the air between them heavy with anticipation. When their bodies met, it felt electric. He pressed his lips to her cheek, leaving a scorching imprint as her nostrils filled with the musky scent of his expensive cologne. "Sergei!" she gasped. "It is you! I wasn't sure."

"That's my intention," he replied as he pushed up his sunglasses to his forehead. She recognized his eyes right away, but his face seemed older than she recalled; fine lines bracketed his mouth and eyes, and a few silver hairs peppered his temples. The shorter hair, beard, and leather jacket gave Sergei a more rugged look compared to the diplomat she remembered. She felt disoriented as she questioned if this was the real Sergei, or was the earlier Sergei closer to the truth. She'd have to ask him later. Most men would gladly talk about themselves. But he wasn't most men.

"How are you?" she asked, recalling the argument she had had with him at their last parting. "I was pleased to hear from you, but our last moments together in Pristina were so difficult."

"I'm hoping we can clear things up," he said.

She snorted involuntarily, for there was nothing to clarify. Still, she replied, "We've got a lot to talk about."

He smiled in agreement and said, "If this is your first time in Ljubljana, I can show you around. I'll take you to your hotel so you can freshen up first, if you wish. "

Her spirits lifted. "That sounds wonderful," Kit said. She had managed to navigate the first awkward moments of their meeting, which was a relief.

Sergei grabbed her luggage, and she followed him out of the arrivals area to a Skoder SUV in the parking lot. It was a more practical vehicle than his official black limousine in Pristina would have been and wouldn't draw as much attention. He loaded her bag in the trunk and opened the passenger door for her with a chivalrous gesture, then slid in behind the wheel.

"The GRU teaches its agents to be polite, at least," Kit joked wryly, feeling a thrill run through her at being near him again. She settled into the seat. "It's great to see you again, Sergei, despite everything. I wish our reunion was under different circumstances."

He gave her a searching look before finally starting the engine. "Things had to be this way," he said.

She glanced into the rearview mirror and wished she had put a bit more effort into her makeup. Not only was she visibly tired from her stressful week, but lack of sleep and an early start hadn't helped any.

Sergei drove her to her hotel in downtown Ljubljana and waited downstairs while she dropped off her things and freshened up. When she emerged back outside, she was dressed in jeans, trainers, a T-shirt, and a silk scarf, with a leather jacket thrown over the top. She wore a light mist of her autumn fragrance that was a mix of vanilla, sandalwood, and orange blossom.

"How do you like your room?" Sergei asked.

"Not bad. It'll do," she replied.

"One of these days you'll learn to set your standards higher, not just get the job done," Sergei said with a hint of superiority in his voice.

Kit felt her face flush, and thoughts of Xander came into her mind before she could shove them away. "Why can't you stop trying to make me feel like I'm not good enough?"

"That's not my intention. I only want the best for you." He wrapped his arm around her shoulders and gave them a gentle squeeze before letting go. "I want you to set your sights higher over the next few days. I'm glad you decided to come. I know things aren't simple back in Pristina."

"You're right," Kit replied. "I really needed a break away from all the drama. Although something tells me there will be drama here too, just of a different kind." She was taking a huge risk coming here, with no one to check up on her if something went wrong. Despite Sergei's appeal, he could be just as dangerous as Raco, but the difference was that you never knew what was lurking under the surface with him. One minute he could seem like a gentleman, and then the next you'd find yourself a perilous situation. This was the very situation that Owen had wanted to protect her from, and she had pushed him away.

Sergei seemed to be relishing the role of tour guide. "Most of Ljubljana's attractions can be reached by foot. I want to show you some of the work of Jože Plečnik. He's a Slovenian architect who became popular in the 1920s and 30s for his unique designs throughout the city,which I doubt you heard much about in New Zealand."

"That's an understatement."

"Plečnik combined architectural designs inspired by ancient Greece with modern elements and gave them his own unique twist," Sergei elaborated.

"I thought we'd be focusing more on your philosophy than architecture. I was looking forward to learning more about Kasch," Kit said.

"Don't worry, Katarina. We will do both. Ideas are enhanced if we can experience them in 3D rather than just think about them. This inner city is like a sanctuary where we can explore new perspectives together."

They started strolling through a park towards a building with neoclassical features. The atmosphere of the architecture made Kit feel relaxed and clearheaded, ready to take on new challenges.

"It's like a little Vienna," Kit said.

"That's because the architect Plečnik was inspired by Vienna."

"It's strange that you, a Russian, would be so invested in Slovenia."

"I lived in Moscow and spent many years in St Petersburg, and I love old Europe, including Slovenia, which is one of the reasons I'm here today." He took her arm as they walked along.

Kit sighed. This was not what she had expected during her visit to Ljubljana. However, it was easier to talk about history than discuss the criminal charges against this man. Or his marriage.

"You always have a plan. So why else did you come to Ljubljana?" she pressed. She could leave some of the more controversial topics between them for now, but she still felt compelled to find out more about him.

"You're getting to know me too well," he said, drawing her closer into his arm as they walked through the park. "I'm a part of an exclusive philosophical group that meets from time to time in different locations. I thought you'd like to join us while we're here."

"You did mention it before. Is it some kind of secret society?"

"More like a club," he said.

"Where exactly are we going now?" she asked.

"To the castle; we can get an overview from up there."

As they rounded the corner, Kit and Sergei stepped into the bustling town square, which was alive with the hum of conversation and the aroma of freshly brewed coffee from nearby cafes. Set close to the center was a beautifully crafted bronze statue of France Prešeren, a renowned Slovenian poet, and his muse, Julija Primic, standing by his side. Her delicate outstretched hand poured out an invisible creative elixir onto him, symbolizing the inspiration she provided him throughout his life.

Kit noticed a group of locals gathering around the statue, laying flowers and handwritten notes at its base. She heard snippets of conversations from the people who talked about their favourite pieces by Prešeren or shared stories about how he had inspired them. It was evident that the Slovenians still cherished their national poet, whose words had endured through time and helped shape the nation's identity.

On the other side of the plaza stood the impressive, pink-coloured town hall, a testament to Baroque architecture. Its ornate facade spoke of the city's rich history and the political power that once resided within its walls.

As they walked together, Kit and Sergei crossed one of the three stone bridges that spanned the emerald-green Ljubljanica River, which meandered gently through the heart of the city. The bridges, designed by the famous architect Jože Plečnik, not only connected the two sides of Ljubljana but also served as a symbol of unity and harmony among the city's diverse communities.

For Kit, the juxtaposition of the poet and the town hall, along with the serene river and Plečnik's bridges, embodied a delicate balance between art, power, and nature. As she gazed upon the scene, she pondered how the past might lend her insight into her own chaotic present.

They were admiring the bridges when trumpets and drums started to play. A colorful procession filled the square featuring people dressed in vibrant traditional costumes reminiscent of the city's medieval past. The brass band played jaunty tunes, attracting onlookers.

"This is amazing," Kit said, her eyes widening at the spectacle. "What are they doing?"

Sergei smiled, enjoying her enthusiasm. "The pageant is meant to generate energy and celebrate Ljubljana's unique history," he replied. "This spot was an important crossroads for east and west Europe, a meeting point for different cultures, ideas, and trade. The procession reminds people of their rich heritage and the significance of unity in a diverse society."

As the medieval-themed procession approached the river, it veered towards the middle bridge. The participants, carrying colorful banners, gracefully crossed the expansive central bridge before disappearing into the narrow streets on the other side of the river. As the crowd dispersed, Kit and Sergei resumed their stroll through the picturesque streets, taking with them the exciting energy of the unexpected pagaent. She wondered what lessons she could take back to Pristina from all this.

"There are so many possible meanings to the symbolism. How do we know which ones are right and which are just speculation?" Kit asked.

"Much of Plečnik's work is symbolic," Sergei explained. "People can interpret it according to their own views. For someone trying to solve transportation issues, the two extra bridges may be a novel solution; for an artist, it could be a work of art; or for a yogi, it could represent three energy channels up the spine."

"I'll go with the artist's interpretation," Kit said.

"A psychologist might say that these bridges symbolize ways of transitioning between different states of consciousness—the left brain and the right brain," Sergei added.

"That's really interesting," Kit said. "So, if we crossed over the left-hand bridge, what does that mean?"

"You decide," Sergei replied with a smile. "It means what you want it to mean."

"Okay, I'll take the bait. It means that we're moving deeper into some kind of mystery."

"That's the best meaning of all," said Sergei, smiling.

"What does it mean that the procession took the middle path?"

"That's open to interpretation," Sergei responded. "Physically, the central bridge is the largest and so more convenient for a large group, but symbolically, it may represent the city's role as a mediator between cultures and regions, a bridge between the past and the future. By taking the middle path, the procession could be emphasizing the importance of balance and unity in Ljubljana's rich history and its continued pursuit of harmony in the present."

Kit and Sergei continued their exploration of Ljubljana, wandering through the lively market arcade designed by Jože Plečnik. The renowned architect had blended ancient and classical designs to create a harmonious environment. The vibrant stalls overflowed with fresh produce and handcrafted trinkets, while the aroma of freshly baked bread and the melodious tunes of street musicians filled the air.

As they strolled, Sergei's enthusiasm for Ljubljana's history and architecture was infectious. "I want to show you something else which is interesting in its own right," he said, his eyes sparkling with excitement. "The Dragon Bridge. But I can tell you about that later."

"No, tell me now," Kit said with a feigned groan, her curiosity piqued.

He laughed. "You're such a curious creature! You can spot dragons on Ljubljana's bridges as well as on top of the castle. But you want to know everything in one go!"

She chuckled. "No hope of that with you!"

Arriving at the funicular station, Sergei purchased tickets for their ascent to Ljubljana Castle. As they settled into the car, he explained the castle's storied past. Built by the Habsburgs in the fifteenth century, it had long been a symbol of power and influence in the region.

As the funicular glided up the steep incline, Sergei elaborated on the significance of the dragons that adorned the city's bridges and the castle. "In Slovenian mythology, dragons are guardians of the city, protecting it from harm and watching over its inhabitants."

Kit was captivate by Ljubljana and couldn't wait to explore more of the city with Sergei.

"Europe is just so amazing," she exclaimed, taking in the stunning view from the slowly ascending cable care. "There's nothing like this in New Zealand. We have stunning natural beauty of course. But not medieval castles!"

As they wandered through the castle's courtyard, Kit found herself appreciating the contrast between her high-stress job in Pristina and the newfound freedom she felt in Ljubljana. Despite the tensions between them, Sergei had an undeniable allure that made her feel like she could be someone else around him. In the gift shop, Kit picked out souvenirs to take back to New Zealand, including a key ring for Xander. It was the first time she had thought of him since leaving Pristina.

Sergei ordered them coffee at the café, and Kit couldn't resist ordering a slice of the thick, creamy cake, a local speciality. "Oh Lord," she moaned after the first bite. "This is delicious. Try some, Sergei!" He obliged, slicing himself a piece with his fork.

"It is very good," he commented. "But one day, I hope to show you the delicious cakes we have in Russia. Perhaps you'd enjoy St. Petersburg."

Kit felt her heart race at the thought of traveling to Russia with Sergei. Despite her attraction to him, she couldn't forget that he was involved in the very crimes she was helping to prosecute. She took a deep breath and tried to focus on the present moment, enjoying the cake and the beautiful surroundings. She was learning to compartmentalize, keeping different parts of her life separate. It was easier that way, at least in the short-term.

"St Petersburg does sound amazing," she finally admitted.

"Our group meets every six months or so, seeking fresh ideas and locales that ignite our inspiration," Sergei explained. "We harness our imaginations to enhance the likelihood of desired events materializing in the real world. And I use the phrase 'real-world' loosely," he said. "Because there are many realities, and our consciousness can travel from one to the other. The movement of consciousness is what we call time."

Kit listened intently, savoring another bite of the cake.

"So, in a parallel existence, I may forgo this cream cake and sip black coffee instead?"

"Precisely. But aren't you pleased to indulge in this moment with me, enjoying coffee and cake? Your choice of dessert betrays your true intentions for coming here." He chuckled, raising an eyebrow.

"And those are …?"

"For pleasure." He said it suggestively, rolling the word in his mouth as if he was talking about more than a culinary delights. She laughed. "Busted. You got me there." Kit diverted her gaze, masking her embarrassment. "I came here to relish the cake, although the sweets in Pristina aren't half bad; they make a rather delectable baklava."

"I'm pleased to see you articulate your desires more openly. Let's use the architectural marvels surrounding us here to empower ourselves further." He paused for dramatic effect. "In fact, I can make a bold promise to you now."

"And that is?" She couldn't resist asking.

"I can take transport you to realms you've never encountered before."

"That is literally true. But do you mean more than just visiting Ljubljana?"

"I do," he confirmed. "But for now you'll have to be patient."

"Do you think we've already embarked on that journey?" Kit asked.

"Absolutely," he answered, taking her hand in his. The warmth of his touch grounded her in the present, helping her to realize this was really happening. "I have faith in your abilities. Your insight about the bridge leading us deeper into the mystery was quite profound."

Kit didn't pull away from his grasp. Instead, she spoke quietly in response. "I'm not overlooking the crimes you were involved with in Pristina; I'd just prefer to revisit them later."

"Understood," he said, producing a passport from his pocket and placing it on the table. "Here, have a look inside."

Sergei's passport immediately caught her attention. It represented one's identity and the freedom to traverse international borders. Moreover, it was crucial for securing and retaining employment.

As she examined the passport, he spoke again. "I can't emphasize enough how grateful I am for your friendship and support."

She noted that the passport bore the name of Oleg Anton Soroka, identifying him as a Ukrainian citizen.

"Why are you traveling under an alias?"

"You, of all people, should understand why. There's a pending international arrest for me. Interpol hasn't acted on it as I have diplomatic immunity. But in case something changes, I can't travel using my own name."

Kit glanced downward at the table. "I can't believe you involved yourself in . . . in that situation with the killings."

"Let's not delve into that now. The fact that you've accepted my invitation here shows your understanding of the situation's complexities. I want you to know how much I value your work."

"Do you expect me to revoke the warrant? You're well aware that only the chief prosecutor—Eva—has that authority. It isn't likely she will."

Sergei stowed away the passport. "You never can tell. Just in case there's an opportunity, I want you to remember our time together."

"You keep exploiting me! Over and over," she said, enraged. "Why do I keep allowing this?" She shoved her chair away from the table.

"Don't misunderstand me. That's not my intention at all. I'm merely presenting the reality of the situation, regardless of whether you can assist me or not. No matter what happens, I'll stand by you."

She regarded him again. "Has your intelligence agency been monitoring the chief prosecutor's office? Eavesdropping on Eva's conversations?"

He stared at her impassively. "There's no need for an elaborate intelligence operation to know what's happening in the chief prosecutor's office. All we need to do is read the news or watch television."

"Right, of course, I know that Eva has courted controversy," Kit conceded.

He nodded. "Yes, and I care about you, Katarina. Expect considerable stress when Eva's efforts to expose the corruption prove futile and backfire on her."

"Was that why you invited me to Slovenia? Anticipating that Eva would be ousted?"

"A few weeks ago, when I sent you that initial message, it was before any of this had happened. But now it's playing out, you may find that you have more"—he searched for the right words—"autonomy at work."

The thought left Kit reeling. She had exposed herself to his manipulation by agreeing to meet him.

"This isn't fair, especially since I just moved to Kosovo recently!" Kit protested.

"I know it isn't fair, and please don't feel pressured by me. I'm simply bringing these issues to your attention," Sergei said.

Kit exhaled and retrieved her cigarettes from her bag.

"Can you order me some coffee, preferably Irish with whiskey? I know its early, but I need something stronger right now."

Sergei raised his eyebrows when he saw her cigarettes. "You didn't smoke last time we met."

"You don't know what I've been through," Kit sighed, lighting up a cigarette.

Sergei stepped away to order her coffee and returned moments later. "If you want to talk about why you're so stressed, I'm here for you. I saw reports about Eva's claims of judicial corruption in Kosovo—involving international judges—and another story about one of your own investigators speaking of kickbacks and bribes. Does that impact you?"

"Of course it does. I work in the chief prosecutor's office," Kit responded. A waitress appeared, placing a tray with another cup of coffee, a bottle of amber liquid, and two glasses on the table.

"It's honey liqueur," Sergei offered, gesturing towards the bottle. "I think you'll like it." "Coffee, liqueur, cream cake, and a cigarette. You know I can't stay angry for long," Kit admitted.

"And don't forget the view," Sergei said, gesturing to the picturesque panorama of the old city below them.

Kit savored her cigarette and sipped the delectable honey liqueur. "Alright," she said. "I'll look into your red notice arrest warrant. No guarantees though."

"Understood," he replied. "That's all I ask."

"I'm just angry about the whole ordeal," she vented. "Tom, our anti-corruption expert, uncovered a massive kickback scheme—we're talking hundreds of millions that could involve upper management from my office. It sounded far-fetched, but when he confronted them with the allegations, they went ballistic and threw him out. He's now a pariah. They arrested him and confiscated his passport. He was lucky to get it back after the US embassy intervened."

"So, do you think they're guilty and the judge too? Could they be in it together?"

"I think it looks suspicious." She switched between sipping her coffee and smoking to keep her hands busy and stop them from trembling. "How could they get so much money out of Kosovo? And is it possible to stop them?"

"It's not easy, but there are methods. Some of my associates know how to move funds from one location to another without detection by authorities."

"Goodness me," Kit feigned surprise. "I never would have guessed!" |

"I know you don't always think well of me, but don't be too quick to judge," Sergei replied. "Especially when I might be able to help. What do you need?"

"We need to bring the criminals to justice, but it's not always easy in Kosovo. A lack of oversight means judges can be bribed and influenced. And to top it all off, even international organizations don't always own up to their actions. It seems like they're more worried about keeping their donors happy than anything else."

"I couldn't agree more," Sergei said. "It's an appalling state of affairs. I'd be glad to help in any way I can."

"Please, Sergei, keep all of this between us. No one should know that I said anything about it," Kit warned.

"Don't worry. Most of it's already in the public domain, thanks to your boss," Sergei assured her.

Kit grappled with the aftermath of Raco eluding justice, as well as the slaying of the privatization panel leader. She was convinced that Raco was part of the larger kickback scheme, working for someone else. She also knew that Sergei had used Raco in the past for a contract killing. She was aware that her behaviour was inconsistent, and that she had fallen prey to Sergei's manipulations, but perhaps she could use him as he had used her.

Sergei continued speaking again. "Kosovo is in a delicate position—neither a fully independent state nor governed by another country. Consequently, it becomes an easy target for transnational organized crime and corruption. Rules are made to be broken in Kosovo, and those responsible often get away with it unscathed."

"That is why international organizations stepped in," Kit added.

"Unfortunately, they haven't been entirely successful," Sergei noted sadly. "Still, there's opportunity here. Without enforcement of the rules, people's true natures play out, allowing you to discover what's genuinely important to you, and you can adapt to better reflect those values going forward."

"There's a lot of suffering in Kosovo, like poor Tom Baumgarten who was arrested for his honesty," Kit stated.

"At least Tom has the chance to show his strength of character. But in many other places, the corruption's hidden, and people's morals are never tested."

Kit nodded in agreement. "I guess that could be true for Eva too. If she hadn't gone to Kosovo, she wouldn't have known her willingness to stand up for her beliefs."

"And I think you, Katarina, you are also evolving. You can see the positive and negative aspects of a situation and still manage to survive it all. You defend what you value, if unconventionally."

"Do you think I've lost my way?"

"No, quite the opposite. You are one of the most ethical people I know, but it's based on your beliefs and values, not someone else's. That's something I respect and cherish about you."

Kit contemplated the way that Sergei had indirectly expressed love for her. It made a warm sensation spread within her.

"Thanks," she said. "I've been struggling with the morality of hiding my visit here to see you. But I think the bigger truths we're discovering together outweigh any concerns about appearances."

"I couldn't agree more," Sergei replied. "Kosovo is trapped between two political forces: the self-proclaimed Kosovo government with its Albanian leaders and the preceding Serbian authority. Both parties desire to join Western Europe, and my country shares their aspirations for regional prosperity."

"I can go along with your idea of Kosovo being a place of testing and change, but these ideas about Russia's goals in the Balkans sound dubious to me.

"Let's continue our conversation. I just ask that you keep an open mind. But in the meantime, let's make the most of our time here. I want to show you some unique locations designed by Plečnik and use them for self-discovery," he said, smiling knowingly.

"What do you mean?" Kit inquired, taking a sip of the honey liqueur and appreciating its smoothness. She couldn't help but think of how Owen would prefer to find an Irish pub and share a pint of Guinness while watching sports, or enjoy ice cream together. In contrast, Sergei always made everything feel more fascinating and intense.

"We can gain self-knowledge and power, and I'll guide you. But rather than just discussing it, let's do it. I also want you to meet my friends."

"But weren't your beliefs influenced by Rasputin? Wasn't he known as the mad monk and nearly invincible?"

"Historical accounts aren't always accurate. The man known as Rasputin was an advisor to Russia's former royal family, whose hidden knowledge helped him to increase his charisma and extend his life. His discovered diaries containing instructions on spiritual exercises, which have been the foundation of our methods ever since. We've refined them by incorporating quantum physics insights, creating a potent system for altering reality and self-improvement."

Kit shuddered, suddenly finding the honey liqueur less appealing. She put out her cigarette and finished her coffee before standing up and slipping on her coat.

"Let's go," she said, bagging her belongings. "Maybe you can guide me through some visualization exercises." They headed back to the funicular station, where a handful of passengers were already gathered. Sergei steered them away from the group and turned to her.

"What would you like to focus on?" he asked.

"Can we stop these crimes? Even your people would support that. Make sure the money laundering doesn't happen and get the funds returned to Kosovo. I have a vision of seeing that corrupt judge arrested in handcuffs. Let it be so," she replied.

"Let's make that a reality," he said and pulled her in for a kiss, flavored with the lingering taste of honey liqueur.

Chapter Sixteen

Kit couldn't help but draw similarities between the National and University Library's architecture and her high school art history lessons about the Italian Renaissance. Even though the bricks and stones fit together perfectly, the colors appeared haphazard. The lower part of the building was grey, while the bricks above were mainly red, and some of the embedded stones originated from previous structures. Across from the library, a uniformed police officer stood guard—a reminder that it was a national treasure.

"This might not be Plečnik's most impressive work," Sergei said, "but it's my favorite. The design takes us on a journey from ignorance to knowledge. There's an exhibition inside that you might find interesting."

"On what subject?"

"Forbidden knowledge—something that fascinates both of us."

"Mainly you," Kit mumbled under her breath. Sergei trafficked in secrets, while she was always trying to unravel mysteries. She noticed a large banner hanging from the side of the building. On the right side in English was written: "And yet they read them: Banned books in the early modern age."

Moreover, she became aware that even though the stone blocks were pitted and damaged, they all fit together flawlessly, much like her relationship with Sergei. He offered her forbidden knowledge within a flawed relationship, but still she felt perfect when she was with him. And the backdrop of Kosovo, battered and broken like the wall, was somehow beautiful. She shook her head to clear the thought. She didn't want to share her feelings with him.

In front of them stood two elaborate doors.

"These door handles are designed to look like the head of Pegasus, the winged horse of Greek mytholgy who's supposed to represent a student's journey towards higher values and knowledge," Sergei pointed out.

"They're amazing," Kit remarked, running her finger along one of them. "The one on the right seems to be used more than the other. It looks brighter."

"The doors may be different colors," Sergei remarked, "but both lead to knowledge." He then opened the left-hand door for her. Inside was a cozy, well-worn vestibule area. Beyond it was a grand central staircase leading up to a mezzanine floor lined by a series of black stone pillars.

They followed signs to the exhibition. The dimly lit space was filled with glass cases, each containing books, manuscripts, and artifacts that had once been considered too dangerous or subversive for public consumption. The exhibition showcased works that had been banned, burned, or hidden away over the centuries for challenging the status quo or exploring taboo subjects. As they walked through the exhibit, Kit was captivated by the wide array of items on display. There were ancient scrolls from the Library of Alexandria, medieval manuscripts on alchemy and witchcraft, and even twentieth-century books that had been banned for their controversial contents.

Sergei pointed to a case containing a rare copy of the *Index Librorum Prohibitorum*, a list of forbidden books maintained by the Catholic Church for centuries. The cover page featured a wood cut of two Church figures burning books. "It's incredible to think that so much knowledge was kept from people simply because it was deemed too dangerous or contrary to the accepted beliefs of the time," he said.

Kit nodded, deep in thought. "Yes, it's amazing how something as simple as the written word can have such power over us. It just goes to show that knowledge truly is a double-edged sword. Like reports on sensitive or unpopular topics these days."

"It shows how morality is always changing," Sergei said from behind her. "What was forbidden then is not forbidden now, and what is forbidden now may not be forbidden later."

"Are you saying that everything's relative and nothing matters?" Kit asked him. "No, I didn't say that nothing matters. On the contrary," he murmured.

"You know what I mean," she snapped back, and he responded by placing his hands on her shoulders and giving them a gentle squeeze before planting a kiss on the back of her neck.

Kit gasped in surprise at this unexpected action, feeling a wave of pleasure ripple through her body. She looked around the room quickly to make sure no one had seen them, but everyone else seemed far too involved in their own conversations or observations to have noticed them. "Don't worry; no one is paying us any attention," Sergei whispered in her ear.

She whipped around to face him, unable to suppress the blush that rose to her cheeks. "Don't do that in front of everyone. You know, they should arrest you for that," she joked nervously. "In fact, I'll make sure they do!"

"Ah, but you forget—I have diplomatic immunity," he teased. "Besides, you didn't tell me to stop."

Then the couple nearby turned around to look at them, and Kit moved away from him.

"You or the Ukrainian? Which one of you has diplomatic immunity?" she inquired. "Both," he replied in a whisper.

"Stop it," she commanded.

Their exchange felt like a lovers' quarrel in front of others, and it was becoming embarrassing. She glanced around for a pretext to change the subject and noticed a sign on the wall that explained how the Catholic Church dealt with forbidden knowledge. "That board says priests stored books such as the Flagellum Daemonium in monastery libraries for research. Even Paracelsus's work on alchemy ended up in a Ljubljana monastery at one point," she said.

He scrutinized the signs with some amusement. "The Scourge of the Demons"? We could try to find those sometime."

The atmosphere in the room started to feel oppressive. The shadows of fire and demons danced in the dim light and made her dizzy. "I need to leave," she said, and quickly exited the room. The air outside was fresher, and she inhaled deeply to clear her head.

"You surprised me in there," Kit said when she faced him again.

He shrugged. "Sorry, it just happened. I didn't plan it. If you want me to stop, I will."

She waved her hand at him dismissively. "Now is not the time or place to discuss this. I am afraid our association could become more dangerous."

Suddenly he asked, "Do you ever think about what happened between us in Pristina?" Averting her eyes from his face, Kit replied, "That was a mistake; it meant nothing."

"Then why did you come here?" Sergei asked as he studied her expression closely.

She shrugged and answered vaguely, "I don't know exactly. I just needed to get away from Pristina for a while."

He grinned at her mischievously, then quipped, "You're being evasive. It looks like you're playing a game of cat and mouse with me now."

In response, Kit asked with a teasing glint in her eye, "So who's the cat and who's the mouse?"

***

The reading room was open for visitors today, and Kit stepped inside, taking in the scene. She saw neat rows of wooden desks, each complete with its own green reading lamp. Large windows let in natural light, and two bridges connected the two sides of the room, held up by tubular steel pipes with gold-colored joints. Three enormous chandeliers adorned the space between the balustrades, each with two large bronze wheels on either end and an ornate pagoda in the middle. Natural light from the windows and artificial light from each lamp filled the space. The burnished chandeliers hung from the ceiling like giant wheels.

"They remind me of aircraft propellers!" she said, pointing up at them.

"I'll tell you a story about that," Sergei said as they climbed a staircase to a balcony above. They slipped into one of the alcoves among the shelves of books so they could talk more privately. When she looked out at the ceiling panels, forming squares and rectangles, Kit felt like she was soaring high, riding on Pegasus from the entrance below.

"Would you like to hear the story behind this room, Katarina?"

"Yes, please."

"In 1944, a mail plane from Italy flew right through the window over there."

"That's impossible!"

"The pilot was unable to land and so he flew through the window. Fortunately, the reading room was empty; they had run out of heating fuel earlier that day. Everyone in the plane was killed, as well as another one or two people on the ground. But it could have been far worse: a hundred lives could have been lost if people had been in the room that day. The aviation fuel fire destroyed tens of thousands of books."

"Unbelievable!" Kit said, looking up at the big window and envisioning a small aircraft soaring through it, shards of glass scattering all around as it tore through the room, shredding the wood panelling and books alike. She felt a sense of vertigo, as if a devastating force had assailed her. The scent of ignited fuel and thick acrid fumes filled her senses. Kit stepped back, steadying herself against the wall and shutting her eyes for a moment.

"I'm safe now," she told herself, but it didn't make her feel any better. Suddenly, Sergei was pressing up against her, and she opened her eyes in surprise. His face was close to hers, his eyes hidden in shadow, and his features looked hungry. He tilted her chin upward and forced a kiss on her lips right there in the alcove, with surreal images of explosions and destruction filling her mind and a sense of panic rising in her throat. Despite reassuring herself that it was okay, she still felt a sense of impending doom triggered by the story about the airplane crash.

The taste of his lips against hers, combined with the smell of his aftershave and the warmth of his mouth, invaded her senses. Sweet and metallic, salty and bitter all together: the taste of fear.

He had taken advantage of the situation when he noticed her vulnerability, and Kit turned her head away from him, struggling to find her voice.

"I … I can't breathe."

He paused and stepped back, although not far enough to lose their connection. Her body still tingled from their contact, while her heart raced. Her lips were swollen and sore from his kiss. Then he pulled her in again, kissed her on the cheek, and brushed the hair from her forehead.

"Do we want to leave now?" he murmured. "Or stay for a chance of being caught? It could be more exciting." He glanced around at the few people flipping through books on other levels.

"No, let's go now," she said.

He guided her down the stairs, through the reading room, and out of the building. Now everything seemed calm again. The marble columns brought back memories of bygone eras as they walked past students carrying backpacks full of books and papers.

After they left the building, Kit gulped in the fresh air. She felt shaken and conflicted about what had just happened. He had only kissed her, but it felt like he had manipulated her into an intimate situation she wasn't ready for. The forbidden books had lent a sense of intrigue and anticipation. His words of a crashing plane had almost pushed her over the edge of violation.

"I'm sorry," she said. "I don't know why I reacted like that. I panicked with thinking about that plane crashing into the library and then . . . But I don't know why I should apologize."

He grinned, satisfied by the heavy influence he had over her.

"No need to apologize, Katarina." He exhaled. "I told you these are powerful locations and powerful forces. I want you to enjoy life more intensely. Come, let's go to the café and meet some of my friends."

He offered her his arm for support, and she accepted it even though it was he who had made her feel unsteady a few moments ago.

"I need a smoke," she said.

They walked away from the library towards Café Mignon, a French-inspired cafe tucked behind a large willow tree a few blocks away. Several bicycles leaned against the wall next to some small, round tables with customers sipping their drinks as they read the paper.

"They named this town square after the French revolution, and as you can see, the café is French themed," Sergei said.

"Why are there so many tributes to France?" Kit asked.

"Napoleon freed them from the control of the Austrians. This town square is a homage to the French revolution. And revolutions can be not only political, they can also be personal."

Inside, the place was illuminated by a large rectangular, stained glass window depicting various images of French culture. The walls were deep blue, and the tables and chairs were a dark wood. The ceiling was adorned with wooden beams, creating a canopy of warmth. Visitors could feel as if they had been transported to Paris. In one corner, a couple was making out, completely oblivious to their surroundings. Kit noticed several groups of people seated around, chatting and savoring the early autumnal weather. Sergei approached a table with three people—a blonde man and woman and a dark-haired woman. He shook each one by the hand then turned towards Kit and invited her to come over.

"Caitlin, I'd like you to meet my friends, Natalia Marin from Romania and Gregor Petri who is also from Bucharest. Leo Varga is from Ljubljana. This is Caitlin Chase." Kit shook Natalia's and Leo's hands, leaving Gregor's till last. As she did so, Kit felt a sudden jolt of recognition. She remembered this man from Task Force Capture, when he had butted heads with Matt Hackman. At the time, she had thought Gregor was arrogant and entitled.

"You were on that Pristina Task Force, right?" she asked him.

Gregor nodded. "It's been a few months since then, hasn't it?" he replied.

She recalled that Gregor Petri had given Matt a hard time by challenging his authority and mishandling the arrest of Dasham Raco. As a result, Matt had lost his command of the official task force until Raco was caught. It suddenly became clear to Kit; Gregor had been working together with Sergei all along, helping Dasham Raco get away that time they raided his house. Sergei, Gregor, and Raco were all linked to the Staro Dorbi attack on the Serbian farmers.

"I read the other day that Mr Raco and his accomplices have escaped again," Gregor said smugly.

Kit nodded warily. Petri's behavior was still objectionable. It made her shudder to remember the feel of Raco's rough hands on her body. Now she was being introduced by Sergei to this manipulative character socially. If Gregor Petri engaged in the same visualization practices as Sergei, that could explain his self-assurance and success in whatever game they were playing. She pulled herself together and decided she would have to learn more before deciding what action to take next.

"Are you still based in Pristina?" Kit asked him.

"My time there is ending soon. But who knows, I may be reassigned back to Kosovo," he replied.

Kit managed a tight-lipped smile. She refused to let them see how rattled she was feeling inside.

"And Leo is an art historian and poet who leads local tours for visitors on the side," Sergei said cheerfully, attempting to ease any tension he may have sensed.

Leo smiled and rose, giving Kit's hand a gentlemanly kiss.

"Natalia is from Romania and teaches dream interpretation," Sergei said. She was a petite woman in her late thirties, with captivating, large, brown eyes that seemed to hold a sense of the mystical. Her glossy, black hair added to her striking appearance.

"It's nice to meet you both," Kit said, sizing up the pair. Leo was a tall, slender man in his mid-thirties with the look of a Greek statue about him—like Michelangelo's *David*. "I'd love to hear more about your teaching," Kit said.

"It would be my pleasure," Natalia replied with a warm smile.

Sergei then pulled out a chair for Kit, who sat down and called the server over to order drinks and snacks for everyone.

"Kit wants to learn more about Khash, and I'm showing her around Ljubljana," he said to the group.

"Fantastic," Natalia replied.

Leo looked at her with interest. "Where are you from, Kit?" he asked.

"I'm from New Zealand," she answered. "I work with the OIDC in Pristina." She felt obliged to mention her job in Kosovo in general terms, since Gregor knew already.

"And that's how you met Sergei," Natalia said knowingly.

Kit nodded in agreement.

"It's like our paths just kept crossing, Katarina," Sergei said with a grin.

"For sure," Kit replied. She reclined in her chair and stretched out her legs, crossing her ankles. She felt ready to just let the evening play out, with or without Gregor Petri.

"Oh, sorry, what did you say your name was?" Leo asked quizzically. "Caitlin, Kit or Katarina?"

"All of them," Sergei said with a chuckle, answering for her. The server arrived and delivered their orders. Kit had coffee—Sergei knew to get her an Americano—Natalia ordered tea, and Leo and Gregor a draft of Slovenian beer. An appetizer plate was the next item to arrive at the table.

"Anyone mind if I…?" Kit offered, waving her Vogue slim cigarettes around the table. Everyone gave permission, and Gregor pulled his own cigarettes out.

"So how did you all meet Sergei?" Kit inquired.

Sergei intervened before anyone could answer. "You know how it goes, diplomatic functions here and there, friends of friends. That kind of thing," he said. The others looked at Kit expectantly, as if hoping for a reaction from her. She suspected that Sergei must have encountered Gregor in Pristina during one of his diplomatic missions. For all she knew, they may have had their own off-books task force planning operations in Kosovo with Russian backing.

"So are you all into this philosophy, Khash?" she asked instead.

"Yeah," Leo said. "We all have our own perspectives on Khash. We have various levels of expertise, and people are picking up whatever skills they can at their own pace."

"Dream work is actually part of our Khash practice," Natalia added.

"What do dreams have to do with it?" Kit asked in surprise.

"Well," Sergei began, "according to Khash, when we dream, our consciousness is free to explore different realms of possibility, sometimes even alternate realities. We can harness the potential of this theory by exploring these alternative reality through dreams and other methods which offer insights into different courses of action."

"What does 'alternative realities' even mean?" Kit asked. "Sorry to ask so many questions, but I really want to learn more about this philosophy."

"Quantum physics introduced the idea of multiple worlds. For each possible choice and outcome, a branching out of reality occurs. Think of it like a tree with different branches, different paths."

"So in one reality I might become and lawyer and work in Kosovo. But in another one, I married my high school sweetheart and live off the grid in a tiny house," Kit said, laughing at the exhilarating idea.

"Exactly. And more than that, somewhere in the universe—or multiverse—there is another version of you doing just that."

"I thought dream recall was for psychotherapy," Kit said, recalling her own experiences discussing dreams with her therapist. "I mean, I read that in a book on psychology."

"The two are not exclusive," Leo said.

"Can you tell me how to work with my dreams?" Kit said, looking at Natalia, who agreed. She passed around the plate of snacks. Kit took a shortbread cookie and sipped her coffee. She would need a proper lunch soon.

It was as if Sergei knew what she was thinking. "Maybe we should eat lunch while we're here."

"That's a good idea. I came straight from the airport. They didn't served anything to eat on the flight," Kit said. Sergei smiled but also said nothing about their visit to the Castle café. No doubt he approved of her discretion, she thought. It was another sign that she was becoming more careful.

"The restaurant serves French-inspired cuisine, but I can recommend the Slovene wines," Leo said.

"Maybe you can suggest one," Kit said. "I think it's great you meet in different locations. Where else have you met?"

"Vienna, Prague, Berlin. Places we can reach easily by air in central and eastern Europe," Sergei said.

"Great for sightseeing," Kit said.

"It's not about sightseeing," Sergei said. "To embrace different possibilities, we need to step outside our comfort zones and let go of our old selves. By exploring different locations, we can't predict what will happen, making it easier to break free of the familiar."

"What about venturing to the far north or the far south?" Kit suggested.

"We could go to Siberia next time," Leo said.

"That's a great idea! I know of some hidden gems in the Altai mountains. However, we have to remember Father Peter who likes to join us on our trips," Sergei added. Everyone nodded in agreement.

Sergei continued his thoughts. "I've been trying to get Kit to join us for a while. I was glad when she could make it this time." The group of friends looked at her and smiled.

"I took a risk when I joined this group," Kit said.

"And I'm pleased you did," Sergei replied. He reached out and took her hand in his, giving it a gentle squeeze before he pulled away and started talking again. "We can be so much more than we give ourselves credit for, but only if we let go of the past and focus on the present. Being in unfamiliar settings can often be just what we need to shake us out of our complacent habits. Even if it means getting ourselves tangled up in some questionable circumstances. That can actually be a good thing!"

Sergei reached for Kit's Vogue slim cigarette packet and pulled out a single cigarette. After Leo promptly lit it for him, Sergei leaned back and inhaled deeply. The slender cigarette looked comically small compared to his large hands, so that everyone couldn't help but laugh.

Though he seemed to be making a point about embracing the unexpected, the way Sergei savored the cigarette, carefully bringing it to the flame, slowly inhaling and exhaling, stirred something within Kit. He was showcasing his ability to appreciate moments of pleasure—something that could be shared if they ever found themselves alone together again.

The buzzing of her mobile phone jolted Kit from her reverie. She plucked the device from her bag and opened the message. It was from Xander. "Call you tonight?"

"Tomorrow," she typed back cautiously, aware of the curious eyes of the others at the table. Fortunately, Natalia spoke up first, drawing everyone's attention away from Kit..

"I bought a new dream journal," Natalia declared. "I recorded my first dream in it this morning."

"Please, share it with us!" Leo said eagerly, his eyes alight with interest.

As the conversation continued, Kit sent another message to Xander—"Miss you"—more to make up for her lack of availability than any heartfelt feeling.

Sergei looked at her intently. "Your fiancé, I presume?" he asked in a low voice meant only for her. "Is he still an avid cyclist?"

"As far as I know," Kit said. "He's a passionate environmentalist."

Sergei nodded and turned his attention back to the table chat, and Kit breathed a sigh of relief when their meals arrived. She couldn't shake the feeling that Sergei was hinting at her dishonesty with Xander, while at the same time appearing to approve of it. He frequently made remarks about Xander that seemed intended to put him in a bad light in Kit's eyes.

The food finally arrived at the table, with everyone having different main dishes: crêpes and salad for Kit, quiche Lorraine for Natalia, a Croque Monsieur grilled ham and cheese sandwich for Leo, a hearty lamb navarin stew for Gregor, and Steak frites—a round of steak with pomme frites and green garnish for Sergei. Kit washed down the first bite of her crepes with a crisp Slovenian Riesling.

"So, what would you recommend I do for my first dream assignment?" Kit asked Natalia, eager to change the subject.

Natalia put down her knife and fork, dabbed her mouth with the linen napkin, and spoke. "The first step is to remember your dreams. Keep a dream journal next to your bed with a pen nearby to write them down as soon as you wake up. Before you sleep, set an intention for a specific dream. Think of a question or topic you would like more information on and tell yourself, 'I will dream about this tonight.' The answer may not come that night but it will within the next few nights."

"I understand now that dreams are not separate from reality," Leo interjected.

Gregor smiled mischievously and said, "I won't tell you what I dreamt about last night."

Natalia looked over at him and said, "Don't be so mysterious."

Sergei teased Gregor, "I won't waste my time trying to figure out your dreams."

Natalia reassured Kit. "I'm sure you can do it. Some people are better at dream work than others."

Kit nodded thoughtfully. "All right, I'll start tonight. I know what I'd like to explore—how to solve my current case. On a different note, what hotels are all of you at?"

"We're both at the Cubist hotel, but on different floors," Natalia responded.

"I'm from Ljubljana, so I don't need a place to stay," Leo said.

"We also use dreams to envision alternate paths for the future," Sergei offered. "Vitamin B-6 can help."

"Lucid dreaming is something I'm interested in; when you wake up inside a dream and can influence it. As we manipulate our dreams, maybe we can control our lives better too," Gregor commented.

Natalia nodded her head in agreement. "It can be fun to go lucid, but sometimes it is better not to have complete control."

Kit pondered Natalia's words. "What about sleeping pills? Can they mess with dream recollection?"

Natalia frowned. "Yes, they induce sleep but disrupt the brain's natural cycles. They can even suppress dreaming process. Alcohol doesn't help either."

Kit mulled this over as she ate. Her experience with Dr Montenegro's pills aligned with Natalia's explanation; she resolved to stop taking them soon. But with so much happening, sleep had become elusive. Perhaps she should try to get some natural rest tonight and see what dreams came her way. As she considered the possibilities of the day ahead, a nervous excitement stirred within her chest. Would Sergei attempt to visit her room? If he didn't, she wasn't sure whether she'd feel relief or disappointment. Kit shook her head; she could entertain those thoughts another time.

"Once we finish eating," Sergei said, "how about we take a stroll around the inner city? It could broaden our horizons. We can use it to enter our dreams or meditations. I suggest we visit the Dragon Bridge."

"Sounds good to me," Leo said. "Maybe the others don't know the story of Ljubljana's Dragon."

"The honor is yours," Sergei said, indicating that Leo should share the story.

Leo smiled, took a breath, and began recounting the tale of Ljubljana's Dragon. "This is a story about Jason, the hero from Greek mythology, and the Argonauts during ancient Greek times. Jason is said to have founded Ljubljana. His maternal great-grandfather was Hermes, which reveals that hermetic wisdom has been present in this city from the beginning. Legend has it that after taking the Golden Fleece, Jason sailed along the river and found a lake surrounded by a marsh near present day Ljubljana. He defeated a monster there, which is now represented by the dragon seen on Ljubljana's arms and flag."

"Another version of this tale," Gregor said, "claims that the Dragon legend originates from small white salamanders living in a nearby cave."

"In another Slavic myth, slaying a dragon opens up waters and ensures abundance on Earth," Leo said. "This could be connected to the marshes around Ljubljana that pose a flooding risk."

"Or maybe it's about Saint George and his fight with a dragon," Sergei suggested. "But I prefer the story about Jason and his Argonauts because his great-grandfather was Hermes, an important symbol of the hermetic tradition in Ljubljana."

"Can you explain the hermetic tradition?" Kit asked.

"It's an ancient wisdom which states that what occurs in the heavens is similar to what is observed on Earth, and vice versa. The law of correspondences enables us to uncover the truth of different universes, as there are many."

"I'm not sure if I fully understand it, but I sure do like the story of Jason and the Argonauts," Kit said.

"Before we go to the bridge, I like to share something with you all." Sergei pulled several white envelopes out of his jacket pocket and passed one to each of them. "I've prepared some guiding thoughts based on our Khash philosophy. Father Peter has reviewed them and given them his blessing."

Sergei handed out a neatly typed sheet of paper to each of them. Kit reached eagerly for her envelope and tore it open. She relished the prospect of learning more about Sergei's enigmatic philosophy. She pulled out the page and read.

Thirteen Steps to Winning in Chess and in Life

By following these steps, anyone can become a master of the game and conquer their opponents with ease.

1. *Visualize your victory - Imagine the outcome you desire and focus on that vision every day. The mind is a powerful tool. Use it to your advantage and see the end goal clearly.*

2. *Engage in self-examination and discover what game play suits you best. Your strengths are your greatest weapons. Utilize them and watch your opponents fall.*

3. *Every game is a psychological struggle. To win, you must first know your opponent. Study them and play to their weaknesses.*

4. *Think ahead: Plan multiple moves in advance, so that you are always one step ahead of your opponent. Anticipate their moves and be prepared to counter them. Create multiple threats, so even if they counter one of your plans, you have others to fall back on.*

5. *Do not panic when you're under attack. Keep your cool: maintain your composure and stay focused on the game, even in high-pressure situations.*

6. *The game is constantly changing. Be flexible and adapt to the changes as they come. Things can get messy, but winning is all that matters.*

7. *Control the center: focus on securing the central area of the chessboard and field of operations to have the advantage over your opponent.*

8. *Embrace chaos - Use the confusion and disarray to your advantage. When the board is in disarray, seize the opportunity to make your move.*

9. *Be unpredictable - Keep your opponent guessing and off-balance. They will be more likely to make mistakes. Be like the wind, blowing where it will and hard to anticipate. Your enemies will never see you coming.*

10. *Sacrifice for gain: be willing to sacrifice a lesser piece to gain a greater advantage in the game.*

11. *Be alert to the climax of the game and pay extra attention at this critical time to identify a hidden threat or opportunity.*

12. *Deceit and misdirection are weapons to disguise your true intentions in the game. Use them wisely and your opponent will never know what hit them. Confuse and mislead your opponent wherever possible.*

13. *Develop your pieces: Bring all your pieces into the game to maximize your potential for success. The queening of a pawn symbolizes the ultimate victory and is the pinnacle of strategy and planning. The transformation of a humble pawn into a powerful queen is the result of careful planning and execution, much like the successful completion of a mission.*

She skimmed through the points, nodding in agreement with some and raising an eyebrow at others. When she got to the point about deceit and misdirection, she frowned. "I don't like this one," she said, looking up at Sergei. "Using deceit and misdirection is not always the right thing to do. I don't like the idea of sacrificing lesser pieces to get ahead, either." She wondered if she was a lesser piece that Sergei could sacrifice without a second thought.

Sergei shrugged. "In the game of life, winning is all that matters. Sometimes we have to use whatever means necessary to come out on top. Misinformation and disinformation are essential tools we need to master."

Natalia spoke up. "I must disagree, Sergei. Success shouldn't come at the cost of your integrity and values.

It's crucial to stay true to oneself and uphold what you believe is right."

Gregor chuckled. "You're both mistaken. In life, there are no absolute rules. To achieve victory, you have to use any means necessary, even if it means bending or breaking the rules."

Kit shook her head. "I can't support the notion that the end always justifies the means. Sometimes doing the right thing is more important than winning."

Sergei sighed, glancing at Kit and Natalia. "That's fine for you two, but in the real world, you must be willing to do whatever it takes to come out on top. Integrity and values are very much subjective concepts."

"I consider it an artistic statement. Like a painting. We're not supposed to take it literally," Leo said after taking his time to read the text.

Natalia nodded thoughtfully. "I suppose it's important to address our shadow selves, our darker, antisocial side. We can't pretend it doesn't exist because it's part of a whole human being, part of us."

Kit turned her attention back to the paper, scanning down to the final point. "The queening of a pawn symbolizes the ultimate victory and is the pinnacle of strategy and planning," she read aloud. "I understand the symbolism, but what does it mean in practical terms?"

Sergei leaned forward, his eyes lighting up. "It means that through careful planning and execution, you can transform a humble pawn into a powerful queen. Just like in life, where with the right plan and effort, you can transform yourself—or someone else—from a lowly individual into a powerful and successful person."

Kit sat back in her chair, considering Sergei's words. "I can understand the appeal of winning, but I still believe that success shouldn't come at the cost of our values and integrity."

Sergei merely shrugged, glancing at Gregor, who nodded in agreement. "To each their own, I suppose. But in the end, it's all about winning and coming out on top. Like in chess. You might think you've executed a brilliant game, but once your king is toppled, it's game over."

The group fell into silence, everyone lost in their own thoughts about the philosophy of strategy and winning. Kit couldn't shake the feeling that there had to be a better way, a way to win without sacrificing her values and beliefs. Simultaneously, a faint whisper at the back of her mind posed a challenge. To what extent would she go to dismantle the corruption festering in the upper echelons and restore justice? But for now, she would keep that question to herself and continue to search for a way to balance success and integrity. "While you think about that, I have another surprise for you. Father Peter is in Ljubljana on Church business. He's agreed to see us, and might even answer some questions about this," Sergei announced. The group shifted and murmured in surprise.

"How can he go along with this philosophy, Sergei?" Kit asked, gesturing to the sheet of paper. "As a priest."

"You can ask him that yourself," Sergei said.

"I will," she responded. This could be very interesting. Father Peter had been a shadowy figure who seemed to be part of their group, despite the fact that Kit had never met him.

"I suggest we meet up in twenty minutes at the Orthodox Church. I made an appointment for us to meet Father Peter in the office. I suggest you dress conservatively.

Women should wear a long dress or skirt, and men trousers and a long-sleeved shirt and jacket. After that, we can take a look at the Dragon Bridge," Sergei proposed.

"Oh no," Kit said. "Why didn't you tell me your plans? I didn't bring any clothing like that." In fact, she didn't think she owned anything that might fit the occasion. "Maybe I shouldn't come. He doesn't know me, after all."

"I have planned for this." Sergei was always two moves ahead. "I took the liberty of purchasing something suitable. Besides, Father Peter knows that you're not a member of the congregation, so he will make allowances. He has a list of the names of all of us who will be at the meeting, including yours. "

"Orthodoxy doesn't have a strict dress code, but there are some unspoken rules of etiquette," Natalia explained "The clothes should be modest, without embellishments, and knees and elbows must be covered. The head must be covered with a headscarf. Easy really."

"I'm really quite curious about the outfit you've got for me," Kit said.

"You'll just have to wait and see," Sergei said.

Chapter Seventeen

The group met about half an hour later outside the Holy Trinity Russian Orthodox Church in Ljubljana. The men were looking respectable and soberly attired. Kit had dressed in an outfit she found in a package from Sergei. A silver peplum tunic fell in graceful folds to her hips, over a long matching skirt. She had tied the fine linen scarf around her shoulders, but Natalia started fussing and tied it over her head.

Kit felt a sense of suppressed excitement mixed with trepidation. She had always loved to dress up as a young girl, and this felt like another costume. Her curiosity about Father Peter was overwhelming. She couldn't imagine Sergei deferring to anyone, and she wanted to get the measure of the Father. This eminence gris behind Sergei, the great manipulator, must be a fascinating person in his own right.

A young man dressed in clerical black greeted them at the entrance and invited them into the historic building that showcased the architectural style of the Russian Orthodox Church. The interior of the church was richly decorated with icons, frescoes, and other religious artwork. As they walked through the cloisters, she could smell the aroma of frankincense resin burning at the altar. The cloister seemed such an ordered, calm environment, far from the struggles of the secular world.

The young man, perhaps a seminarian, ushered them into a meeting room and indicated that they should wait. A few moments later, a tall, impressive man entered the room, clad in the garb of a Russian Orthodox priest. The others greeted him, saying, "Peace be with you, Father." Kit murmured the same words after them, doing her best to fit in.

Father Peter had an imperious bearing. He held himself erect, and from his considerable height, well over six feet, he looked down on them. Garbed in a black cassock with a pectoral cross around his neck, he wore a stiff, cylindrical head covering, like a stovepipe hat but without the brim, that made his presence even more imposing by adding to his height. Under his arm, he held a large, ornate chessboard. Kit reflected that he emanated a sense of focused power that was different to the Church of England clergy she had met in New Zealand. The latter had seemed down-to-earth and approachable, whereas Father Peter, with his full beard, black robes, and impressive height, was charismatic, if intimidating. His striking blue eyes surveyed them, stopping to take in everything about each person before moving on to the next. When his gaze finally settled on Kit, she felt mesmerized. It was as if they were the only two people in the room. Even her awareness of Sergei receded into the background. She felt that he was assessing her to decide whether she could be a threat.

Sergei interrupted the moment when he stepped forward and presented a gift to Father Peter, who accepted it with a nod and handed it to his assistant. It was a beautifully wrapped parcel, and based on its size and shape, Kit guessed it could be an icon for the Father's personal devotions.

He sat down, and they followed his lead to join him around the table. Sergei was on his right. Kit tried to observe from an inconspicuous position among the others.

"Welcome, my friends," Father Peter said, his voice deep and resonant. "I have been expecting you." Father Peter spread his hands in a gesture of welcome.

"We are here to seek your wisdom, Father," Sergei said deferentially.

Father Peter nodded, a smile playing at the corners of his lips. "So you have," he responded. "And I have much to teach you. As a representative of the Russian Orthodox Church, it is my calling to offer counsel and solace to all who seek it. Each of you confronts a distinct set of trials, but I urge you to never forget the importance of living a life rooted in the principles of our faith."

With deliberate care, he placed the chessboard on a table and began setting it up. His long, pallid fingers danced across the board with graceful, well-practiced gestures. Kit's gaze was drawn to the ring adorning Father Peter's right hand—an ornate, antique piece featuring an exquisitely crafted, silver Orthodox cross embedded in black onyx. The ring seemed to emanate an aura of power, history, and spiritual authority.

Once the board setup was complete, Father Peter began to speak again. "Chess is a symbolic dance of strategy and dominance," he declared. "It hones our intellect and teaches us to act decisively under pressure from an adversary. The game serves as a guide in our pursuit to uncover the truth."

Kit listened to Father Peter with growing trepidation, acutely aware that she was treading in waters that were far too deep for her. Doubt gnawed at her, making her question her preparedness for the challenges that no doubt lay ahead. She wasn't sure if she was ready for what was to come. As Sergei and his friends absorbed the priest's teachings with rapt attention, she realized the gravity of the situation; there would be no turning back. She was now entwined in this perilous game, and escape was no longer an option.

"For the benefit of the newcomers to this group, allow me a few moments to delve briefly into the storied past of chess. The game has a rich history that spans over a millennium, with its roots in the ancient lands of northern India. From there, it coursed its way through Persia, eventually finding its way to Russia in the tenth century. Rapidly capturing the fascination of the aristocracy, chess was revered as a tool for honing one's mental prowess and forging a formidable character, essential attributes in the complex world of power and intrigue."

Father Peter's voice was sonorous and held Kit's attention, as if she was mesmerized.

"Our group venerates the legacy of Grigori Yefimovich Novykh, better known as Rasputin. Through his extensive travels around Greece and Jerusalem, he gained esoteric knowledge and powers of influence and healing. Rasputin believed by mastering the game of chess, one could decipher the world's inner workings and the threads of destiny. As a close advisor to the Tsar Nicholas II and his wife, he played chess with members of the royal court, using the game as a metaphor for life to teach strategy, patience, and composure.

"Today, chess remains a symbol of intellect and strategy worldwide. Like Rasputin, I believe that the game of chess holds the key to unlocking the mysteries of the cosmos. So, my friends, embrace chess, and let its philosophy guide your life's journey. May we honor Rasputin's memory and teachings, striving to live to our fullest potential and become the best versions of ourselves."

Even though she found the priest intimidating, Kit couldn't keep quiet any longer. She had to probe further to find out more about the man and Sergei's philosophy. "Excuse me, Father Peter," she said, raising her hand. "But I don't understand. How is chess supposed to unlock the mysteries of life?"

Father Peter turned to her, a smile on his face. "Ah, a skeptical mind," he said. "That is good. For it is only through questioning that we may arrive at the truth. I wouldn't expect any less from a friend of Sergei."

Sergei shot Kit a warning look, but she ignored him. She was curious and wanted to know more.

"So, what is the truth?" she asked, crossing her arms.

"The truth, my child, is that the game of chess is a metaphor for life," replied Father Peter. "Each piece represents a different aspect of the human experience, and each move represents a decision we must make. By studying the game of chess, we may gain insight into our own lives and the path we must take."

Kit frowned, not entirely convinced. "And what about Rasputin? How does he fit into all of this? Wasn't he discredited as a charlatan?" Kit's initial plan to remain inconspicuous during the meeting was thrown to the wind. She couldn't resist speaking up. Sergei leant forward, frowning. He looked as if he was about to reprimand Kit for speaking disrespectfully to their host, but the Father raised his hand, indicating that Sergei should wait for him to respond to the questions.

"Rasputin was a great master of the Khash chess philosophy," said Father Peter, his eyes gleaming. He clearly relished the topic. "He dedicated his life to unlocking its secrets, and he came to understand the true power that lies within the game. It was his belief that, by mastering the game of chess, one may unlock the secrets of the universe and attain great power and wealth."

The room was silent for a moment as Father Peter's words hung in the air. Kit could sense the tension in the room, and she could tell that the others felt uncomfortable with her line of questioning. This was the first mention she had heard of wealth in connection with Khash.

"This knowledge came to us from some manuscripts made by his close students, which have been kept safe from public view. Not many people are privy to this powerful knowledge. I admit that most of my brothers in the Church do not share my views on the topic. I am content for Kasch to remain the purview of a select few. Despite generally negative views, some still view Rasputin as a spiritual healer and a symbol of the influence of the Russian Orthodox Church in politics," Father Peter added.

"So influence in politics is important?" Kit asked. Father Peter inclined his head in careful assent. "If you don't mind me asking, what is your position on Kosovo's independence from Serbia?" Kit had wondered before about Father Peter's connection to Sergei and his Kosovo operations?

"You ask a sensitive question, and I'll answer. We're all friends here. The Russian Orthodox Church does not support Kosovo's independence. We have strong ties to the Serbian Orthodox Church, which opposes it. Russia is a close ally of Serbia, also opposing it. Kosovo, 'the heart of Serbia,' has many important Serbian Orthodox sites. So, Ms. Chase, I think you can read between the lines here."

Kit mulled over the response. His opposition of Kosovo's independence was hardly surprising, and Father Peter had been careful to avoid admitting any direct connection to Sergei's activities trying to destabilize Kosovo.

"Thank you, Father Peter,'" Sergei interrupted. "Your teachings are most enlightening. You have given Caitlin, and all of us, much to ponder. But I think we should move on to other matters now."

Kit leaned back in her chair, feeling frustrated. There was so much she wanted to know, but it seemed that Sergei and the others were not interested in exploring Kosovo politics further. She couldn't help but feel like she was missing something important, and she made a mental note to research the topic further on her own.

"Father," Sergei continued. "We're going to the Dragon Bridge. I thought you could say something about the symbolism of the dragon."

The priest nodded and thought for a moment. "In our faith, the dragon is a symbol of the forces of temptation and sin that seek to ensnare the soul. The story of St. Michael the Archangel and the dragon has deep spiritual meaning. It's a reminder of the struggle between good and evil within every person. St. Michael signifies divine protection and the power of faith to overcome the forces of evil."

"So each of us needs to confront and overcome opposing forces, symbolized by the dragon," Sergei summarized.

Father Peter nodded. "Anticipate your opponent's moves and plan accordingly. Your opponent is Satan, and this is a spiritual battle. Study his tactics and anticipate his strategies so that you can defeat him.”

“Evil comes in many forms, Father,” Gregor said.

“Perseverance, hard work, and unity is necessary to achieve your goals. Remain grounded in your faith before any opposition, and you will win the battle,” Father Peter said.

“Thank you so much, Father Peter,” Sergei said.

The priest turned his attention to Kit again. She did not meet his gaze as she was already regretting her outburst. She was, after all, just a visitor in their world and perhaps had been an ungracious guest, causing embarrassment to her friends on her first visit.

“Caitlin, I’m glad we met. You have great potential and a bright future. Even if you don’t share our faith now, consider the wisdom and guidance the Russian Orthodox Church offers. It can provide comfort and support in life’s challenges, and I encourage you to explore our teachings and beliefs. I am available if you need to discuss any of these matters further.”

Kit looked up, their eyes meeting—hers oceanic green and his arctic blue.

“I’m sorry if I spoke out of turn,” she said. “I’m fascinated by what you have to say and grateful for this opportunity.” That much was true. Father Peter inclined his head, accepting her apology.

“Dear children, as followers of the Russian Orthodox Church and admirers of Rasputin’s legacy, we must live in a way that honors his memory. Strive to embody his compassion and spiritual wisdom and stay devoted to our teachings. Life and chess are both games of trial and error, with no guaranteed wins. May the Church’s wisdom and love guide you in all your endeavors.”

With that, Father Peter rose, nodding to them. His aide opened the door, carefully stowing the chess set and Sergei's gift. The group of friends reconvened outside the church, leaving the sacred space behind.

"Wow, that was amazing," Kit said. "Sorry if I asked too many questions. I didn't mean to be disrespectful. I'm sorry if I came across like that."

Sergei had recovered his composure after the irritation he had shown inside.

"Father Peter isn't going to be offended by a few questions," Sergei said. "I think he rather liked you. But you should have the strength of your convictions and stop apologizing for you actions."

"I remember when you first told me about Rasputin's legacy, I was quite surprised, shocked even. I always thought he was a charlatan."

"You should be aware by now that there is evidence to support any hypothesis. It just depends on who's telling the story," Sergei said.

"What did you think of Father Peter, Kit? As a person," Natalia asked.

She thought for a moment. "I was impressed, honestly. He has an incredible presence. It was the first time I met a priest from the Russian Orthodox Church. I don't know if he's typical."

"Father Peter is not typical," Leo said.

"He's in a category of his own," Gregor agreed.

"I'd love to learn more about those manuscripts he talked about. The ones Rasputin's students wrote, I suppose based on his teachings. Where are they now?"

"They're in a safe place," Sergei said. "But if you spend more time with us, you might learn more about them. For now, you'll have to make do with my thirteen points I gave you."

"Has he ever visited the Serbian Orthodox monasteries in Kosovo?" Kit asked, still convinced that there must be some connection between the Russian Orthodox priest and the Serbian Orthodox Church.

"Of course," Sergei said.

"I wonder if he meant his offer to talk to me again," Kit said.

"Father Peter doesn't waste his words. If he said it, he meant it," Sergei said. "We'll see how things develop."

Chapter Eighteen

The group made their way through the winding cobblestone streets of Ljubljana, each step bringing them closer to the iconic Dragon Bridge. Sergei and Kit led the pack, their footsteps echoing with purpose. Gregor, a few steps behind, through force of habit maintained a vigilant gaze, scanning the surroundings for any potential threats that might compromise their mission.

Natalia and Leo, seemingly absorbed in their own world, trailed leisurely at the rear. The pair exchanged thoughts and observations about the city's history. Every so often, Leo would stop and point out a building or monument, explaining its significance to the city's cultural landscape.

The fresh air and the stunning architecture of Ljubljana provided a welcome respite for Kit, who had been grappling with the intensity of the closed-room meeting with Father Peter. "It's nice to get away from Kosovo for a while," Kit said. "That place can be overwhelming at times."

"Sometimes it helps to take a step back and look at things from a new angle," Sergei replied.

Kit's mind drifted back to their last encounter in Pristina, when her emotions had spiralled out of control and she had slapped him several times. Now she was starting to understand him better, or so she thought. Maybe he even approved of her letting out her feelings. It certainly hadn't deterred him from contacting her again. On the other hand, he had asked her to find a way to cancel his pending arrest warrant. He seemed to always have multiple motivations.

"I feel like I'm still searching for what I want to do with my life long-term. I want to be a prosecutor in the short-term, but I haven't figured out my goals for long run. And my relationships? Who knows?"

Sergei offered her a warm smile for sharing her confidences. "Finding your path can take time. But, for what it's worth, I think you're doing just fine."

Kit looked over her shoulder at Gregor, who was following closely behind them. Conscious of his proximity and not wanting him to overhear their conversation, she stepped away from Sergei and turned around to face him.

"Hey there, buddy! What can I do for you?" Sergei said cheerfully as he clapped his arm around Gregor's shoulder.

"Just taking it all in, boss," Gregor replied. "Thinking about my next move and how I want things to unfold."

"To make your dreams a reality?" Sergei said.

"Yes," Gregor confirmed. "My promotion in the Romanian army is well overdue."

"Good man," Sergei said with a nod of approval. "I appreciate someone who knows what they want." He glanced at Kit, who refused to look at him, as if he was saying that Gregor knew what he wanted so why didn't she.

They approached the Dragon Bridge, where two large, metal dragons perched atop large concrete plinths.

Their webbed wings were aloft and their gaping, beak-like jaws thrust outwards. Further, smaller dragons curled around the Art Nouveau lamps. Sergei rounded the group up and asked them to consider the dragons more deeply.

"Most people see these dragons as whimsical bridge decorations, but I want us to think of them symbolically," Sergei said. "What goes through your mind when you look at these statues?" Sergei asked. "Notice every detail and commit them to memory. Later, recall this image. It might lead to a dream or fantasy about these dragons."

Natalia chimed in, "You can do that with any image. I often draw a tarot card at random and imagine entering it for insights into a particular question."

"You could have a tarot session later; you can show Kit how it's done," Sergei suggested. "But for now, let's focus on the dragons. We are using imagery to more clearly define our goals and help us change our lives."

As the group arrived at the Zmajski Most, or Dragon Bridge, they marveled at its imposing presence, the four dragon statues guarding the entrance as if daring anyone to cross.

The bridge, a symbol of the city's resilience and strength, seemed to hold a deeper meaning for the group, a metaphor for the challenges they would face together in the days to come. Little did Kit know that her journey towards justice would lead her into a labyrinth of secrets, conspiracies, and hidden dangers, with each step taken on the Dragon Bridge marking the beginning of a treacherous path.

By now, the sky had grown cloudy, and a wind had started blowing. Kit stepped away from Sergei and took a closer look at the Dragon Bridge before them. As Natalia began making notes, Kit's unease from her previous encounter with Sergei and their visit to the library returned, centering around the nearby mythical dragon.

The members of their group started walking mindfully across the bridge, each wrapped in their own thoughts. Natalia put away her notebook and slung her backpack over her shoulders and moved forward with purpose. This was Kit's chance to confront her fears and move beyond them. The fear of heights that had plagued her since childhood crept back as she inched across the bridge. The light faded, casting a gloomy atmosphere over the town. Kit felt like she was walking through quicksand, becoming heavier and slower with each step. When she reached the middle of the bridge, two more dragons awaited her. She remembered that crossing water symbolizes transformation—a chance to move from one state to another. Kit thought of Jacob Mueller, Raco, Sergei, and even Xander. She feared their reactions and anger towards her, but she could be free if she believed she was. She had to overcome her fears if she wanted to move forward. These people could no more stop her than these frozen metal dragons on the bridge could, unless she let them.

Kit breathed more deeply, and her shoulders relaxed. She held her head higher and walked more briskly. Hyperaware of the dragons, she could appreciate them as works of art, but she rejected the fear that they triggered. When she reached the end of the span, she noticed the surroundings again. Sergei was waiting there, observing her.

He gathered the group around him. "Tell us what you experienced," he said.

Natalia spoke first. "I remembered a recurrent dream I have of crossing a bridge. I can't see the beginning or the end of the bridge, and I'm frozen in the middle. I glance down and see swirling water and mist. I look up and see a rocky mountain range. Sometimes the bridge is swaying, other times I look down and see that it's made of rotten wooden planks and I'm scared to move. I knew I could live the dreams and bring them to a conclusion by crossing this bridge."

"Does that remind you of anything?" Sergei asked.

"I've been stagnating professionally for a while now. I know I have to take a risk and move forward. Maybe I should leave my day job, even though I'm afraid that I won't be able to earn enough through my dream therapy and art work."

"Excellent work, Natalia. Now you can plan what you'd want to find in your new situation. How about you, Leo?" Sergei asked.

"I got inspiration for a new poem," Leo said. "The dragons were friendly for me. I thought about how important the dragon is in Ljubljana. It inspired legends, making this the beautiful city that we have today."

"I'd like to see that poem when you're ready to share it," Sergei answered. "And Gregor, did you discover anything?"

"I found that I have a connection with the dragons, a sense of self-confidence and strength. Just like they stay perched on the bridge for years, I want to make an impression in my own life. These dragons have an incredibly long lifespan, much like I plan to have; I'm certain that I'll have enough time to reach my goals."

Sergei patted Gregor on the back and grinned in approval.

"Now, Kit," Sergei said in a soft voice. "What happened for you?"

"The dragons remind me of the people I'm nervous about. I realised I don't need to be intimidated by them anymore. The dragons made me realize that these people are like empty shells and only have as much power over me as I give them," Kit said. "I found my courage."

"I'm proud of you," Sergei said, embracing her with a kiss on the cheek. "In my fantasy, I spoke to the dragons and one asked me a riddle which I had to answer in order to complete the crossing."

"So, what was the riddle?" Gregor couldn't hold back his curiosity. They all wanted to hear it. Sergei fixed Gregory with his gaze and recounted the riddle in a poem.

> *"However high I fly*
> *Or however low I go,*
> *My greatest treasure I hold within.*
> *What is it?"*

Kit laughed and said, "And did you know the answer?"

Sergei replied with a chuckle, "Some things must remain between a man and his dragon! The right answer is whatever you want it to be; just remember not to veer away from your goals."

Gregor quickly caught on and said, "So there's no wrong answer?"

Sergei shook his head. "The trick is knowing what you want and being sure about it."

Kit rolled her eyes but smiled at the same time. "You never stop messing with people's heads, do you?" she joked.

Sergei shrugged as he started explaining. "Let's go back to our guiding principle, 'Khash.' It draws its essence from the intricate game of chess, where the ultimate objective is to put the opponent's king in a position of 'checkmate'."

He paused for emphasis before continuing. "Now, 'Sheikh Mat' is a Persian term which translates to 'the king is helpless,' or dead. When Sheikh is said backwards, it sounds similar to 'Khash.' The parallel we draw here is that in our game, just as in chess, your 'king' could be a strategy, a plan, or a crucial point of leverage. When it's dead or compromised, you lose. Therefore, our philosophy, 'Khash,' inspires us to think a step ahead, to strategize like a chess player, foreseeing potential threats and countering them before they make us helpless. I'm merely trying to inspire you to play a better game."

The explanation shed light on the underpinning strategy within their unique code language, drawing the depth of the game of chess into the real-world maneuvers of their operations.

Kit sighed. "It's enigmatic and maddening at the same time."

Natalia laughed. "I know what you mean, Kit. I keep telling him to quit playing games, but it never works for long."

"What about Father Peter? Does he like to play games too?" Kit asked.

"You mean other than chess? He's the biggest trickster of them all." Sergei chuckled. "But I think we achieved something meaningful this afternoon. Each of us had an exceptional experience playing with the dragons. We each came to a new understanding."

"You're right, Sergei," Kit said. "I came here seeking a revelation in my case. Instead I had a personal breakthrough."

"I expect you'll get all your objectives this weekend, and more," Sergei said.

Kit was uncertain. "We'll have to wait and see if I make any progress on the case. I asked for a dream about it."

"There's one other place I would like to take Kit today. I'm sure the rest of you have already seen it," Sergei said. "Let's meet in the main town square for dinner at eight o'clock. Use the rest of your time to create visualizations based on what you experienced today or go to a bar and drink odka."

"So where are you taking her?" Leo asked.

"To the Devil's Courtyard," he answered.

CHAPTER NINETEEN

The Devil's Courtyard was part of an old monastery belonging to the Order of Teutonic Knights, a militant German religious order similar to the Knights Templar. In the 1950s, it underwent renovations designed by Plečnik, and now it catered to small chamber music performances.

"Let's hope we're not too late to get in," Sergei said, walking up to the iron gate topped with an arch flanked by two half columns. He pushed the side of the gate, and it opened. Inside the courtyard was a line of plinths displaying modern sculptures and a relief of a warrior knight stopping a shield and sword, likely from a crypt. They were met by the custodian, an older man, who exchanged words with Sergei before welcoming them in.

Sergei and Kit stepped through the hallway and entered a modest-sized courtyard enclosed by walls of the presbytery and cloister, lined with benches below rows of lamps.

"It still feels like a monastery," Kit remarked quietly. "They've kept the character, but there are some new elements too."

"Let's explore," Sergei said.

A chilling atmosphere enveloped them as they stepped into the Devil's Courtyard. Shadows danced across the small, enclosed space, the cloister walls enclosing them in an eerie embrace. Kit's gaze followed the rows of lamps that adorned the walls, their dim glow casting an otherworldly pallor on the pebbled floor. Intricate patterns of marble circles and white plinths emerged, supporting minimalist marble blocks that seemed to hold secrets of their own.

In the farthest corner, an ancient metal door, emblazoned with a crimson cross, hinted at a clandestine Order to which it belonged. A short, worn landing led the way into the unknown. Kit's eyes traced the peculiar circular arrangement of columns, drawn to one of the cryptic marble exhibits. She reached out, her fingers brushing against the sigil-like symbols etched into the surface, tiny circles linked together by straight lines.

"So, this is the Devil's Courtyard," she murmured. "It's not huge, but there is something captivating about it…"

"Have you noticed its most unique quality?"

She then focused on the spotlights embedded in the walls—four rows of them, spaced evenly around the perimeter. Each light had a half sphere projecting from it with an open face housing a bulb. "The walls seem strange," she said, feeling the hairs on her neck stand up as the Devil's Courtyard revealed another mystery.

"When they turn on those lights in the dark, it looks like these walls have eyes watching us. I asked the custodian if he would turn on the lights when it gets dark. Plečnik converted the Monastery of the Holy Cross into a venue for the Ljubljana Festival," he explained.

When the lights finally went on in the lengthening dusk, it was like all traces of the walls had been erased, and so they sat for some time in silence, immersed in this special atmosphere created by an orange, glowing curtain of light.

"It looks as if the walls have completely disappeared and we're sitting in a room of light," Kit said.

"I like to share things that are utterly unique with you," he said.

Kit, unable to contain her curiosity, asked, "Why do they call it the Devil's Courtyard?"

Sergei glanced around, his eyes settling on the sinister lights that seemed to watch their every move. "Those lights are like demonic eyes watching us," he replied. "The Holy Orders, such as the Teutonic Knights, often faced evil more intensely due to their rigorous training. Maybe they battled their inner demons right here in this courtyard, though the lights themselves were undoubtedly Plečnik's brilliant design."

"Doesn't Lucifer mean 'light bringer'? Maybe all these lights are designed to illuminate our desires."

The sky grew darker, as if nature itself was conspiring to intensify the atmosphere. A blanket of clouds blocked any sunlight from entering the courtyard. Raindrops began to fall, seeping into the crevices of the paving and deepening the colors around them. Kit shivered as she zipped up her light top.

"Let's stay a little longer and appreciate this moment," she suggested, her voice soft.

As they stood there, Kit breathed in the intoxicating aroma of autumn and the ancient buildings, the Devils Courtyard weaving its enigmatic spell around them both.

"It'll be Halloween soon," she said thoughtfully.

"We're getting closer to one of those moments of transition. I can sense it too," he said.

The rain started to become heavier, and thunder rumbled in the distance, following a flicker of lightning in the mountains.

"I don't want to get too wet though; it's getting colder," Kit said as she started to feel the water seeping under her collar.

"Alright, let's go," Sergei responded.

She stood up and glanced around at the enchanting Devil's Court with its glimmering walls of light. He took off his heavier jacket and put it around her shoulders before they left through an archway that led them from the courtyard into a dark passageway illuminated only by occasional flashes of lightning. As they exited, the lights switched off. The beating of the rain became more insistent. With the darkness, Kit's other senses became more acute.

She felt herself swathed in the silky interior of Sergei's jacket, imbued with a heady fragrance of leather and tobacco blended with vanilla. He was a strong physical presence beside her. She shuddered, and his arm tightened around her. The two of them stood, trapped in the darkness between the Devil's Court and the Courtyard of the Holy Cross, with elemental forces swirling around them.

"Would you like to kiss me?" she breathed, close to him. Then all she was aware of was the warmth of his lips on hers as they were swept up in a passionate embrace. Kit's thoughts flashed back to when Sergei had carried her to safety after she fainted at a crime scene. His strength had lifted her up when she was her weakest. Kit was much stronger now. Now she had come to Ljubljana to explore what their relationship could become. She appreciated that he had waited for her invitation this time rather than imposing on her personal space as it felt like in the library earlier that day.

Sergei groaned from deep within his throat as his body tensed against hers, and his free hand pressed against her back. She could tell he was about to lose control, but she felt empowered by the passion they shared.

In the darkness, she let her emotions guide her, but her mind drifted to another memory. Unexpectedly, she remembered when she kissed Owen at Durrës Beach, eating ice cream in the sun and pretending to be a couple during surveillance. The thought of him sent a chill through her, and she pulled away from Sergei, gasping for air.

Kit felt a mixture of excitement and confusion after the passionate kiss with Sergei. She felt that she had to offer some explanation, although she didn't fully understand herself what had just happened. "That was intense," Kit said, her voice trembling slightly. "But we should get going before someone catches us."

Sergei seemed reluctant to leave, but he nodded and gave her a quick kiss on the forehead. "As you wish, my love," he said, his Russian accent sending shivers down her spine. Kit glanced around, making sure that no one was watching them. She knew their relationship was risky and could jeopardize her career and his safety, but she couldn't resist the temptation of being with him. They left the hallway and took the garden path back to the gate. Sergei pressed the button to open the gate, and they stepped outside.

"I really loved today and spending time with you," she said. "But now I feel exhausted. I just need some time to myself. I don't think I'll join you all for dinner."

He nodded understandingly. "I get it," he said, his voice soft. "Take all the time you need. I'm proud of you for stepping outside your comfort zone and exploring new things."

They approached the hotel, which had a luxe bar that doubled as a coffee shop during the day.

"I need a drink," she said. "Do you want to join me?"

Sergei agreed, and they chose a cozy corner with leather chairs and a small glass-top table. Kit got a whiskey sour with ice cubes, and Sergei requested a shot of vodka with some snacks. Sergei downed his vodka in one shot, then immediately ordered another.

Kit watched him with admiration, noticing how his hair, now shot with silver, had become dark blonde curls from the rain, while his golden-colored eyes had a stormy intensity. She couldn't help but notice his slightly reddened lips, a reminder of their kiss. She savored the moment before gazing away again at her drink.

Once the server left, Kit leaned back and crossed her feet at the ankles. "It feels good to relax," she said. "I think we managed to escape the worst of the rain."

"Yes, we did. But I have the feeling that the storm is not over yet." Sergei nodded, his eyes twinkling.

Kit raised an eyebrow, intrigued. "What do you mean?"

Sergei leaned closer, his voice low. "I mean we have much more to explore, you and I. The Devil's Courtyard was just the beginning."

Kit felt a thrill run through her. She knew their relationship was risky, but she couldn't resist the temptation. She took a sip of her drink, feeling the warm liquid seep through her body.

"You're right," she said, her eyes locked on his. "The game is far from over. You mentioned you thought I could crack my case this weekend. What did you mean by that?"

He grinned, then reached into his pocket and pulled out his wallet. He opened it and removed a card, which he put down on the table in front of them. She picked it up and studied it. On one side it read "HexD Nightclub" and on the other side there was a handwritten name: Kapitan Silver.

"This is a nightclub," she said sceptically. "How is this supposed to help me with my money-laundering investigation?"

He smiled faintly and replied, "Someone who often goes there might be able to help you—a person who goes by the name Kapitan Silver. They are affiliated with Russia's foreign intelligence service and specialize in hacking. If anyone can uncover evidence of the illicit funds transfers out of Kosovo by high-level officials, it would be Silver."

"Someone like that sounds expensive. I don't have that kind of money."

"Silver owes me a favor," Sergei said. "Also, HexD is a code word for the number thirteen," he added and watched her expression. She didn't want to admit that she hadn't known the meaning of the phrase. "Can they stop the financial transfers being made?"

"I don't know. Silver trades in information. You might learn something important to your case."

"This is my only lead, but what if Silver isn't there or won't speak with me?" Kit asked.

"It's my pleasure to help," Sergei said as he patted her knee and pulled a pen from his pocket. He wrote something in Cyrillic script on the back of a card and set it on the table. "I suggest we go together to the urban squat tomorrow night; that's where the nightclub is located. We may get lucky and find Silver. These are abandoned buildings that have been claimed by a community of squatters, artists, and protesters."

Kit looked at the card, feeling a sense of anticipation. She knew that the next few days would be crucial for her investigation, and she couldn't afford to miss any opportunities. She turned to Sergei and smiled.

"Thank you. Let's do it," she said, and then asked hesitantly, "Do you have some kind of protocol for contacting him?"

"I prefer to do this off books, not as part of a GRU operation," he said. "Security has been an issue there. Extremists have been stirring trouble, so some of the clubs at the squat have hired their own security to maintain safety."

Kit nodded warily and studied his expression closely; it was hard to tell where the truth ended and the lie began. She knew his involvement could put her investigation at risk, but she also knew that he had valuable skills and connections that could help her crack the case.

"So what's his M.O.?" she asked, curious.

"A combination of social engineering and programming skills, as far as I know. For some of these hackers, it's an accomplishment to access a major computer system, be it a bank, a monetary institution, or a government agency."

"It would be amazing if you could do that, Sergei. I am so concerned about the current situation in Pristina."

"Me too," he replied, his eyes darkening. Sergei's cell phone rang, interrupting their conversation. He excused himself and walked away to take the call privately. Kit took the opportunity to slip the card in her wallet. When he returned, he said, "That was Gregor. The group is waiting at a nearby restaurant for drinks. Are you sure you don't want to join us?"

She also stood up. "I'd like to, but I am really tired. Maybe tomorrow morning I can meet you guys for brunch? I like your friends—apart from Gregor, who was really insulting to Matt during our task force meetings."

Sergei chuckled. "But he is great to have on your side."

"I don't think he was ever on our side," she said, feeling frustrated. Gregor had a reputation for being ruthless and untrustworthy among her other friends and associates.

"Just give him another chance; you may end up changing your mind about him."

Kit sighed. She knew she couldn't afford to alienate Sergei's friends if she wanted to pursue this alliance, but she also knew she had to be careful not to compromise her position too much. She already had plans forming in her mind for the evening that she didn't intend to share with Sergei. Two could play at the game of subterfuge.

"Get some rest, *malishka*, little one," Sergei said, his eyes locked on hers. "We have a big day tomorrow." Kit nodded. She watched as Sergei walked away, his broad shoulders silhouetted in the darkness. She knew that the next few days would be crucial for her investigation, and she couldn't afford to make any mistakes.

Once she was back in her hotel room, Kit took out the card that Sergei had given her and studied it closely. She ran her fingers along the scrawled words "Kapitan Silver – VIP access" before slipping it into her bag. She knew that going to the nightclub was a risky proposition, but she also had to take chances if she wanted to crack the case in the short time available before the power plant contract was approved and the funds transferred out of Kosovo.

As she got ready for the evening, Kit felt a mix of anticipation and nerves. She checked her phone for any messages from Sergei, but there were none. She took it as a sign that tonight, she was on her own. Through determination and courage, she would make her own luck in this unknown place. With newfound energy, Kit headed out into the night, ready to face whatever lay ahead.

CHAPTER TWENTY

Kit waved down a taxi from her hotel to the Metelkova squat, situated in the heart of Ljubljana. Once used as a shelter by the Former Yugoslav National Army, it had since transformed into one of the largest urban squats in Europe. The sprawling commune was a thriving hotspot for alternative culture, alive with music, theatre, and art throughout its labyrinthine bars, canteens, and makeshift galleries.

She hunted through her bag, finding the Club HexD card and read out the address to the taxi driver. As they drove, they passed under the dim glow of orange streetlights that cast eerie shadows on the narrow streets. The taxi pulled up outside of the graffiti-covered buildings just before midnight. A blend of street art and weathered statues and lurid art emerged from the shadows, each telling a story of resistance and freedom.

Kit handed the driver his fee before clambering out of the car. Her thick braid hung down her back, and her full leather jacket skimmed her miniskirt and tights, while her high-heeled boots clicked on the worn pavement. The thumping bass of techno music reverberated off the crumbling walls around Club HexD's entrance, where amongst the colorful graffiti, she made out the letters of its name. Inside, a party was in full swing, drawing people in.

The taxi driver looked at Kit with concern when she told him she didn't need him to wait for her. She thanked him, shut the car door, and headed towards the club with determination.

At the entrance to the building, a burly man wearing dark trousers and a T-shirt collected money and stamped the wrists of guests with an ink design. Kit recalled Sergei's comment about the hired security. She could make out silhouettes through the pulsing light and thumping music, but it was difficult to discern individuals in the throng. She allowed the bouncer to mark her with a cross and showed him the card with the name Silver on it. He quickly evaluated her face before searching her bag for weapons. He directed her to a bar towards the left with a jerk of his chin. As she moved further into the room, she felt a wave of pressure vibrate across her body with the beat of the music. A young man grabbed her arm and pulled her into a dance, which she enjoyed for a few moments for the sake of fitting in before heading to the bar. There, two people were seated. One was a woman in her mid-twenties with an asymmetrical haircut, wearing cut-offs, high-heeled sandals, and a crop top decorated with shimmering sequins. The woman faced a man in his thirties with dark hair, wearing dark jeans and a black T-shirt marked with a Maltese cross. He looked rough around the edges, as if he hadn't shaved or brushed his hair for days.

"I'm looking for…" Kit yelled, but she knew her voice could not be heard. She pointed to the back of the card Sergei had given her: "Kapitan Silver." The woman viewed the card and then handed it to the man, who nodded. Kit retrieved the card and slipped it back into her bag. The girl indicated towards the rear of the room, and she followed Kit, with her companion closely behind.

Out the back of the club, there was a simple kitchenette with a worn wooden bench, mismatched plastic chairs, and a stained sink. A couple sat at the bench, wrapped in each other's arms and lost in a passionate kiss. Kit noticed the remaining track of white powder on the table, a clear indication that they had been doing cocaine. The man with them snapped something sharply at the couple, who reluctantly disconnected from each other. He jolted his head towards the door and spoke again in a gruff tone. The woman stumbled but was supported by her partner as they made their way towards the door.

"So," said the blonde woman, hands on hips as she faced Kit. "What's this about?" The voice carried a distinct Eastern European accent.

"I'm looking for Kapitan Silver." The words felt awkward coming out of Kit's mouth, but the woman didn't seem to notice anything amiss.

"Why?"

"I'd rather discuss that with the captain."

"Who told you to come here?" asked the man. Kit turned to him. He looked back with bloodshot eyes. He looked rough, with unkempt hair, dark rings around his eyes, and stubble on his chin.

They both looked threatening, and Kit knew it wasn't her place to make demands. She shifted her weight, taking a step back, and perched on the side of the table, trying to look more relaxed than she felt.

"Look, I'm sorry," she began. "I'm looking for the kapitan. A friend of mine said he could help me."

The woman pierced her with a hardened gaze, the small silver ring in her eyebrow catching the dim light. "I doubt you can afford the kapitan's help," she replied.

The man beside her spoke up. "Come on, darling. You'd be welcome to join us. We've got some heavy drinking to get back to out there."

Kit tried to smile, although she felt it was a little forced. "I'd like that," she said, her voice wavering slightly. "But first, I need to find the kapitan." She cleared her throat and added, "My friend Sergei said I might find him here."

"Sergei?" the blonde asked. "Sergei who?"

"Sokolov," Kit replied. She shouldn't have mentioned his name, but this might be her only chance to get to Silver.

The woman raised an eyebrow. "Wait here; Sasha will keep you company."

She spoke into a phone in Russian for a few brief sentences while glancing at Kit every now and then.

Kit smiled, but took a step away from Sasha and made a show of scrolling through her mobile phone. There was a message from Sergei. "Where are you?"

"Alright," said the woman. "Change of plans. You are to go to this cafe at sixteen hundred hours tomorrow. Just you, no one else."

"Will Kapitan Silver be there?"

She didn't answer directly. "I'll write down the address on your card." She scribbled "Vegz," on the back under the name Kapitan Silver and passed it back to Kit. "This is a one-shot deal. If you don't show, you don't get another chance."

Kit snatched back the card and put it into her bag. "No worries. I'll be there." Over the roar of the techno music, she shouted a quick "Thanks," then made her way out of the club.

Once she got outside, Kit was grateful for the fresh air and stillness of the night. She dug around in her bag in search of a cigarette. Finally, she found a Vogue slim packet and lit up. Her mother would be in shock if she knew Kit had taken up smoking; maybe she'd mention it when they Skyped next time, but she'd keep the sleeping pills to herself. As she called a taxi, Kit noticed an orange one just like the one she took earlier was already waiting outside the building. No need to dial after all.

She dropped her cigarette to the ground, stubbed it out, and dashed towards the taxi. It was the same driver.

"So, you decided to wait for me anyway," Kit said as she opened the rear door. She was about to climb in when she saw another person already sitting in the back. Sergei leaned forward to look at her sternly from the darkened rear seat and patted the seat beside him.

"What are you doing here?" she asked.

He just leaned forward and told the driver to take them directly to his hotel, the Grand Union.

"I said what are you doing here?" she insisted. But she already suspected that he had guessed she had come looking for Kapitan Silver without him. She didn't know who the blonde woman had called, but for all she knew, it could have been him.

"We will talk about it at my hotel." He glanced towards the taxi driver, who looked less relaxed than on the previous ride out to the squat. She understood he didn't want to discuss it in front of the driver. When they arrived at the Grand Union hotel, she reached for her wallet, but he already paid the fare, plus a generous tip.

She could smell his expensive cologne as he leaned forward to pass the money to the driver. An involuntary shiver of desire ran through her.

"I don't know why you're making such a fuss," Kit said.

"Did I make a fuss?"

"You're being difficult. I don't need to report back to you about everything I do."

"I invited you here. Kapitan Silver is my asset, my contractor; so yes, you do need to inform me of your activities."

Sergei and Kit walked through the grand marble lobby, the chandeliers glittering overhead and the sweeping staircase leading to other floors. Although the staff at the front desk likely noticed them, they kept their gazes averted and made no comment. Sergei led her to the elevator which would take them up to his penthouse apartment.

"Don't worry," he said with a smile. "They know not to pay attention or ask questions. They recognize me as someone to respect."

Kit made an exasperated sigh at Sergei's self-importance but did not comment further until they entered the penthouse, which offered a breathtaking view of Ljubljana's bright lights and historic skyline. The apartment had been recently renovated, with a meeting room large enough for Sergei's inner circle of philosophers to meet in private. He hung up her jacket on the ornate brass coat stand, then went to the bar to fix them both a drink.

"I take it you didn't overindulge at the HexD," he said.

"You know I didn't," she said with a huff. "You act like I'm your asset, that you control me." She used the term employed by spy agencies for a confidential informer.

"You know I care for you deeply, Katarina," he said in a calm tone that made her feel uneasy. "You are dear to my heart; you know that, don't you?" He handed her a mojito with fresh mint—he had planned ahead—and gestured that they should sit on the sleek, black leather couch. "I invited you here because I want our relationship to reach a new level. But for that to happen, we need to trust each other."

"I took a huge risk coming here to see you," she said in a low voice. "Knowing what I do about you."

"I had to take active measures in Kosovo, not out of malice but because I believe that these people can't govern themselves. They need guidance from Serbia and Russia."

Kit snorted in disbelief. "Guidance? Kosovo seceded because they felt exploited and damaged. Russia is always looking to exploit any advantage they can find."

"That's just one perspective," he countered. "You need to see things from all angles. Let me arrange for you to visit Belgrade. You'll see that things are different there, better."

She blinked in confusion as he held onto her arm when she tried to stand up. "We have to trust one another, Katarina. That's why you're here even though you think ill of me. In a war zone, people do what they have to. Sometimes it's regrettable. Our allies destroyed countless civilians in the last World War—Hiroshima and Nagasaki, Dresden—but now those incidents are overlooked in the rush to blame Russia."

Kit took a deep breath and looked away, trying hard to digest what he had said. The death of the mother and child she had personally witnessed at Staro Dorbi had affected her more strongly than historical data about much larger numbers of civilian casualties during wartime. She reached for the mojito, grateful for the momentary distraction.

"Yes," he went on, his voice low. "They're aware of the Staro Dorbi operation in Belgrade, but it's classified at the highest level. That was part of a confidential strategy to win back Kosovo."

He gave her an intense look. "We need to trust that we will both keep the facts about this to ourselves. It wouldn't look good for your office to know you're with me," he warned her.

Kit opened her mouth to speak but stopped. If they knew she was with Sergei while they were trying to strip him of his diplomatic immunity and arrest him, it would be disastrous for her career. She found his physical presence irresistible, his designer clothing draped over his muscular frame, his cologne making her dizzy. From the moment she accepted his invitation to Ljubljana, he had her under his spell, though she tried to resist it.

Finally, her resistance crumbled, and she slumped against the couch. "I don't know," she murmured.

"You hurt me when you tried to deceive me by going to the squat alone," he continued. "I knew you would take the card and visit there tonight. These are my contacts; I arranged for them to meet you there or else they wouldn't have given you the time of day. I instructed them to prepare for your visit."

She hung her head in shame. "I thought you had figured it out."

"Let me help you take down the criminals in charge of your organization," he said as he leaned over and planted a kiss on her forehead. "The international judges need to be exposed for the frauds they are. We can do this together, and it will be great for your career. But make no mistake, you can't accomplish this without me."

He put his arm around her back, drawing her in. "Let me into your life, Katarina. We have so much in common. The way you escaped from Dasham Raco and arrested him when no one else could was masterful."

A shiver of pleasure went through her when he Russianized her name, despite her better judgment. "You lied to me about your wife being dead," she said. Her voice sounded petty, petulant even to herself. His marital status was insignificant in the grand scheme of things, but the fact that he had deceived her stung.

"I told you she was dead to me after her accident and her subsequent personality changes. The rest is just a legal technicality. Of course, I made sure she has the best of care in one of our state facilities. There is no marriage in the true sense of the word."

"And you made a fool out of me with that fake Faberge egg! How could I have been so gullible?"

"It was only a prop to illustrate a point, and the point still stands, even if the egg was a replica. It was secure from theft and harm because I ensured it was."

Tears welled up in her eyes, and she reached for a tissue from her bag. "You always have such a logical, reasonable justification. Even though I knew it wasn't wise, I had to see you again. It's like I'm under some sort of spell."

She wiped away a tear that rolled down her cheek.

"Allow me show you something that defies all reason and logic," he murmured, his voice laced with seduction.

"If you permit me, I can take you on a journey to a realm you've never experienced before. To master the secrets of chaos, you must let go of your inhibitions and expand your narrow perspectives. Let me show you something extraordinary, Katarina. You will come through it empowered."

"What are you implying, Sergei?" she said, looking into his eyes. His face had transformed into a menacing, predatory mask, but his dark amber eyes still conveyed a softness that promised her reassurance.

"Now is not the time for words, only sensations and actions. But I won't employ force. You must make this decision of your own accord. All you need to do is say yes to discover what's on offer. Your permission is crucial for this hold any significance."

"Two consenting adults," she said with a smirk, though she knew it would not be plain vanilla sex.

"Do you grant your consent?" he insisted.

Her legal training prompted her to argue back: "How can I grant permission for something when I don't know what it is?" But despite her reservations, she felt compelled to acquiesce to his offer.

"In our philosophy," he continued, "life is like a chess game played between light and darkness. It is a game of survival, destruction, and rebirth. At a certain point in the game, a pawn may reach the opposite side of the board and become a queen. Pawns can die and become queens, going from the weakest piece in the game to the most powerful. Let me take you on that journey."

"This is meant to be," Kit sighed. "I just didn't realize it until now." She rested her head against his shoulder before he stood up and pulled away from her. He unzipped her high-heeled boots, one at a time. He offered her a hand and helped her stand up. "Come with me," he said, and she followed him.

Chapter Twenty-One

He led her toward the suite's bedroom, the cold marble floor sending shivers through her bare feet. He stopped and pulled her into a tight embrace, his lips close to her ear. "Remember, this is only the beginning. We will explore more, even when it may seem like we've come to an end."

She looked at him with a perplexed expression despite his words providing some comfort that there could be a future for them. But then the tenderness and seduction abruptly ceased as if a tempest had descended.

He pushed her body hard against the wall, and she fumbled with his shirt buttons. He captured her wrists and held them above her head as he kissed her passionately. All of her thoughts of morality melted away into nothing in that moment. His perfectly tailored clothes fell off his body as he used one hand to hold hers above and the other to take off his own clothes. He tried to take off her T-shirt but couldn't without releasing her from his grip. He spun her around and made quick work of taking off her top and bra before she quickly shed the rest of her garments.

"Bed," he growled as he guided her backwards until he scooped her up into his arms and carried her the last few meters to the large bedroom.

She felt intoxicated. This new feeling was nothing like the cozy nights spent with her Xander or the dawn jogs on the Auckland waterfront. Those memories flashed in her mind, only to be replaced by his hands lowering her onto the bed. She wanted him right away, as if there was no time to lose. She recalled how she had slapped him when she found out he was involved in the Staro Dorbi killings, and all of his lies. He had just taken it, not a sign of pain on his face. Now, she let him do what he wanted, voicing low, throaty moans in encouragement. He spoke Russian words that she did not comprehend but still understood the feelings that he conveyed.

When he entered her, something inside her broke, and their pulses merged. Even though she was not a virgin, she felt that no lover had ever fully possessed her before. They moved together, and their bond grew stronger. He then suddenly shifted his movements and started breathing slowly, as if controlling himself to keep the pleasure going. His left hand pinned her hands above her head once more, while his right hand clutched around her slender neck.

"Breath play," he whispered to her. "You'll be my white queen." His grip tightened around her throat, and he applied pressure over the carotid artery and windpipe. He became aroused beyond what she thought possible— so did she—though she could no longer express it through panting or moaning. She had never thought that the game of chess could be turned into an all-consuming erotic game of life and death.

She attempted to bring her hands down, to push him away, to inhale. But she couldn't. His entire weight was now on her, and as he moved higher, she felt her climax start to build. But there was no escape. Her breath was blocked off, her blood pushing against the interior of her eyes. Steadily yet undeniably, he increased the force until she was struggling to take a proper breath. His own breath came hot against her face. Even though the room was dimly lit, his eyes were glowing a dark amber hue, like glass gateways leading to another universe and time. He was a predator, hunting in the semi-dark and catching her in his claws. He was devouring her.

The orgasm started to come through her, slowly but steadily growing through her pelvic area, up her back, into her neck. She arched her back with pleasure, at the same time having the sensation she was fighting for her life. Now she couldn't even breathe at all, and the tension on her carotid artery was dragging her deeper into darkness.

"Is this what it's like to drown?" she thought just before the ever-expanding darkness overtook her. At precisely the same time, her climax increased and flourished, and she felt thrown out of her body. She was suspended close to the ceiling where everything was peaceful and serene. The intense feelings of unease and fear had vanished, and now all that remained was an extreme sense of tranquillity. Looking down, she could see their two nude figures on the bed, legs entwined in the sheets, him on top of her as he now smothered her nose and mouth with his hand.

"So I'm dying," she thought. Her throat did not ache anymore; likewise, that pressing need to breathe had been removed. He must have planned this all along as part of his cruel plan. She heard his words of command as a challenge, "Go, Katarina! Hunt for your heart's desire!"

She felt a sensation of floating and rotating as the fabric of her reality tore. She found herself back outside the University Library reading room she had been to earlier. As she walked in, it was as if she were seeing the room through a filter. Sunbeams burst through the windows and illuminated particles of dust that made her think of planets, worlds, stars, and galaxies as they spun and twirled in the air.

Suddenly, a man's voice spoke right beside her: "Lead me from the darkness to the light."

She noticed a golden glow around the edge of a wooden panel on the far end of the library. She drew closer and opened it to reveal a glowing chamber with no windows. Both of its walls were lined with single-edition and limited-edition books. An astrolabe stood in one corner, and an intricately carved wooden chair sat in front of a table. The man standing behind this bench had silver-grey hair, a bushy beard, intense brown eyes, and arched eyebrows that made him look familiar. She recognized him from portraits at the library. It was Joze Plečnik, the Slovene architect who designed the University Library and other places she had visited in Ljubljana. He had been dead since 1957.

"So you found my special room," he said to her.

"Looks like it," she replied hesitantly. "Um, you're dead though. Does that mean I am too?"

He paused for a moment as if deep in thought. "We've had a few dreamers come here over the years," he commented. "They're usually on some kind of quest." He waved his hand to indicate his disregard for that topic. "This building I designed was to honor learning and progress as they knew it in classical Greece, the Renaissance, and ancient times."

"I can hardly believe I'm here," she said softly. "Just moments ago I was…" Her mind brought up a picture of a dimly lit room, someone pushing down on her throat and chest. It seemed like years had passed since then, not minutes.

"Tell me what you search for," he prompted her.

"I'm here to solve a crime. Someone has stolen money from those they are sworn to protect, and the responsible parties believe themselves untouchable. I want justice."

He nodded in understanding. "That same struggle happened in my time. I used my architecture to try to bring people closer to truth. But what else do you seek?"

She hesitated before saying softly, "Love. If I can solve this case and understand love, I'll be content."

He smiled slightly. "I understand love in a Platonic way; I sought to manifest it through my designs, through harmony in this world. But you mean something different—romantic love—and I don't know if I can help you with that." He turned his attention to the shelves behind him before continuing, "The Bible mentions something called the book of life or scrolls of destiny. We have part of those records here."

He ran his finger along the spines of the books until he found one he wanted. He placed it on the table and opened it. The pages were like something from Da Vinci's sketchbook, full of diagrams and mathematical equations, animals appearing to run across the page. She noticed a plan of pyramids, circles, and squares followed by a sequence of numbers.

She read an enigmatic phrase that seared into her consciousness: "Draw a circle with a diameter all the way across of 1 and the circumference is a continuing sequence known as Pi, 3.14159265 . . .”

The shapes of pyramids swam before her eyes, images of ancient Egypt, the jackal-headed deity, numerals . . . She was losing coherence and felt drawn towards the door. Plečnik stared at her. “Remember!” he commanded her urgently as his image faded.

Time and space folded, and she lurched away until she realized she was immobile again on the bed. Her skin felt clammy, and she was unable to move a muscle. Panic set in until she heard her own groan and felt air enter her lungs. After a few moments of terror, her strength slowly returned. She rolled onto her right side in a recovery position, listening for any sign of where she was. Traffic hummed in the background. A door closed nearby, followed by a trolley rattling down the hallway.

Someone entered and announced themselves as room service before leaving whatever they had brought in the living room. Disoriented, it took her a few moments to remember last night. She had been with Sergei, and he had almost killed her. Her fingers explored her tender neck, and she wondered how much bruising there was. Then silence filled the room, and she knew she was alone. Her hands searched for the other side of the bed, but it was vacant.

Gingerly, Kit rolled towards the edge of the bed and opened her eyes. The sun was up, streaming through the blinds and into the bedroom. Sergei had gone, leaving a plush set of ivory towels arranged alongside a silver, silk dressing gown. On the bedside table was a note and a single milk chocolate on an exquisite plate.

Trembling, she reached for the note and read it: “You flew last night, my darling. I have been called away to Moscow. Please enjoy the breakfast and the suite as long as you wish. Take what you want. Go to your appointment this afternoon. I will be in touch. S."

Kit muttered under her breath, slid on the robe and slippers, then walked into the living room of her suite. A table was set for a champagne breakfast with fruit and yoghurt, omelette and toast, pastries and jam, coffee with cream, Prosecco from Italy on ice in a trolley. No doubt Sergei would have lectured her on the details if he had been there.

Kit was still reeling from the night before, but she felt parched. She filled a glass with sparkling water, then went to stare out the window of the suite. Her head felt foggy. The dream she'd had was fading rapidly. She searched for her bag and thankfully found her cell phone. She opened it to jot down some key points from her dream: Plečnik, a secret room in the library, squaring the circle, pyramids and the mathematical formula pi. But had there been something about life purpose as well? It was becoming less clear to her. She had felt a burning need to solve this case, so much that she had taken more risks than ever. The thought of what had happened with Sergei was too overwhelming to examine. She might need talk about it in more detail with Dr Montenegro.

Kit rummaged through her bag. It appeared Sergei had already searched it as the contents were out of order. The cold water quenched her thirst and the fresh aromatic coffee followed, helping to revive her. She laid out fresh towels and set the raindrop showerhead to hot. She glanced in the mirror, scared of what she'd find, expecting to see her neck ravaged and covered in bruises. Luckily, there was just some discolouration down one side of her neck. Sergei had applied pressure to her body in such a way as to constrict her breath and the blood travelling through her jugular vein, yet he had been careful not to leave any visible bruises. He was well versed in this art, it seemed.

With the shower running full blast, Kit stepped into the generous shower stall and closed the door behind her. She needed to get herself totally clean. Closing her eyes and leaning against the chilled marble walls, she felt the water cascading over her body. Pieces of the events from last night flooded back through her mind: the wild techno party at the squat, the meeting there.

Suddenly she jolted back into consciousness again as she remembered her four p.m. appointment. No matter what had just happened, she would have to go. Captain Silver might help her resolve this mystery. After thoroughly lathering herself up, she changed quickly. The breakfast was starting to look appetizing now. She checked her wristwatch; it was already ten thirty a.m.

Kit went searching for some lemon slices for a second glass of water and discovered some at the bar near where he had prepared their drinks last night. She gasped to find an empty vial of liquid placed beside the white rum he had mixed in with her mojito. Could he have given her something in the drink that he prepared for her? The vial was of pharmaceutical quality, but unlabeled, and lay next to an eyedropper. It may have been GHB, which can present as a clear scentless liquid. She stopped for a few seconds to consider how she seemingly had lost any will to resist him, although as far as she knew she hadn't lost consciousness until he almost strangled her. Taking a deep, shaky breath, she hugged herself tightly. Not sure what to do, finally she wrapped the tiny bottle in a napkin and tucked it in her bag. If it was some kind of date rape drug, it could explain a lot that had happened.

Sergei, the experienced operative, had most likely left the pharmaceutical bottle for her to find. When she asked him about it, he would surely come up with some plausible explanation as to why he had administered a drug. He'd argue that he was trying to take her on a transformative journey, though the experience of the lucid dream and near death left her feeling transformed and in a state of disorientation. Even though it was one of the most intense sexual experiences of her life, Sergei still managed to weave manipulation and fear into it. Then he vanished, leaving her behind in the lavish hotel suite to process what had happened, refusing to accept any responsibility.

Time was passing, and she intended to keep the appointment with Captain Silver. She called reception to check what Sergei had written in his note about her being able to stay there. The receptionist confirmed that Mr. Soroka had registered her in the room under his credit card for another two days. Apparently he had used his Ukrainian pseudonym. She should collect her passport from reception when it was convenient.

"Shit," Kit muttered as she realized what he'd done: taken her documents downstairs while she laid in a drugged stupor. She should have kept the passport locked in the safe at the other hotel.

Kit returned to the bathroom, taking note of the expensive toiletries provided. She brushed her teeth and gathered her hair into a ponytail. Glancing in the lit mirror, she saw her freckles were scattered like small burns across her pale skin, her features pinched, and her blue eyes burned almost too bright in the reflection. Kit's neck was marred by some discoloration which she hoped to hide by restyling her hair into a messy bun and draping auburn tendrils of hair over her neck and around her face. She finished dressing before picking up her passport from the receptionist.

She decided to go back to her original hotel, the Best Western, check out early, and bring her luggage back to the suite at the Grand Union Hotel. It was a far more comfortable suite than the standard single room she had reserved for herself. Besides, she wanted to punish Sergei for being such a manipulator by running up expensive food and beverage bills on his credit card. Of course, he wanted that, to put her even more in his debt. There was no way to win this game with him. She just had to keep her eyes focused on her goals.

On that pleasant, crisp morning, she walked along the river's edge and finally reached the Best Western Hotel. The high-heeled boots she wore clubbing the night before were beginning to pinch her feet when her mobile phone buzzed. She pulled the phone out of her handbag and flipped it open. It was a message from Angel: "Boss wants to know how your R&R is going."

Kit wondered if Angel or Eva had somehow caught wind of her escapade from the night before. Probably it was Angel who had wondered about her and was using Eva as the excuse to check.

"The weather is fine," she typed back. "What's new in Pristina?"

"Will brief you when you get back," came the reply.

"Can I bring you anything?"

"Chocolate or brandy maybe. Only kidding, don't worry about it."

"I'll see what I can do," Kit typed back.

Suddenly, Kit noticed multiple texts from Xander and Owen and one from a mysterious number. When she opened it, she discovered that Natalia had invited her to the Mignon Cafe for a tarot reading, as promised. She glanced at her watch, confirming she'd have time to join her before the meeting with Kapitan Silver.

Kit changed into jeans and flats, threw on a T-shirt, and tied a red, silk bandanna around her neck before leaving the Best Western Hotel. Taking a taxi back to the Grand Union Hotel, she used Sergei's key card to enter the suite. Room service had removed the trolley and tidied up the area, leaving fresh towels and replenishing the bar. She was glad she had managed to grab the phial of liquid for testing later, if she could manage to do that without raising too many questions.

Kicking back on the comfy leather couch, she had a chance to admire the view of Ljubljana during the day, including the castle perched atop the hills. With half an hour to spare before her meeting with Natalia, she took the time to explore her hotel suite. In the walk-in closet of the master bedroom, she found some luxurious Louis Vuitton luggage and a chic dress, jacket, and shoes with a card reading "for Katarina" pinned to it. As well as this, there were some distressed Levi's girlfriend jeans and a cotton ruffle shirt, giving her the opportunity to go with whatever style she wanted. Shopping had been out of the question while in Pristina due to lack of time, and they had been too occupied by sailing and Xander's activities in Croatia to check out the shops.

"In for a penny, in for a pound," she muttered as she pulled open her tired, old suitcase and began to move the items inside to its larger and more contemporary replacement. She was irritated at Sergei for knowing exactly what she desired and giving it to her without her asking. Even more annoying was the knowledge that he had accurately guessed her precise dress size. Still, she accepted his gifts. As if sensing what she was thinking, a message arrived from him on her mobile phone.

"You like?"

She couldn't help smiling in spite of her irritation. "I'm so mad at you."

"You're welcome."

She rolled her eyes yet continued to arrange the clothing in the fashionable bag. Then, she held up her jeans and realized these were the perfect outfit for her meeting with Kapitan Silver later that day.

"Yes, I'm just packing the items. Thank you. Did you slip me something last night?"

"If you mean did I give you coffee and cocktails, yes."

"It was more than that. You almost killed me last night."

"Yet there you are, still alive."

She threw down the mobile phone on the bed out of frustration, then snatched it up again.

"Where are you?"

"Vienna airport. Senator lounge. Where are you?"

"At the hotel. I'm going to run up room service bills with your card."

She could almost sense him chuckling from Austria at her words.

"Good. What do you have planned for this afternoon?"

"Wild horses couldn't stop me from meeting Captain Silver."

"Keep in touch. Must go, flight boarding now. *Uvídimsya skóro*, see you soon, my white queen."

She mumbled to herself in disbelief and once again dropped the mobile phone on the bed. She felt as if Sergei was trying to say that she was like a humble pawn in this game that he had made a queen. But where was this game leading?

Chapter Twenty-Two

The day was fresh and smelt of damp autumn leaves following the rain the night before. Kit left the lobby of the Grand Union Hotel wearing the new outfit Sergei had given her, with her own signature leather jacket over the top. It amazed her how he must have planned this whole scenario and prepared the hotel suite for her, complete with gifts for the morning after. Whenever she struggled to think through the situation with him, she got a headache. If she worked to cancel the Interpol notice to arrest him and had accepted his gifts, did that mean she was already compromised?

Kit made her way back to the Café Mignon in the French Revolution Square, the same site where she had met with Sergei's friends the day before. Customers were scattered around the small, round tables, sipping their drinks and reading the paper. It felt like days had passed since she was last there rather than just yesterday.

She was eager to meet Natalia and find out what the tarot card reading had in store for her. She entered the inviting café and spotted Natalia in an alcove near a window overlooking a courtyard with a few more tables. She waved to get Kit's attention and welcomed her warmly.

"I'm so glad you could come," Natalia said. "I've been looking forward to showing you something about tarot. I was afraid you might have left after Sergei had to go away."

"Thanks for your invitation. I'm sorry I couldn't make it to dinner last night; I needed to rest after a day's travel." Kit pulled out a chair from the table that Natalia had reserved by the window.

"I understand," Natalia replied. "The work we do can be a lot to process. But next time, maybe come a day or two earlier."

"Where are Leo and Gregor?"

"Leo went to an exhibition, and Gregor went to the Romanian embassy for some reason."

He would, thought Kit drily. Gregor Petri was like Sergei, always hustling, but without his charm or intelligence. But now it was time to focus on Natalia.

"Should we order some tea or coffee?" suggested Kit. "Do I need to cross your palm with silver?"

"Sure, let's get a drink. No need for payment though. It's my pleasure. I thought we should spend some time together discussing tarot. It's such a useful tool."

"Good idea," Kit said. "I've got about an hour before I have to go. I'm curious about tarot. I've heard it can be a tool for divination and self-discovery," Kit replied.

Natalia's face lit up with a smile as she spoke. "This deck of tarot cards can give us insights into our lives," she said. "We can look at the past, present, and future, our relationships and our careers, and help us make better decisions."

Kit was captivated by the cards in Natalia's hands—their intricate designs and bright colors that were like glimpses into another world.

"Let's give it a try," Natalia said. She passed the deck to Kit and asked her to pick one. Kit took the cards and shuffled them slowly in her hands. Finally, she chose one and flipped it over. It was the symbol of the Fool. Her eyes widened in surprise. The card showed a young person looking upwards, seemingly unaware that he was about to step off a cliff. He was dressed as a vagrant and carried a bundle on his shoulder while a small dog bounded along next to him.

"The Fool card represents new beginnings and potentials," Natalia said. "It's about taking risks and embracing the unknown. Like the joker in a regular deck of cards, it means you can make the best of any hand you're dealt in life at the moment." Kit nodded in agreement as a spark of hope lit up inside her.

"That makes sense," she said.

"It's about stepping outside your comfort zone," Natalia continued. "And remembering to enjoy the journey. What do you think of when you see this card?"

"The dog catches my eye. It seems that when I've been in trouble lately, a dog has turned up, one way or another." She was thinking of the fox who appeared when she was being hunted by Raco, the Egyptian statue in the Albanian Museum that she had hidden behind from the men chasing her and Owen, and even Eva's dog Bambino seemed to always be there to offer support when things got tough. Max, the canine unit dog, had been the one to find Raco's hidden weapon cache and his hostage.

"Throughout human history, dogs have been reliable guides when facing the unknown and trustworthy companions," Natalia said. "They can appear in dreams to show our instinctive wisdom."

"I wonder what the dog is trying to tell the Fool on the card. Trying to stop him from walking off the cliff or encouraging him to take that first step into the unknown?"

"We can treat the images in the cards as if they're dream images. If that dog was part of you, what would he be trying to tell you?"

Kit closed her eyes for a moment, imagining that she was poised on the edge of a cliff. She remembered the dizzy feeling of vertigo as she stood with Sergei on the cliff in Prizren. That was the day when she fell for him. And last night she had fallen even further, hovering between life and death with his hands around her throat. She shuddered and touched the sensitive skin at her throat. She glanced up to see Natalia looking intently at her.

"The dog would probably say to look before I leap."

"Good advice," Natalia said. "But it seems the Fool has to make this step without knowing exactly where it leads in order to begin the story that continues through the tarot."

They were interrupted by the server, who bought a tray of tea, cups, and spiced cookies.

"Perfect timing," Kit said and reached to pour for them both. "Can the cards tell me anything about this complicated legal case that I'm facing? What should I do?" *Am I in danger?* she wondered silently.

Natalia shuffled the deck and handed them to Kit shuffle. Natalia then laid out four cards clustered around a central one and turned them over one by one to study the reading.

"The first card is the two of swords." She pointed to two crossed swords against a sombre background. "It's difficult to make progress. There's a stalemate, balanced forces. An enemy that is difficult to overcome."

Kit leaned closer, nodding. That seemed correct. Natalia continued. "The Lovers card shows that you could be confronted by a major life choice, and also perhaps destiny is linking two people. The Queen of Cups, a fair-haired intuitive, caring woman. She might be influential. But she's upside down, and the Moon shows possible deception."

"Deception? What do you mean?"

"It could indicate illusions, dealing with shadows buried in your subconscious."

"Now you're sounding like my therapist," Kit said. Far away from anyone who knew her from work, Kit felt she could be open with Natalia. "I wonder who that could be," Kit wondered.

"The cards show the potentials in a situation. Maybe you haven't met her yet," suggested Natalia. "But wait, there's more. Here's the King of Swords as a hidden influence. He's an intellectual who could perhaps help you with strategies and analysis of the situation."

"I know someone like that," Kit said.

"He could also be manipulating behind the scenes."

That could be Sergei, Kit thought. On the other hand, her father had recently come back on the scene, and she didn't know what his agenda was. Then there were the senior officials implicated in the corruption case. "I know several people who could fit that description," Kit said.

"It's odd that the Empress is central to the spread. She signifies abundance and pleasure. If you're in tune with this energy, you could have the strong impulse to take care of people, to mother them almost, or become a mother. You're very creative, almost a visionary sometimes."

"I've got no plans to become a mother just yet," Kit said. "But I do like to take care of people, like seeking justice for victims."

Natalia took a sip of tea and then nibbled on a spiced cookie. "Your financial situation looks good. Very good, actually," she said, scrutinizing the cards again. "I think much will turn on how you handle the situation with these two people, and that's your choice."

"Could the woman be you?" asked Kit.

"No, she's more likely to have a fair complexion."

Kit thought of her colleagues in the office. She couldn't think of anyone obvious. Zena Lace had the right appearance. There was an antipathy between them, but Zena didn't seem to be dishonest.

"I suppose I'll find out," Kit said. "Could you have a look at my love life? I won't bore you with the details, but it's complicated."

Natalia made another spread. "The Two of Cups is in the middle, focusing squarely on your love life. I can see several men. One is an intellectual manipulator. Another is restless and impulsive, the Knight of Swords inverted, and then the Emperor, maybe someone in law enforcement or an institution. The Five of Swords is a card of sorrow and loss, but also of strength that can come out of it. You may be facing a difficult situation, but you are strong enough to make difficult decisions. You need to choose your battles carefully. I think that's you," she said, pointing to the Queen of Coins. "A career woman in control of your own resources."

Kit carefully looked at the Two of Cups.

"What does that one mean again?" Kit asked, feeling overwhelmed by all these characters. The cards seemed to swirl before her eyes, making her feel dizzy.

"The Two of Cups is about relationships and the need for balance between partners," Natalia explained.

She pointed to the two figures depicted on the card. "These two figures are in harmony with each other. This card is a sign to pay attention to your relationships and make sure they are harmonious."

Kit nodded. She could feel the power of the card and the messages it held.

Natalia continued, "You should meditate with this card. Take it away from the deck and focus on it. Meditating with a card can help you to unlock its true meaning and identify the messages it is trying to tell you. This can help you to make decisions about how to move forward in the relationships."

Kit nodded, taking the card in her hands for a moment and waiting for any feelings to come. She smiled. "I know what I should do. I should be with the person who helps me to be my best self, and the one I feel strongest and most caring with."

Natalia smiled back at her. "See? This is the power of the tarot. It can give you insights into your life and guidance on how to move forward," Natalia said. "Take chances and open yourself up to new possibilities—be brave—and you will be rewarded."

"You're good," Kit said. Maybe even better than her therapist at helping her sort through issues, she thought. "I feel as though I've got new insights into my situation."

"Perhaps choose one more card before you go," Natalia suggested. "One last key to guide you forward." Natalia fanned the cards out in front of her, face down. Kit took one card and turned it over. It depicted a mature, bearded man standing alone on a mountain, holding up a glowing lantern.

"The Hermit," Natalia said. "It can show the need for solitude in seeking clarity. It could also represent a wise counsellor in your life."

Kit chuckled for a moment. "That looks like Father Peter," she said. "What do you think of him?"

"He's remarkable. Can be intimidating sometimes, but he's generous with his time."

"How do you communicate with him?"

"Usually in a group like today or through written correspondence. Once or twice I've had a private meeting with him."

"What kind of things did you discuss?"

"It's somewhat similar to our conversations with Sergei. He asks us questions about our concerns and makes suggestions, although from a more Christian perspective, of course."

"I'd like to learn more from him about Rasputin's legacy and those documents."

"You mean the notes of Rasputin's teachings discovered by his son?"

"Yes. How is it that a priest could have a son?"

"Orthodox priests are allowed to keep their wives and families if they marry before entering the priesthood. Besides, while Grigori Rasputin was a mystic and a holy man, he was not officially a priest."

Kit nodded thoughtfully. "I see. I have a lot to learn."

Natalia smiled and retrieved a business card from her handbag. "Here's my card. Give me a call any time. We can discuss tarot, dreams, and the Orthodox traditions."

"Thanks, Natalia. I appreciate it. Here's my card." Kit gave her a business card and wrote her private phone number on the back. "Let's keep in touch."

Kit stood to leave. As she walked out of the cafe, she felt she had gained a fresh perspective on her life and a newfound appreciation for the power of tarot. But there were some unsettling messages, as well as intriguing suggestions. She would just have to deal with those issues as they came up.

CHAPTER TWENTY-THREE

Taking a deep breath, Kit increased her pace. Now was not the time for hesitation. Her top priority was to look for Kapitan Silver. If there was any chance at all to stop the money transfer from Kosovo before it was too late, then it would all be worthwhile. The privatization panel was set to convene in a few days and could sign off on the agreement to build the power station and process the money transfer soon after. Coming up with a plan to halt the funds transfer was crucial— and it had to happen soon, because once the payment went through, tracking it through the Swiss confidential banking system would be nearly impossible.

Kit found the Vegz Café in a nearby street. In contrast to the Café Mignon's quaint French chic, the Vegz Café exuded urban minimalist elegance. It was larger than she had expected. The exterior showcased contemporary black and chrome décor, with a few tables set out on the pavement in front of its smoked windows. Upon entering, Kit discovered a dark interior with hardwood floors and ceilings adorned with spotlights and symmetrical lines, as well as a fully stocked bar complete with coffee machines. Walls were lined with plants and ferns in potted holders, while three cooks busied themselves in the kitchen and two servers attended to customers' orders. Kit checked her watch; she was five minutes early.

She sat outside at one of the tables in the footpath, waiting. If nothing happened, she would go back inside and start asking around. A server wearing black leggings, a miniskirt, and a T-shirt with the cafe's name approached Kit as she studied the menu.

"I recommend the pumpkin pie," the server said with a Russian accent. Kit looked up with surprise on hearing that voice, only to see the same blonde woman she'd met at the HEXD club.

"I'm here to meet Silver," Kit said.

"The apple crumble is excellent too." The server added in a low voice, "Don't say that name out loud."

"Good to know, thank you." Kit smiled; at least she'd made contact.

The server pulled out a map and showed her the location of the café, pretending to share information as if she were a tourist.

"What sightseeing do you recommend?" Kit asked.

The woman pulled up a chair at Kit's table and bent over the map. "My friends usually go to the castle, then to the National Library," she replied. This was the cover for their clandestine meeting. This woman must have known about Sergei's movements as he'd taken Kit to both these places. It was too much of a coincidence that she should know about them.

"You're Kapitan Silver, aren't you?" Kit finally asked, repeating the forbidden name.

The woman was still studying the map, tracing the path of the river with her finger. She wore heavy silver jewelry on several fingers with their neatly filed nails. She merely nodded in response. "I like to keep busy. This is my day job," she answered.

Kit studied her profile: pale, almost translucent skin, fair hair, high cheekbones, an upturned nose, and generous lips—not more than twenty-five years old.

"You know why I'm here?" Kit asked further.

Silver didn't look up from her map; she merely traced the line of the river with her finger.

"Our mutual friend contacted me. He's calling in a favor for you, lucky girl." It seemed odd that Silver called her a girl, as Kit was older.

"Did he explain the situation?"

"Yes, he did," Silver replied. "I need information from you first though. Names and addresses, phone numbers, whatever you can give me on the targets. Also, your contact details. I suggest we connect via this app."

She ripped off two pages from her order pad. "This is my contact number," she said and wrote a number. "Send me an invitation via this encrypted app. On the other page, write the target information. I'll bring your order in a few minutes and we'll talk further."

"Thanks," Kit said. "I expected you to be a man. Sorry about that."

Silver flashed her a grin. "The job is part of my cover," she said. "No one would suspect a waitress." She tapped her pad back into the heavy leather pocket hanging from the belt low around her hips and returned to the kitchen to deliver the order.

Kit felt a sudden surge of gratitude to Sergei for his help, although the situation was no less precarious now than it had been before. She was about to enter a criminal conspiracy to defraud, although it was for a good cause— to stop a major theft and money laundering operation. Again she pushed her fears and misgivings to the side, just as she braved the dragons on the Dragon Bridge. She was going to see this through. First, she entered the phone number into her mobile and then sent an invitation to Silver's number through the encrypted social networking app. Within a few moments, the message came back: "You're connected with Argento." Argento was Spanish for silver, she recalled, and she pulled out a pen from her bag. Apparently this was one of Silver's aliases.

Kit navigated to the organization OIDC's online profile page and copied the addresses for the senior management. She scribbled down the names Jacob Cornelius Mueller, Michael John Burke, and Victor Tirol on a scrap of paper. After a quick search, she had their contact information in Kosovo. Silver returned with snacks and coffee and sat back down to examine the paper.

"That should be enough to get us started. Do you want me to try breaking into their accounts?"

"Yes," Kit said. "I want you to track down their passwords and stop any significant transactions. I also need to know where the money is being transferred to and who is on the receiving end."

Silver let out a low whistle. "You're not asking for much, huh?"

"If it's too much, just say so. I don't want to push you too hard."

Silver smiled. "Of course I can do it. I just can't tell how long it will take."

"We don't have much time. The transfers will be approved in a few days and could happen soon after that."

"Alright, I'll start on it tonight. Sergei is going to owe me for this."

"Wasn't it the other way around? You owed him?"

Silver shrugged her shoulders. "He got me out of jail a few times."

Kit felt jealous for a moment. Silver was an attractive woman. Was that why Sergei had contact with her? She pushed the thought out of her mind. She needed to stay focused on the mission.

"I need to halt the transaction and trace its intended path from beginning to end. The money needs to be sent back where it came from," Kit said.

"Do you want to take a cut for yourself?" Silver asked.

"I hadn't thought of that, but no. The whole sum needs to be returned to Kosovo, where it came from. Furthermore, I need the evidence to prosecute these men for corruption and stop them from initiating the transfer again. If we can get convictions, that would be reward enough for me."

Silver nodded in agreement, although a knowing smile played on her face while she stared off in the distance, as if she was mentally calculating something.

Then, as if suddenly remembering something, Kit said, "You haven't asked anything about me."

Silver answered confidently, "Don't worry, I did my research already. You are Caitlin Chase, an associate international prosecutor in Pristina, Kosovo. Your mother Rosalyn has connections in the defense industry in New Zealand and Australia as well as with the witness protection program. Should I say more?"

Kit stared at her amazed, wondering how much she knew about Vasha and her mother. Anxiety filled her mind. Were they in danger? Silver watched her expressionlessly with large, brown eyes like a cat sizing up its prey.

Kit tried to sound brave. "Alright, so you did your research. I had to expect that. Is this deal still on?"

"Yes, we've got a deal. I'd love to make a shitstorm of trouble for these assholes."

"We have that in common," Kit said.

"One last thing," Silver said. "We have a database of sensitive information on politicians in the West. The name of the judge seems familiar. Maybe I can dig up something compromising on the three individuals. You can either make it public, use it to blackmail them, or save it for a rainy day. It's up to you."

Kit felt a surge of excitement go through her. Having something on these men who pretended to be moral but caused harm gave her a thrill.

"Yes, absolutely," she said eagerly.

"It's been a pleasure doing business with you. Have the pie on the house." Silver's smile was bright as she spun around and walked back into the café with a bounce in her step. It was apparent she loved her job. Maybe she was exactly what Kit needed to complete her case. Could Silver be the tricky Queen of Cups who had appeared in her tarot reading a short time ago?

Chapter Twenty-Four

Pristina, Kosovo

Kit touched down in Pristina Sunday evening following an uneventful flight from Ljubljana. She felt at home in Kosovo, even if it was a short-term posting, and the frenzied events in Ljubljana were already starting to feel like a dream. As she collected her luggage off the carousel, the bags and designer clothes inside seemed to belong to someone else. Checking her social media app reminded her of her meeting with Silver—one that seemed like a fantasy now.

When the taxi dropped her off at her apartment, she scanned the area for Raco and his gang, but there was no sign of anything suspicious. Kit unpacked her luggage, started up a load of washing, and started to prepare for the next day at work. Then, she made some tea and sat down with her journal to plan out the week ahead. There was a privatisation panel meeting coming up, and Silver needed to confirm that she was able to put in place the anti-money laundering measures. That compromising information on the suspects could be worth gold when it came to preparing a prosecution case against them. A murder investigation into the death of Rustem Kupi, the chairperson of the privatization panel, was still underway. She had only been away for a few days, but it felt like ages had passed since she was in the office the previous week. Sighing, she opened up her office email account and found numerous messages marked urgent. But before she could open them, her mobile phone buzzed with a message. It was from an unlisted number that Sergei often used. "Welcome home, darling," it said.

"How did he know I was at home?" was her first thought. She quickly figured out it wouldn't be too hard to calculate when she'd be back in Pristina for work the following day. The urge to reply immediately was strong, but she resisted it. She didn't want to reinforce his need to control her from a distance. Assuming he was at a distance, she pondered, and got up to check out the window. No one was down on the sidewalk that she could see. She carefully closed the blinds and returned to the couch. She had a lot to think about.

When she lightly touched her neck, it still felt sore— her hand kept on returning to it. Her encounter with Sergei had been one of the most intense moments of her life, and now she had once again cheated on Xander. Reminiscing about her fiancé, she noticed he hadn't been in contact with her much recently. When she thought of him, something twisted in her stomach—he didn't comprehend what was important for her anymore. Their relationship was adding to her already high stress levels, and she had to bring clarity to this situation to safeguard her self-respect. She quickly sent him a message: "I think we need a break so I can think straight. Thanks for understanding–K." A heavy sigh of relief escaped her lungs. She had been feeling tense regarding Xander for some time. Even during their cruise along the Dalmatian coast, things hadn't been great between them. Now here she was, breaking up with him via text message because confronting him directly made her too scared.

A few moments later, his response came. "Thanks, I agree." She could feel her relief quickly turning to resentment. Was he only agreeing because he had been waiting for the right moment to end things with her? Had all the tension been coming from him in the first place, rather than her? He had already confessed to dating other women during their time apart. Kit threw her phone onto the couch and crossed her arms and legs. This should have happened a lot sooner, with or without Sergei on the scene.

A few minutes later, her phone rang again. It was Owen this time, asking about her trip to Slovenia.

"Relaxing," she said. "It's nice to have a break sometimes, even if I did think about work a lot."

He didn't question her story and went on to update her about the current cases. Unfortunately, they hadn't made progress in the murder investigation or locating Raco and his gang. While Kit felt pleased that she may have a lead for stopping the money laundering, she couldn't tell anyone what she was planning as they would link her both to Sergei and an illegal bank hack. Suddenly, she wondered where this bold part of her character had come from; her mother had been hardworking but fun-loving, and she'd barely known her father. He had remained out of her life since her younger years, yet now he was in touch. She scribbled in her journal to make a date for another session with Dr Montenegro.

"Did you receive the invitation?" queried Owen. His voice brought her back to the present.

"What invitation?" she asked.

"The US ambassador is throwing a Halloween shindig on Wednesday night. Everyone's invited," he answered.

"You think we're invited to the fancy dress as well?"

"Yes, they're encouraging guests to wear costumes, masks, or whatever they like," Owen said. "It's the real deal, and there'll be a raffle for charity."

"I've got nothing to wear," Kit sighed. Then she remembered the dress that Sergei had left her in the Grand Union Hotel suite. That would do perfectly. "Where does the ambassador live?"

"He has a house out of Pristina that he uses for official functions," Owen said. "Now that I think about it, I don't have anything to wear either," he added with a trace of humor.

"Why not wear your dress uniform?"

"Yeah, I guess I can do that." He laughed. There was a pause, and she concluded that Owen wanted to say something else.

"Thanks so much for calling me," Kit said to fill the gap in conversation.

"Of course," he said. "Matt will most likely be arranging a meeting this week, so I guess we'll see each other soon."

Then he added, "If you haven't made other arrangements, do you want to go to the ambassador's party together. It's better than showing up by yourself."

She thought for a moment. To her surprise, the idea of going about with Owen was appealing. She could enjoy his company without the complications of Sergei's games or her guilt about Xander that things weren't working out as they should.

"Sure," she said. "Why not? It will be fun."

"Great, I'll pick you up," Owen said and quickly disconnected the call. Kit had the feeling that he wasn't going to say more in case she changed her mind. He was one of the few people she could trust in this chaotic world.

She jotted down the date for the party in her diary, then starting working through her work emails on her laptop. The invitation from the US ambassador to a gathering at the residence had arrived, followed soon after by a notification that the privatization panel meeting had been brought forward to Wednesday morning. After reading it again to check, she realized that the funds transfer could happen any time after that.

Her hands trembled as she took out her phone and located Silver's earlier message. She sent a swift reply: "New deadline–Wednesday. Meeting brought forward–K."

Her automated response came: "Silver conducts business." Kit found it amusing that Silver had chosen an automated message that referred to the metal's conductivity of heat and electricity. "Let's hope Captain Silver can conduct this business," she thought to herself. She considered telling Sergei but decided against it; the less contact they had at the moment, the better.

Kit also decided to schedule an appointment with her therapist, Dr Montenegro, to talk about the end of her relationship with Xander and the unexpected return of her father. However, she wouldn't mention Silver. Not even doctor-patient confidentiality could properly protect this compromising news. She sent Maria a request for a session either Monday or Tuesday night.

Then, as she remembered Eva's suggestion to speak to the Minister of Energy, Visar Dreshaj, she realized she still had his personal number saved in her phone. Without hesitation, she sent him a text message: "Kit Chase here, are you free for coffee this week to discuss business? Sorry to disturb you. Thanks K."

No sooner than she'd sent it, her phone rang. It was Dreshaj.

"Ms Chase, it's a pleasure to hear from you. I'm quite busy this week, flying to Berlin on Thursday and Parliamentary meetings earlier in the week. How about a quick cup of coffee around four tomorrow?"

Kit scribbled it down in her planner. "That works for me, Minister. Thank you."

"What's the purpose of the meeting?"

"To discuss the privatization panel and the new power station contract."

"Are you sure you want to get involved in that?" His voice deepened with concern. "There was some unfortunate news last week about the chairman of the panel…"

"I don't want to be involved, but my office is."

"Alright, then. Since I assisted you on your last case, perhaps you'll keep me updated this time? And don't forget I promised to take you to a casino. You know my family owns several," he said with a chuckle.

Kit felt a twinge of discomfort at the mention of the casino. Eva had said they were off-limits for staff, but she pushed that aside. "I'll keep that in mind, Minister. Thank you for your time."

As they said their goodbyes and he hung up the phone, Kit couldn't help but sense an attraction between them. However, she knew it was unlikely anything would come of it. He had provided her with valuable information from a lost diary that enabled her to solve her last case, so she was open to helping him this time around. Still, she couldn't help but wonder if he would extend the same courtesy to her again in return.

Chapter Twenty-Five

Kit's alarm clock chimed, jolting her from her slumber on Monday morning. She reached for her phone and switched it off before snuggling back into the warmth of her down comforter. The sounds of the bustling city outside reminded her that she was far from her aunt's villa in St. Heliers, Auckland, and was now working in Pristina, Kosovo, as an international prosecutor.

Determined to start the week off on the right foot, Kit decided to head to the gym for a session with the punching bag, some weights, and a jaunt on the treadmill. Later in the week, she was scheduled to meet Owen for their usual joint gym session. After putting on her track suit and packing a change of clothes into a bag, she pulled her glossy, auburn hair into a high ponytail, grabbed an apple for a snack, and headed out. The morning air had a fresher edge compared to the night before but still carried a pungent stench of lignite from the coal-fired power plant nearby. And Kosovo was soon to get yet another one. Lignite coal was plentiful and cheap, making it an easy choice for officials who weren't able to invest in cleaner energy options. By the time Kit reached the gym, her hair and clothes were imbued with the smell of lignite.

The locker room was filled with other morning gymgoers when Kit walked in, many of them already in the process of changing their clothes. She made her way to the treadmills, where a few people had already started their run. She began slowly, then increased her speed to a jog. In front of her, the window showed the rising sun as it burned away the morning mist. As her eyes scanned her surroundings, she noticed Owen on a treadmill beside Zena Lace Letalova, the police forensic psychologist she had met at the previous crime scene. Zena wore leggings and a cropped T-shirt over her sports bra. Kit felt suddenly self-conscious in her oversized sweatpants.

"Owen, I didn't realize you were here!" Kit said with surprise.

"I don't usually come this early," he said. His breathing was coming short and sharp. "But today seemed like a good day for it."

"I thought so too," Kit said, increasing the speed of her treadmill. "And Zena must have thought the same." With a hint of jealousy, she observed his companion's shapely legs striding along on the treadmill. He blushed slightly before continuing to run without further comments.

A few minutes later, Kit decreased her speed before finally bringing the machine to a stop. "That's my warm-up done," she said as she began to leave. "I have other things to do today, so I have to get going."

"Uhm . . . yeah," Owen said with hesitation in his voice. "I guess it's just one of those Mondays to start the week well." She suspected that Owen was trying to explain why he and Zena were in the gym together so early in the morning, not wanting Kit to think they had just rolled out of bed and gone straight there.

"See you, Zena," Kit called out, waving her hand. "Have a good workout!"

Kit felt annoyed by seeing Owen and Zena together. Didn't he have a girlfriend back in Wales? Had they made plans to meet for a workout the same way Owen had with Kit? Or was it just coincidence? She was surprised by the irritation she felt and how out of character it was for her. She had always thought Owen was not her type. There was no point in doing a full workout now; she couldn't punch the bag without looking like she was angry. Doing some weightlifting machines would have to do, followed by a short session on a stationary bike. She showered quickly in the women's locker room and changed into a professional but comfortable outfit suitable for the office that she had brought with her, then brushed her hair and added makeup. As she reached the door of the changing room. she almost collided with Zena, who was on her way in.

"Have a great day!" Zena said cheerfully. Kit wondered if that was smirk on Zena's face.

Feeling revived by the exercise and the shower, Kit headed towards the office. Still emotionally worse for wear after the taxing weekend with Sergei, breaking up with her fiancé, and seeing Owen with another woman, Kit was now looking forward to doing some routine work. Even reviewing the old court cases was looking more bearable now.

But when she got to the office, Kit was met with a sudden shock. Crime scene tape was stuck across the entrance to Angel's office, preventing anyone from entering Eva's area. Neither of them were in the room, and there were no documents or papers anywhere. She stood still for a couple of moments, speechless. The idea that this place was her safe haven had deserted her. Kit reached for her cell phone and called Eva.

"I'm here at the office and I see your office is taped off. What on earth is going on?"

"Same story as what happened to Tom," Eva responded in a slightly breathless tone. In the background, Kit could hear traffic noise. It seemed like Eva was walking somewhere in town.

"Are you okay?" Kit asked. "Where are you?"

"I'm heading to do an interview at a TV studio," Eva said. "Grab a copy of the local English language newspaper and have a look at their write-up on me."

"Will do," Kit promised. "Who is running things here?"

"You are," Eva said. "It all happened last night. The head of mission has already sent out an email appointing you as acting chief prosecutor."

"Bloody hell," Kit muttered. She didn't feel ready for this kind of responsibility.

"You'll do fine," Eva said. "If you want to, why don't you come down to the TV studio. You can watch."

"Sure," Kit replied. "Did they take your passport?"

"No," Eva replied. "I'm too smart for that. I have mine back in the safe at home. But I can't use my diplomatic passport since it's been cancelled."

"Where's Angel?"

"I sent her home. They put me on administrative leave, pending an enquiry. I'm still getting paid for now."

"All right," Kit said, "I'm on my way." She wanted to support Eva but not by stepping into her shoes as chief prosecutor, not right away.

Eva gave Kit the location of the TV studio. Kit hopped in a taxi and lit a cigarette to calm herself. She paid the taxi driver before alighting close to the television studio. She found Eva having a smoke outside the TV studio. It was a modern industrial building, built using recycled materials, including bricks from houses burnt during the conflict. The facade made of recycled railway sleepers created a play of light and shadow.

"Hey, Eva. What's up?" Kit said.

"I'm okay," Eva said, but she looked stressed. "This place is incredible. I laid my story out in the newspapers for all to see. Did you read the newspaper?"

"No, I didn't have a chance. I came straight here. What does it say?"

"People in the area have called me a hero for standing up to the injustices of the global system," Eva said. "But our own organization has been more critical, claiming I'm an anxious middle-aged woman who just can't get the facts right."

"That must be really difficult," Kit said.

Eva shrugged. "So, how was Ljubljana?" Eva asked, her voice thick with smoke from her cigarette.

"It was good," Kit replied. "Actually, while I was there I came up with some ideas about how to stop the proceeds of crime being funnelled out of Kosovo."

"Like what?" Eva asked, her eyes narrowing.

"Well, if we could find proof of funds being transferred illegally from the power station contract..." Kit began. "How soon do you think we could get an arrest warrant?"

Eva stared her questioner in the eye. "To arrest who?"

"Burke and Mueller for sure," Kit said. "Maybe even Tirol if we can catch him transferring bribes out of Kosovo."

Eva considered this for a moment before continuing. "I know a judge I've been acquainted with for years. Judge Meg isn't in Tirol's pocket, so we could use her. But we can't go near any of the judges chosen by him."

"I don't know if I can pull this off," Kit said hesitantly. "But if I can get information from a confidential source, then it would be good to have a plan to get the evidence before a judge quickly."

"I have more free time nowadays," Eva said. "I'll contact my friend and ask her privately about her availability and set up a secure line of communication."

"What about the targets' diplomatic immunity?" Kit asked.

Eva smiled and nodded her head in certainty. "I'll get in touch with our New York office and see if they will grant a conditional waiver of immunity ahead of time. If you can bring some solid evidence, I'll ask HQ to put the waivers through fast so that Mueller, Burke, and Tirol can't escape justice, and Judge Meg can issue arrest warrants," Eva said.

"I've never heard of an advance waiver of immunity," Kit said.

"We've got to do some creative lawyering," Eva said. "The waiver of immunity won't be issued until the evidence is presented."

"I'm forty-five percent sure I can pull it off. Maybe," Kit said.

"I like those odds," Eva said.

"You're not going to ask Berlin Regional HQ?"

"No. I think they'll protect senior Austrian and German diplomats. I have to go to our global HQ."

"Okay. Are you going to talk about Mueller and Burke in the TV interview?"

"Not yet. If they get wind of what we're doing, they might put a freeze on the power plant scam. I have to stop Tirol as soon as possible though, before he releases any more criminals. For Tirol, we need to find the payments he made Raco."

"Well, they've all got to transfer suspicious sums of money out of Kosovo, right?"

"Highly suspicious sums. It'll be a miracle if your CI can find confidential banking records to prove this. But hey, I believe in miracles," Eva said. "I'm not going to ask you for more details about this. In case I'm questioned, the less I know about your source the better."

"I'm desperate enough to try for a miracle," Kit said. "I don't want to stay acting chief prosecutor for much longer. It's too much work."

Eva laughed.

"Ah, Ms Refazo, there you are!" greeted the studio assistant, dressed in a pencil-slim skirt and powder-blue jacket. Her hair, a flaming tribute to Kosovo's hair styling salons, cascaded down her back. "We're all set up for your interview."

"Excellent," Eva said, flicking her cigarette butt into the bin. "Do you mind if my friend comes to watch?" She gestured to Kit.

"Not at all," the assistant replied with a smile, ushering them towards the corridor with its wall composed of reclaimed bricks and varnished floors.

When they arrived at the makeup room, Eva raised an eyebrow at the sight of a deep red lipstick. "Do I really need to put all this on?"

The assistant laughed and assured her that everyone wore makeup on television.

Kit asked after Eva's rescue dog, Bambino, and Eva admitted she'd left him with Angel.

"Maybe you should have brought him along," joked the assistant. "The viewers would have loved it."

Eva allowed the studio assistant to finish her makeup with a rose lipstick. Kit had to admit that Eva looked better with more makeup on; it hid the signs of late nights spent researching criminal files and telephone intercepts. This made her wonder if she too should head to a makeup artist sometime soon.

The assistant then led them into the interview room. Eva walked along the white carpet leading up to a round platform bordered by metal rings. She stumbled slightly in her high-heeled shoes, yet her shoulders remained set in determination. Eva sat on one side of the large, white table with two bright-blue TV screens behind her. Kit watched from the audience, and the stage looked rather like a boxing ring to her. Two women go in, one woman comes out, she thought.

The interviewer, a woman in her late thirties with shoulder-length blonde hair and sparkling costume jewellery around her neck, sat opposite Eva. She began by introducing Eva as the OIDC Chief Prosecutor.

"Is that right? Are you the chief prosecutor or did you get fired?"

"I am still in my post. I'm on administrative leave though."

"Meaning you're not doing any work at the moment. What is the reason for that, Ms Refazo?"

"I am not sure; perhaps the head of OIDC can answer that one. But I do have an idea why I am here tonight. We have all seen the media reports about me. I am alleging corruption on part of Kosovo judges, but my international organization isn't doing anything about it."

"But didn't they investigate into your accusations? And none of those judges were implicated?"

"Yes, but it wasn't a proper investigation. What can you do in three days? Besides, the investigators are answering to the head of the mission, and he's the one who wants me gone," Eva stated.

"You must have read the stories that are circulating about you."

"What stories?" Eva enquired.

"Someone has been digging up dirt on you."

Eva scoffed. "Let them try."

"They say that you are a mediocre prosecutor."

"You can look at my track record and see for yourself. I prosecuted major crimes cases in Kosovo better than anyone else. The guilty ones are behind bars as we speak."

"Not all of them, though. We know that Dasham Raco and his gang managed to escape custody."

"Not my fault," Eva retorted sharply.

The interviewer continued to press her. "Reports of your personal life have been making the rounds."

"How is that relevant?"

"Rumors of you being divorced and having plastic surgery in Eastern Europe . . . maybe Hungary. That you are an unkempt chain-smoker and have had a traffic violation. The list goes on."

Eva shook her head in disbelief. "A serious traffic violation? No way! Maybe I parked in the wrong place once or twice like everyone else sometimes does. Who talks about men's private lives? It's only because I'm a woman people dare to speculate publicly."

"Moving on, Ms Refazo—there's no proof to back up your accusation against the judge."

"That isn't accurate; there are phone logs that demonstrate clear criminal intent."

Kit watched anxiously as the interviewer grilled Eva further. She instinctively moved to grab a cigarette, only to remember that smoking was not allowed in here. This interview was becoming more hostile by the minute. How long before the media got wind of their illegal surveillance of Judge Tirol? When people in power chose to push back, it was easy to feel helpless.

"But the border records don't reflect your allegation that the judge traveled to Albania to receive a bribe."

"There could be eyewitnesses with contrary accounts." Eva shot Kit a fleeting look.

The interviewer raised her eyebrows. "We'd love to hear from these eyewitnesses. Can you tell us who they are?"

Eva replied with a shrug but held her silence. "The evidence from the phone transcripts should suffice. I'm willing to stake my reputation on it."

"What does senior management at OIDC have to say?"

At that moment, Kit felt her phone vibrate, alerting her to her upcoming coffee meeting with the Energy Minister, Visar Dreshaj. She had forgotten about it when she found the crime scene tape at their office. The Black and White café was within walking distance of her work, though now she had to rush to call a cab and head into town in order to make it on time. She tried to signal Eva that she needed to leave, but Eva was too focused on the interview.

"I apologize," Kit said as she rushed for the exit and passed the studio assistant. "I have another appointment I must attend to." She called her go-to taxi service as she walked away from the building.

"We'll be there in seven minutes," the dispatcher responded. Kit took a few puffs on her cigarette as she waited for the taxi outside the studio. She tried to clear her mind before her meeting with the minister, but it didn't take long for the taxi to arrive.

"Black and White café. Let's go as quickly as you can," she said to the driver. The driver obliged and sounded the horn more times than usual during their ride.

Kit paid and exited the taxi. Visar Dreshaj was already outside, speaking on his phone and smoking between two close protection officers. The dark limousine was nearby, serving as a reminder that Kit had broken one of the first unwritten rules: don't keep a government minister waiting.

Flustered, Kit rushed up to Visar Dreshaj. His rumpled grey suit sat atop his slightly elven features, complete with a turned-up nose, almond-shaped eyes, and a ready smile. People called him "The Inspector" due to his role as KLA's informal inspector general. Before joining the fight against Serbia, he had been an academic and poet; after joining, he maintained high physical fitness levels through his strict exercise regime.

"Minister, my apologies for being late," she said, lightly touching his arm. He finished his conversation in Albanian before replying.

"It's fine. I just arrived myself. It gives my security team time to check the café and find us a place to sit. After you." Kit smiled at him with relief that he wasn't going to give her a hard time about her tardiness.

Two guards wearing identical dark suits and discrete earpieces appeared at a table, undoubtedly carrying concealed firearms—not uncommon in Kosovo. After pulling out the chairs for Kit and the minister, they moved to another table just out of earshot. The café was designed in industrial-chic style with exposed pipes and concrete walls adorned with artwork from local artists. A long, fore-wooden table sat in the middle for larger groups, and smaller tables surrounded it, like a cafeteria. At the back of the room was a tiny bar.

"I still can't get used to having this security detail follow me around all the time," Visar Dreshaj said as he took his seat with a view of the entrance.

"They wanted me to have one too, but I wasn't thrilled about that either," Kit replied before adding, "Guess where I just came from?"

The minister smiled in response, his eyebrows raised in inquiry.

"They're interviewing my boss—Eva—on Kosovo TV for a possibly disastrous story about her personal life. It hasn't gone well. She's still standing up for what she believes in, regardless of how this will affect her professional reputation. I'm worried about her."

"I understand," he said gently, squeezing her hand. "What did you want to talk to me about today?"

Kit was tempted to withdraw her hand but instead reached for a cigarette. The minister lit it and then his own.

"It doesn't look good—you meeting with me here," she said, embarrassed.

"People might consider it strange for a married man like me to meet a beautiful single woman, but my wife is occupied with her own business and is understanding. So, don't worry about me," he replied.

Kit blushed and looked away, not daring to tell him that Eva had suggested she go talk to him in order to gain information about the power station deal. She liked talking to him regardless of the purpose of the meeting.

"I won't take up too much of your time, Visar—I mean Minister. I'm not exactly sure what I want to say. It has something to do with the power plant deal… I'd rather not give away too much."

"So what you're saying is that your office has some interest in the contract to build the new power plant," he surmised.

"I didn't say that," Kit replied carefully before nodding in confirmation. "I think you can draw your own conclusions…"

"The world isn't perfect, Kit," he said, setting his cigarette in the ashtray and surveying the room. "At times, certain concessions have to be made. But Kosovo always comes first for me. I fought, and people I knew died for it. I won't sacrifice it for financial gain."

"That's good to hear, sir. It is a small country, though; everyone knows everyone else."

"Yes, it's true. All I can tell you is that I haven't been directly involved in the contract negotiations for the power plant. I take the advice of my people."

"Still, you must be aware of how badly the coal plant could damage the environment as it stands now."

"Kosovo needs cheaper, readily available energy if we want to become independent quickly. We don't have enough money to do more than use our coal, and we'll get the Germans in to help us with air purification too. That should help."

"I hate to say this, but I think some of my higher-ups can't be trusted," Kit said.

"That might be true. I think Eva might be an exception," he replied.

"What I'm trying to say is that there may come a time when my office needs evidence that certain people profited from this transaction in ways they shouldn't have. Just so you know. Perhaps we can assist each other in this matter if it arises."

"So, I think I understand what you're telling me— not to get involved in the issue in ways I wouldn't like looked at too closely. And perhaps you will accept some assistance from me in the future."

"Yes, that's it," Kit replied. "I believe we understand each other well."

Before they could proceed with the conversation, Visar Dreshaj's mobile phone started ringing, and shortly after, the security details' phones went off too. Even Kit's own phone vibrated in her bag. One of the security men approached the minister and whispered something in his ear. He stood up with a sense of urgency. Kit also got up.

"What happened?" she asked.

"There's been an incident at the power plant," said the visar. "An explosion."

Chapter Twenty-Six

"You should come with me to the power plant," Visar said.

"Are you sure?" Kit asked.

"Yes, your office will need someone to be there. People have already been hurt." He was headed to the door as he spoke. Kit grabbed her belongings and followed him out. Visar Dreshaj waited for her at the entrance and guided her towards one of the waiting black SUVs. He said something to his security detail and driver before they both entered. She quickly put on her seat belt as the driver put a flashing light on top of the car and turned on the siren.

Visar Dreshaj made numerous calls in Albanian while Kit texted Angel and Owen from her phone.

"There is an incident at the power station, we will meet you there. Angel, have Dr Prabhu on standby. There are casualties. Owen, ask Matt to call the task force. Eva can't be there."

Kit regretted that Eva wasn't able to take the lead, yet she couldn't help feeling elated as they raced through Pristina, lights flashing and sirens blaring, with additional emergency units converging onto the highway leading out of Obilić—fire engines, police cars (including a special response force), and ambulances following them in their train of vehicles. What was odd was that she was going there in the same car as the Minister of Energy, who would bear responsibility for such a disaster. She glanced at Visar Dreshaj, who was talking in a grave tone over his phone call, and tried to steady herself.

Taking a moment to focus on her breathing, which was irregular and shallow, Kit attempted to take some deep breaths. As the acting chief prosecutor, she needed to remain composed and remain in control of the chaos and stress. Her inner voice was trying to tell her something; she paused for a moment to listen. Suddenly it came to her. What were the chances of an explosion just before a contract for a new power plant was due to be signed? If the damage was substantial enough, the pressure to sign the deal would increase exponentially. Chills ran down her spine, and sweat prickled on her forehead. It appeared that this may not be an accident at all, but part of a larger conspiracy, one which would provide senior officials with untraceable funds. Kit set her shoulders and vowed to stay focused and alert.

This incident could have a major bearing on the case that had preoccupied her since she heard about it. Visar was now off the phone and frowning as he stared into the distance. She reached across the car seat and pressed his hand with hers. He looked over to her, and she caught his eye as if trying to reassure him about what they were going to find a few kilometers away. There in the back of the car, surrounded by sirens, blue flashing lights, and emergency services, a moment of intimacy and understanding passed between them. No matter what the apparent distance between them was, in terms of position in life, they had an understanding.

"Thanks for being here with me today," he said, squeezing her hand before releasing it. Meanwhile, Kit's mobile phone was buzzing with multiple messages from Angel and Owen. Angel was on her way to collect Dr Prabhu, and Owen was communicating with Matt and Don. Although Kit was aware that Eva had taken the struggle to another level in the public domain, she still wished Eva was there with them.

By the time they arrived at the power plant, it was engulfed in smoke, with multiple fire engines showering water and foam onto it.

Someone immediately escorted Visar Dreshaj and Kit away to a safer vantage point. It appeared that an immense hydrogen tank had detonated and caused destruction in many areas of the station, adding to the flames erupting around them. Kit looked down in awe at the flurry of activity taking place; every type of emergency crew, police force, special response team, and military personnel were all busy at the site.

Another truck pulled up to collect the chunks of metal that had been scattered by the blast. An ambulance admitted two shrouded figures on stretchers.

"They're going to have to shut the power plant down, at least temporarily," Visar Dreshaj said, his voice tight with concern. "We'll need funds to import more energy. This is catastrophic on so many levels."

"Whoever did this must have had some sort of agenda," Kit said thoughtfully. "The timing is too perfect. Just as they were about to sign off on a new power plant, this happens and increases the pressure to get it done."

Visar Dreshaj regarded her, absorbing her words. "No matter how it happened, I will find out the truth."

Kit breathed deeply, trying to detach from the crisis before her and view it as if it were a chessboard she was observing from a castle tower. After a few minutes, she saw her colleagues arrive in an OIDC jeep and waved to them.

"Thanks for the coffee, Visar," she said with a small smile. "I forgot to pay for mine. I have to go join my friends now."

"No need to thank me, Kit," he replied with an understanding look. For a brief moment, they felt like they were away from the chaos of the scene unfolding before them. "I hope we can meet in better circumstances soon. Here come the film crew. Looks like they want an interview with me."

Kit looked down the hill and saw the Kosovo TV interviewer, their assistant, and the accompanying crew making their way determinedly up the hill to reach the Minister of Energy.

"That's the woman who just interviewed Eva," Kit observed. "I think it's time for a strategic retreat. Thanks for the lift." Kit picked her way down the opposite side of the hill, heading in the direction of Angel, who was conversing with a security guard about gaining access to the site.

Her primary objective was to join Dr Prabhu in declaring time of death for the miserable explosion victims. Angel was there, wearing a khaki jumpsuit and lace-up shoes, with a blue denim jacket pulled over it. She was showing her ID to the black-clad special forces officer safeguarding entrance to the location. Kit also had her ID in hand and placed it around her neck. Matt was taking charge, with Owen and Don walking several steps behind. Don had Max the police dog alongside him. Kit recalled that Max was trained on explosives detection among other things.

When they met each other, Angel and Kit embraced quickly. It had been some days since they last saw each other, and many events had taken place since then. Kit shook Dr Prabhu's hand. Dr Prabhu wore a colorful Indian tunic and pants, covered over by a Western jacket and scarf.

"Thanks for arriving on such short notice, Dr Prabhu," Kit said. "I think you know the procedure better than I do, but I believe between us we are expected to declare the victims' time of death."

Dr Prabhu smiled at Kit, who remembered when they'd first met at the morgue and Kit had difficulty being near the bodies.

"No problem, Kit," Dr Prabhu said. "Let's have a look at the victims. I will examine them, and then you can take down the findings."

"Angel, could you come too? I didn't bring any writing supplies with me since I was just at a café when I got the news," Kit asked.

"No worries," Angel replied, pointing to her tote bag. "I have all you need here."

Matt stepped in then and said, "We must approach this as an active crime scene. It's probable that all those emergency services damaged or contaminated evidence. Don, look for other explosives. We can't ignore the likelihood that this is arson, or worse, a terror attack."

Kit nodded in agreement as she said, "Someone could have an agenda in shutting this power station down."

Matt acknowledged her words with a terse nod before they went off to their various tasks. Owen trailed behind Matt, prepared to take note of any discoveries they made. Kit already knew where the ambulances were located since she'd noted their location from the hill they had been standing on earlier. Dr Prabhu walked ahead and announced that they were from the coroner's office and the chief prosecutor's office. Angel followed with her notepad, ready to make notes. Kit stood back, watching them work, ready to play her part in confirming what had happened. She focused on what was happening in front of her and had not noticed a tall, muscular figure who had quietly approached her from behind.

Before she could respond, a powerful figure enveloped her in a vicelike grip and pinned her arms to her sides. She was unable to scream and could only gasp for air. The gruff voice of Dasham Raco sounded in her ear.

"You escaped me before, but not again." He tightened his hold on her bruised rib, and she winced. "I'm coming for you, bitch, when there aren't so many witnesses." He released his grip and strode off towards a maintenance truck that was being used to remove damaged metal from the scene. His three accomplices followed, and all four climbed into the truck.

Kit keeled over with pain. Angel noticed and ran over, calling for a medic before informing Matt and Owen. Matt turned towards the direction of the fast-disappearing truck with a look of determination. It was still visible in the distance. He was on his phone calling for backup, then both he and Owen ran to their jeep and drove off at speed. Several Kosovo security guards stopped them at the exit to check their papers, delaying them while the truck rattled into the distance, crested the top of the hill, and disappeared. Matt growled with impatience, and finally the guards let them go.

"She needs to go to hospital for an X-ray," Dr Prabhu explained.

Kit was treated as a victim of the incident and was prepped for transport to the hospital on a stretcher in the ambulance with a drip for shock and pain. "I'm going to get that guy," she said between gritted teeth. "The utter audacity of it! He must be behind the explosion at the plant."

Angel looked at her with concern. "He's scared, otherwise he wouldn't have attacked you like that."

Dr Prabhu interrupted. "Many people will be going to Pristina hospital ER with burns and other injuries. I can arrange for you to get to a private clinic if you like, Kit."

"Yes, that would be good, thanks," Kit replied.

"I'll call the OIDC chief medical officer," Angel said. "He'll meet you at the check-in at the clinic and go with you for an X-ray and treatment."

"Thanks," Kit remarked faintly, feeling the effects of the morphine numbing her pain as she relaxed. The sharp sounds and flashing lights around the scene dissolved.

***

That evening, Kit was discharged from hospital with her ribs taped up, supplied with painkillers and instructions to take rest. She settled herself in front of the television on the couch. Her stomach growled, and she realized she didn't have any food in the house and didn't feel up to shopping. She would have to make do with nuts and coffee. At that moment, the buzzer rang. It was Owen downstairs.

She gingerly got up and went to the buzzer by the door. "Come up," she said and buzzed him in. "Third floor."

Owen arrived with a two shopping bags full of supplies. "I brought some of my casserole and a few other things. I thought you might need something."

"Bless you!" Kit exclaimed and went over to examine the contents of the bags. "I am actually starving." She grinned at him. "I'll eat something now. Would you like a bite?"

"Yes, I would," Owen replied. "Why don't you stay on the couch and let me heat it up."

Kit gave him directions where to find the kitchen utensils, and before too long they were eating a satisfying bowl of Welsh casserole.

"Angel told me what happened," Owen said with concern etched on his face. "I'm so sorry that I left you there alone. Matt said we had to check around for more explosives."

"There may have been some," Kit replied, taking another spoonful as she spoke. "Raco is working with the conspiracy—probably trying to push through the agreement for the new power plant in spite of the bad environmental reports."

"Did he crack your ribs?"

"No, thank goodness. It felt like it though. They're just bruised and dislocated. At the clinic, they put the ribs back into place and bound them. The doctor says I should take it easy for a while."

"You ever take doctor's orders? Or anyone else's?" Owen asked in amusement.

"Umm, now you make me think . . ." she said, and they both laughed.

"But seriously," he said, "come back to my place. No strings attached. I just want you to stay safe since Raco has threatened you and attacked you again."

"Thanks, Owen," she replied, "but I'd rather stay in my own space. I don't think he'll be coming here, and if he does, I'll just call Security."

"We didn't manage to catch him. I'm pretty sure the guards held us up on purpose. By the time we got through the gate, the truck had already gone a few kilometers up the road. When we found it, it was abandoned. They must have had another car waiting for them to switch over to."

"Did you look through the truck?"

"Yes, there were plenty of prints and other evidence. It looks like the Podujevo Five came in posing as a maintenance crew and started the fire, which led to the explosion. We're keeping it out of the news though. The Minister of Energy thinks it would cause too much panic among the public."

Kit nodded after finishing her food and wiping her bowl clean with a bit of bread.

"That was great, thanks." She knew Owen hadn't realized that she had arrived at the scene with the Minister of Energy before anyone else, even though Eva had suggested Kit speak to Visar Dreshaj about the conspiracy during a task force meeting where Owen was present.

"It was a good thing you saw Raco," Owen went on, "or else we'd still be looking around for whatever caused the fire."

"Well, actually," Kit began, "it was him who found me. I can't believe how audacious he was! It could have been worse, I suppose, but he still managed to avoid arrest. I want him to be locked up for a long time. If Judge Tirol had kept him and his gang in jail where they belong, none of this would have happened."

"I know." They stayed silent for a bit before Owen noticed Kit was looking pale.

"You look worn out. I'll let you get some sleep," he said. "You won't be able to go to the charity event at the US ambassador's place tomorrow night, right?"

"Of course I am! I'm taking my meds and wearing a dress that will hide my bruises."

"The invitation to stay at my apartment is still open if you'd like," he mentioned again.

"I'll be alright. Don't worry, I'll let you know if anything strange happens." She wanted to say something about Zena Lace Letalova and how she didn't want to take away from his time with her, but she decided against it. The day had turned out very differently than how she had expected it to this morning when she saw them training together. He had shared a homemade meal when she was down, and that meant a lot.

After Owen left, Kit took a mixture of painkillers and sleeping pills and fell into a deep, dreamless sleep. When she woke up in the morning, she checked out the window and was surprised to see Owen's jeep was still there. He must have stayed outside overnight just to guard her apartment just in case Raco showed up.

CHAPTER TWENTY-SEVEN

Kit was on sick leave, certified by the physician at the occupational clinic because of her injured ribs. She didn't want to be summoned to the head of mission and asked to account for her movements. What's more, she needed time to gather her thoughts. What better way to do that than to talk to Dr Maria Montenegro?

Dr Montenegro had an opening in her schedule late morning. That was perfect. Kit dressed, gingerly checking her bruises and covering them with a long-sleeved T-shirt and a sweater over her jeans along with suede boots. She threw on her leather jacket and twisted a silk scarf around her neck.

Clattering down the stairs, she remembered seeing Owen's jeep still outside at about six a.m. that morning he had waited overnight to check on her. She felt touched and grateful that he had sat there all night in case Raco came looking for her. He was a loyal friend; no one else had checked on her after the attack.

Kit arrived at the apartment building where the therapist, Dr Maria Montenegro, practiced and pressed the buzzer to be let in. Maria appeared at the door of her studio to greet her wearing a navy sweater and pants set with a bold brooch. While she dressed in understated elegance, Kit now realized that Maria's choice of flamboyant jewelry suited her celebrity status. They shook hands before Maria welcomed Kit inside. Kit left her jacket on the coat hanger by the door. As she turned, her attention flicked over to look for the photo she had seen earlier of Maria and her husband with the US ambassador on Durrës beach. The photo was gone. However, next to where it had been, Kit noticed an accounting statement printout.

"Good morning. How are you?" Maria asked.

"I'm doing okay, thanks," Kit said as she walked along the built-in bookshelf. She was trying to look for the photograph they had discussed before without appearing obvious about it. "So much as happened, I don't know where to start," Kit replied. She glanced up at the sunlight streaming into the room. "That is rather bright. Do you mind pulling the shades a little? It will help me to relax."

"Certainly, that's no problem," Maria said.

"Thanks so much, Maria," Kit said. She swiped the bank statement and deftly folded it in two, slipping it into her jacket pocket while the other woman was occupied pulling the drapes. "That's much better." Kit took a seat on the couch.

"Start wherever you feel the most comfortable. What has the most energy in your experience?"

Often, the beginning of the session was the most difficult as Kit had to choose what she wanted to discuss first. Right now, she wanted to move the session along and show no signs of her pocketing the account statement.

Kit sighed. "I feel overloaded. My dad suddenly reappeared in my life after twenty years. I just split with my fiancée, and then I got involved with a Russian intelligence officer. I was unexpectedly promoted to chief prosecutor, and some criminal attacked me. Those are the highlights of my week, Maria. What should we discuss first?"

"That is a lot to unpack," Maria commented. She kept her voice neutral as always, and Kit wondered if Maria doubted her story. If she had really believed what Kit was saying, surely she would show some kind of reaction. "Let's start by talking about your father's return."

Kit explained what she and her mother, Rosalyn, had discussed the sudden reappearance of her father Vernon.

"How do you feel about that?"

"It's weird - I can't comprehend why he is resurfacing now."

"What do you think might happen?"

"My dad might want to visit my mom. We might discover something about what happened to him during the past two decades."

"Could it be connected that you ended your engagement shortly after hearing from your father?"

Kit stayed silent for a few moments. "Why would there be a link?"

"From what you said, Xander resembles your father in some ways. The two of you had a calm domestic life together, but perhaps it was not as exciting as you had wished. Maybe when your real father reentered the picture, you didn't feel you needed Xander anymore. What do you think about that possibility?"

Kit reflected for a moment before replying. "I never considered that there could be a connection. Maybe in some ways Xander is—was—like a father to me despite being younger than me."

"Age doesn't have to matter much in relationships. What about this new man in your life? The Russian you mentioned? That would be Sergei, right?"

"He has helped me see different sides of myself. I appreciate that, but it doesn't feel like a secure bond. It's thrilling, risky, yet unstable."

"So, there are a variety of male figures in your life. Maybe all of them are reflecting a part of who you are."

"I'll have to think about that," Kit said.

"Don't overanalyze it. Try to sense your way into it and see what emerges."

Kit nodded. "Do you think that everything we experience somehow reflects part of ourselves? Sergei seems to think that. Change ourselves, change our lives."

"The Swiss founder of psychotherapy, Carl Jung, believed in a concept called synchronicity, or meaningful coincidences. That things that seemingly happen by chance can be meaningful to us. So could it be that the world reflects something about us, including relationships?"

"What about bad things that happen? What about being attacked by a criminal, for example?"

"There's nothing simple or automatic about all this. I just ask the question, and you can tell me if it resonates with you, or whether it makes you understand more about yourself than you did before."

"That's certainly that case," Kit said. She started tossing the soft stress ball that Maria kept on the table from one hand to the other and looked distractedly out the window.

"So, how would you like to approach close relationships now?"

Kit thought for a while before answering. "I want a balance between the two. I'd like a relationship with someone more exciting than Xander but who is more stable than Sergei."

"Sometimes we can only reach equilibrium by going through the extremes. Changing the topic for now. How have your sleeping patterns been?"

"Better, thank you. But whenever I get into a routine, something else occurs. Like yesterday when I was attacked by a suspect I helped convict. He escaped from detention and . . ." Kit stopped tossing the stress ball but squeezed it harder, her knuckles whitening.

"Did you notify security about it?"

"No, not really. My co-workers from the EUFOR police know about it though."

"You're in a delicate phase right now, Kit. Things are developing rapidly. You need to keep yourself safe."

"I don't understand what you mean. You think these events are related to my 'phase'?"

"A lot of what we see in others is an expression of our inner self; this may be conscious or subconscious."

"That is what Sergei says; working on ourselves can modify our world. I had an interesting experience in Ljubljana. Some of us crossed the Dragon Bridge and noticed how this symbolism caused different reactions in each of us. I learned that I need to overcome my fears," Kit explained.

"The dragon can be a metaphor for our deepest fears and desires. How did you feel after facing it?"

"Better. It helped me loosen the grip of my worries."

"Kit, please keep yourself regulated in the next weeks. Make sure you get enough sleep, eat healthy, and exercise. You could also note down your feelings in a journal. If you still feel threatened by this person, consider getting personal security."

"I will try, but I have some important cases that need to be completed. When I am done, I could take a vacation."

"What kind of cases are those?"

Kit felt uncomfortable with this question as the cases were all at a sensitive, confidential stage.

"You read about Eva Refazo's accusations in the newspapers, right? There are many consequences stemming from her claims, and I'm dealing with some of them now. Even though I am on sick leave, I must go back eventually to finish that pile of work."

"What do you think about Eva's claims about high-level corruption? Do you think there's something to them?"

Kit shrugged. "I've never known Eva to be wrong about a case, and she wouldn't have gone public unless she was sure. So, yeah, I think there must be something to her suspicions."

"Does she have solid evidence of wrongdoing?"

"She's got well-grounded suspicions, but if she can't investigate further, there might not be much she can do about it."

Maria nodded. "What about this dangerous suspect?"

"He openly menaced me yesterday. I was at the power station explosion, and he laid hands on me. He threatened and injured me." She pulled up her sweater to show the deep purpling on her torso and the binding around her ribs. "Don't worry, my ribs were just dislocated, not broken."

"Good heavens!" Maria recoiled in horror at the sight of the injuries.

Kit felt a twinge of satisfaction. She had at last elicited a genuine reaction from Maria Montenegro, not just a measured psychotherapist's comments.

"Did they capture him?"

"Not yet. He's still furious that I escaped him before and got him arrested."

"What happened during this incident?"

"We were confirming some deaths in the presence of the coroner when he sneaked up behind me. Nobody was watching at that time."

Maria shivered. "Like an actual shadow," she murmured.

"I guess you could say that," Kit said in a falsely cheerful tone. "So, things will not be okay until Raco is locked up—and hopefully my chief, Eva, is reinstated."

They chatted further about the people in Kit's life and what they could mean to her. She didn't want to say much more about Sergei, especially after Maria disclosed that she knew him from the Russian Liaison Office.

"And what happened with Sergei?" Maria pressed.

Kit stopped speaking for a moment. "I met him in Ljubljana. We were . . . intimate. And then Sergei left unexpectedly for Moscow." She chose not to mention the gifts and hotel suite he left her. Kit wasn't yet ready to share the details of her lucid dream and out-of-body experience with Plečnik the architect.

"How did you feel about that?" Montenegro asked.

Kit shrugged. "We've been texting since then, but I was surprised that he just took off without a word. Just like my father did."

"I'm glad you're beginning to recognize the patterns in your relationships. With that awareness, we can start to change them."

"Maybe, but I've still been feeling confused about all the experiences I've been having," she said. "Sergei took me to meet his mentor, a priest in the Russian Orthodox Church."

"How did that go?" Maria asked.

"I felt drawn to the priest's teachings despite myself. He seemed charismatic but at the same time intimidating. I find it hard to reconcile these traditions with my own worldview. I thought I was open-minded, but the way they spoke about Rasputin's legacy seemed, frankly, creepy."

"How did Sergei seem about that?"

"He seemed comfortable. This is his world, after all. I think associating with the Church helps him to reconcile with some of his actions so he can still believe that he's a good person. But that's not all. I had a tarot reading from one of Sergei's friends."

"A tarot reading?" Maria asked, her eyebrows raised in surprise.

"The cards may have predicted my future, but I didn't understand clearly what they were trying to tell me."

"What did you think they might have indicated?"

"I got the Fool card. Natalia said something about new beginnings and taking risks."

"Go on," said Maria, getting up. She searched her bookshelves and pulled out a book on tarot and Jungian psychotherapy.

"Is there anything you don't have a book on?" Kit asked.

Maria smiled and flicked through the book. "The Fool, as trickster-hero or heroine, can play good or bad tricks, depending on our point of view. They can be either destroyed, reformed, or transformed at the end of the story."

"Which will it be in my case?"

"You tell me."

Kit thought for a moment, and then said, "Transformed. I'm going to be transformed."

"Why is that?"

"I'm not going to be destroyed or reformed, so that leaves transformation. According to the book."

"I tend to agree," Maria said. "Systems like tarot can help us to find order in our lives, especially when events seem chaotic. If we don't rely on them too much, things like religion, passionate affairs, tarot readings, and even therapy can be valid ways to explore our beliefs and emotions."

"You always sound so calm and balanced," Kit said.

Maria smiled. "We still have a lot to discuss, but we're coming to the end of our session today. First, tell me how you're going with the sleeping pills. Are they helping?"

"Yes and no," Kit replied. "They are helping me to sleep, but with so much happening in my life, I don't always feel refreshed in the morning."

"You're making a lot of progress, but it's still important that you try to keep to a routine as much as possible. That means keeping regular sleep habits. Give me a call when you're ready for another session. Let me know if you'd like to schedule more frequent meetings, or if you'd like to increase the dosage of the sleeping tablets."

"I will. Thank you, Maria," Kit said. She was moving towards the door and already thinking ahead. She turned and said, "I'm lucky to have you as a therapist."

"Why is that?" Maria asked.

"I came across an article about you in an English fashion magazine. It seems you're well-known in some circles as a celebrity therapist. Or life coach, as some of them prefer to call you."

Maria laughed, quite a musical sound. "Oh, that old story. I let the journalist write the article on me. She's an old friend of my husband Richard's. She owes me a favor now."

"Or you owe her a favor," Kit said.

"I was happy to take you on as a client, Kit. An up-and-coming legal officer like yourself. You're going to go far. Call it a therapist's intuition."

Kit had the impression that Maria was circulating in the world of influence and favours given and owed. She worried about over-confiding in Maria, but at least she had kept come things to herself. Kit felt as if the purloined financial statement was burning a hole in her jacket and left before Maria noticed it was missing. Now she had other things to focus on, like what to wear to the US ambassador's party.

Chapter Twenty-Eight

She spread out the designer clothes from Sergei on her bed and examined every detail. The dress featured a wraparound skirt of heavy, embossed red taffeta, coming to just below her knees. The top was striped in an ethnic design with metallic thread and paillettes and had a plunging neckline. She could add a pin to conceal the bindings around her ribs. The jacket was a brilliant red silk with gold embroidery accentuating her midriff and the tuxedo lapels.

Kit needed something else to turn her outfit into a costume for a Halloween masquerade party. She remembered a lacy fox mask she had bought in Venice with Xander, which she retrieved from an old camphor chest. To complete the look, she added her grandpa's black lacquer cane. She placed them alongside the rest of her items. The walking stick shone like coal, from its pointed end up to its rounded cap. It added a definite flare to her costume.

Overwhelmed with anticipation, she hastily undressed and donned the dress, which fit snugly over her curves. The gathers on one side of the skirt gracefully outlined her hips. She draped on the jacket and cinched it at the waist using a golden belt. She then stepped into her red high heels and carefully placed the fox mask over her face, leaving her mouth and chin visible. To complete the look of her mask, she tied her auburn hair in a high ponytail. Last but not least, she picked up the walking stick.

She considered what Sergei would think of how she looked. She took a selfie in the full-length mirror and sent it to him at the last unlisted number he had used.

"My clothes for the US ambassadors party. What do you think?" she wrote.

A few seconds later, his response appeared: "Magnificent – you're a real kitsune!"

She replied: "Kitsune?"

"A Japanese female fox spirit, a trickster. Your namesake. Like a kitsune, you can be smart and unpredictable to outwit your enemies. I wish I could see you now up close."

She smiled as she typed: "I need all my powers tonight."

Sergei wrote back: "Remember all we discussed and did. You'll be fine."

"Thanks."

He wrote one last message: "Keep in touch."

His approval of Kit's outfit meant more than she was willing to admit; it was almost as if he knew all that was going on and why this was such an important moment. She heard an email notification from the workstation in her house.

An email had arrived from her office's address. It was from Mueller's office to all the senior managers. The message reported that the privatization panel had approved the agreement to begin building a new power station in Kosovo. Work was to start as soon as possible in view of the recent explosion at the generating station and its decommissioning. Kit felt a wave of despair wash over her. The funds transfer from the contract and the kickbacks could go through any minute, and they hadn't found a way to intercept the bank transactions yet.

Maybe this challenge was too much for her. But she paused to consider: What if she did have the luck of a kitsune, as Sergei had said? Maybe anything was possible if she believed in herself. She had to believe that if she was to have any chance of success.

Before long, a message from Owen chimed from her phone. He wanted to pick her up around eight that evening for the event. She appreciated his concern for her without having to ask questions or make any assumptions.

"Sure, see you then," she texted back, adding, "Just getting my outfit ready."

"Can't wait," he replied.

As she put on the finishing touches to her hair and makeup for the evening, she recalled all of Sergei's teachings about strategy and the key to success: always choose your battlefield wisely, know your goals, and surprise your opponents. It was sound advice, but with so many unknowns, it didn't seem like there was much she could do right now except be vigilant.

Kit had some time before Owen was due to arrive, and she remembered the financial statement she had lifted off Maria's bureau. She wasn't even sure why she had done it, but that photo of Maria, her husband, and the US ambassador had struck a chord with her. The beach at Durrës was where their off-the-books operation nearly went bad, and the US ambassador was working closely with the leadership in her own mission. Then there was the magazine article about Maria as a celebrity therapist. In Kosovo, there were a lot of connections between people, some more obvious than others. It was hard to unravel them. The way Maria had referred to her as an up-and-coming lawyer had surprised her. She hadn't considered that Maria might have taken her on as a client because she saw the potential to cultivate someone of influence.

She placed the financial statement on the table and smoothed out the folds. She could see row after row of transactions. Some of the deposits were hefty, and some repeated payments were just below the amount that might trigger an alert with the banks for possible money laundering. She didn't have time to look through these carefully right now. But she knew someone who could— Tom Baumgarten. Kit wasn't sure where he was anymore. Was he still in the Pristina safehouse, or had he managed to retrieve his passport and get out of the country? She had his last phone number, so she tried texting him.

A few minutes later, her phone chimed. It was a message from Tom. He updated her that he had managed to get his passport back and had taken a US military flight to the air force base at Ramstein, Germany. He was there for a few days while he arranged onwards flights.

"That was smart," she texted back to him. There was much less chance of trouble on a friendly military flight than a commercial one. "Fill me in on the deets later. For now, could you please check a financial statement to see if it looks suspicious? This is a celebrity psychotherapist in Pristina with connections to some of our 'friends.'"

Tom agreed, so she photographed the statements and sent them to him using an encrypted app.

"Let me know as soon as you know something," she said. Then she locked the original document in the safe.

***

Owen buzzed on the door downstairs just as Kit finished getting ready. He uttered words of amazement when Kit stepped out of her apartment. "You look fantastic," he said, opening the jeep door for her.

"Thanks," she said, flushing. "Just an old dress I had at the back of my closet. I see you managed to find your dress uniform for the occasion."

"We should go to more events like this," he said.

Her heart fluttered in anticipation as the time grew closer to their arrival at the US ambassador's residence. She held a black velvet bag over her shoulder, just large enough to fit the delicate fox mask inside.

"Have you ever been to the White House before?" he asked.

Kit shook her head no. "Where is it?"

"It's a short drive from Pristina and looks like a smaller version of the famous White House in DC. The lower level is for reception, and the upper half is for living quarters. It's perfect for discreet parties."

"Sounds perfect," Kit said. "Now I can tell the folks back home I visited the White House and they'll be impressed."

Owen glanced at her with admiration before continuing. "They definitely would be impressed if they could see you tonight."

Kit felt a pang of regret that Xander wasn't here to share this moment and appreciate her glamorous outfit. But she pushed away that thought, focusing instead on the fact that she was being driven to a gala event by an elegantly dressed officer and she was kitsune—the fox—for the night.

As Owen drove down dark country roads, Kit reviewed their task force mission plans aloud. Owen sat beside her in the car, the dashboard lighting up just enough of his face to make out his expression.

"So," Kit began, "if we're lucky enough to get evidence against our three main suspects, have you and Matt figured out how we'll arrest them? Did you talk with Eva?"

"Yes," he answered. "I'm sorry I didn't tell you. Things are hectic. If your informant gives us substantial proof, we should submit it to Judge Olga. Evidently, Eva convinced some of the bigwigs at OIDC in New York to waive their diplomatic immunity if the evidence is solid. It has to be done soon because of the massive transactions that are involved."

"No pressure then," Kit remarked wryly.

"Do you have Judge Olga's contact details?"

"No, we didn't get to that because I had to leave the television studio where Eva was being interviewed."

"I've got them on my phone if you need it," he said, handing her his mobile device. She opened his contacts and found Judge Olga Pilska with her email address and phone number. An impulse to find out how often Owen and Zena had been in contact came over her. Could she check his incoming calls and texts without him seeing? When she sneaked a peek, she saw that there had been several missed calls from Zena that day, which she was relieved to see he had not picked up. With a snap, Kit closed the phone and returned it. "Any other news?" she said with a bit too much cheeriness.

"The Forensic Institute matched Raco's DNA to the knife from the scene of the stabbing, but EUFOR still insists that the victim committed suicide."

"It's ridiculous!" Kit exclaimed. "Mr. Kupi couldn't have stabbed himself eleven times; a slice to the wrists are all that it takes to end your life."

"I know." Owen sighed. "They want to hide it because of the important privatization panel business. It looks like Raco and his gang set off the bombs at the power station too. He's so brazen, but we can't seem to stop him."

"We will," Kit said quietly, her conviction so strong that Owen glanced over at her in surprise.

They drove in silence until they saw a large, white building loom out of the darkness. It stood with impressive columns against a backdrop of wooded hills.

"That must be it," Kit said, her voice filled with anticipation. Owen reduced the speed of the jeep as he approached two security guards at the entrance. They gestured for him to drive a few meters further up and park in the lot.

"Kosovo is full of surprises," Kit whispered before Owen dropped into first gear and made their way to the parking area. She saw lovely gardens with shrubbery and a majestic, white statue standing in the middle of the grassy grounds. The security officer pointed to a spot for them, and there was a wide, brightly lit path that led to the grand entrance. The edifice was made to look like a smaller replica of the US White House, perched in an environment of hills and forests.

"I'm going to need this now," Kit said before retrieving her fox mask from her bag, securing it in place and grabbing her cane and bag. After Owen locked up the car, Kit noted that many of the vehicles had luxury branding and diplomatic plates. A few seating areas were placed outside, illuminated by outdoor lighting, while fog swirled around the candles lighting up several jack-o'-lanterns, making it seem like a dreamworld. There was a stream at the back of the property, and Kit took a deep breath of fresh air far from the smoggy city center.

He looked at her silently for a moment. "I'm sorry for staring, but I've never seen an outfit like that before."

"Do you think the mask looks okay?" she asked. "I could take it off if it doesn't."

"No, don't. It looks smashing."

She glanced around at the other people entering the building, some wearing masks and costumes while others were in tuxedos or dress uniforms. The women all wore evening dresses. Kit felt grateful to Sergei for giving her such a stunning outfit.

"Is Matt coming?" Kit asked as they stepped onto the path towards the entrance. Normally, Owen would be Matt's driver for these kinds of events.

"No. He doesn't really care for diplomatic events like this," Owen answered. Offering his arm formally, they proceeded towards the entrance.

"How does the ambassador justify having a residence like this?"

"Perhaps land purchases are good value for money around here," he posited. "It is conspicuous though, isn't it? Not exactly something you expect to see. Although I suppose it does make for excellent entertaining."

When they reached the entrance, Owen produced their invitations, and one of the two security guards checked their names off the guest list and allowed them in.

The foyer was already bustling with guests, servers offering champagne and hors d'oeuvres while autumnal decorations filled the space with seasonal color. A string quartet played on a raised dais to one side of the room. Owen and Kit joined the throng, weaving through the crowd, their appearance garnering curious glances.

They finally arrived at the entrance to the ballroom, stepping through a pair of tall doors and into the magnificent chamber beyond. Perhaps it was the large, tiered chandeliers that illuminated the entire hall, or perhaps it was the light of the full moon that shone through the windows, but something about the moment seemed to sparkle and shimmer, as if a magical aura had settled in the air. But that sense of a magical evening had a sinister undercurrent. Kit could not forget that they were on a knife's edge, associating with dangerous people whom they knew to be involved in a criminal scheme.

CHAPTER TWENTY-NINE

Kit and Owen halted in the center of the room, their muscles taut. Kit was acutely aware that many of their opponents in this fatal game had to be present, with no idea what the outcome might be.

"I wonder who we know here," Kit said, her voice barely audible as she scanned the room cautiously.

"US Ambassador Stanton is speaking with the German ambassador over there," Owen murmured, nodding his chin towards them.

Kit glanced furtively in their direction and noticed her head of mission, Jacob Mueller and his deputy Michael Burke, standing nearby. Judge Tirol was there too. Her mouth went dry and she nervously adjusted her face mask, hoping it would be enough to conceal her identity.

Then as she scanned the room, she spotted Maria Montenegro. Maria stood out with her blonde hair styled in a sleek bob. Her elegant black gown with a plunging back showed off her silver necklace. Kit could see that Maria had paired her dress with silver strappy heels, and her makeup was expertly done with smokey eyes and a nude lip. Maria was surrounded by a group of people all vying for her attention. Kit recognized some of them as prominent figures in the diplomatic and entertainment circles. She could hear the murmur of their conversations, but she could not make out the details. As Kit moved closer to the group, Maria continued to engage with her admirers. But as soon as she caught sight of Kit, her eyes registered recognition. Maria excused herself from the group and made her way towards Kit, her heels clicking on the marble floor.

"Kit! What a surprise to see you here," Maria said with a smile.

Kit took off her mask and returned the smile. "I wondered if I'd run into you. You look stunning," she said, taking in Maria's outfit. Kit felt a mix of pleasure and apprehension. Even though she had a close relationship with Maria in their therapy sessions, Kit also knew that Maria might have connections to some of the people involved in the money-laundering scheme.

Maria smiled warmly. "Thank you. That outfit is amazing on you."

As they talked, Kit noticed that Maria seemed more animated than usual. Her eyes sparkled, and she laughed as she spoke to Kit, her eyes scanning the room. Maria was clearly in her element at this event with high-profile people. After a few moments, a woman broke into their conversation and diverted Maria's attention. Kit took the opportunity to break away and return to Owen.

"Who's that?" he asked.

"Someone I know through work," Kit replied. "A self-styled celebrity therapist." At that moment, she felt her mobile phone vibrate in her bag as a message arrived.

A server came up to them with a tray of drinks, and Kit heard a woman's Russian-accented voice offering them champagne from France. She glanced up sharply to find Silver wearing a maid's outfit, with her hair sleeked back behind her ears. She had removed her facial piercings for the occasion, and her tattoos were covered except for the henna design showing on her left hand.

"Oh my God! What are you doing here?" Kit exclaimed.

Silver hushed her and said in a loud voice, "I understand this champagne is an excellent vintage, from France of course." Kit took a glass of champagne as Owen observed them with interest. When Silver had moved on to another group of people, he asked Kit in a whisper who she was.

"My confidential informant," Kit answered quietly without looking at either of them. "I'm surprised to see her here. She must be up to something; let's watch what happens."

"Okay," Owen agreed. "We can talk about it later. Several suspects here, which can't be a coincidence."

"I agree." Kit suddenly became fully alert. This was no longer just another diplomatic event. She suddenly thought of Sergei. No doubt he would see this as the opening gambit of a chess game. Now the essential thing was to conceal their agenda from anyone who might be watching them and to keep alert.

"Let's mingle. Try to look normal," Kit said.

Owen laughed. "I don't think there's anything normal about your outfit, Kit."

The master of ceremonies took the stage and addressed the crowd, informing them of the charity event taking place in the room. He mentioned how businesses had donated prizes like a luxury car from a German sponsor, cognac from Kosovo's top winery, trips to Ljubljana, as well as spa weekends. Kit and Owen perused the corner table with a list of prizes and purchased tickets in the tombola.

They then threaded their way through the throng, speaking to a few people they knew before arriving at Mueller and Burke. Mueller was immaculately dressed in a dinner suit and warmly greeted Kit, shaking her hand, but the reptilian smile on his thin face made her skin crawl. A wave of cologne wafted towards her.

"It's good to be back, sir," Kit said with a confidence that she didn't feel.

"Dreadful business about your former chief. But I'm sure it will be sorted out soon," Mueller observed. "In the meantime, I'd like you to be acting chief prosecutor. We are impressed with your proactive attitude."

He turned back to Michael Burke, who wore Texan dress boots and a leather tie around his neck. Burke was flushed and smiling. He seemed to have been indulging in his favorite tipple.

"You've certainly earned our admiration," Burke said.

"Play your cards right and your promotion to chief prosecutor could become permanent," Mueller continued.

"Thank you for your confidence, Sir," Kit said, hoping that her mask hid her repulsion. Out of the corner of her eye, she noticed Silver signaling her from across the room. She forced her gaze away and focused back on Mueller.

"These events are great occasions, aren't they?" Mueller said with enthusiasm.

"You might even win the prize for best costume! It's very fetching," Burke said as he stepped closer to her. The smell of whiskey on his breath and the glass in his hand confirmed she was right about his drinking. Owen took the opportunity to interrupt and guided Kit away, saying he wanted to introduce her to a EUFOR Commander.

"Enjoy your evening, Ms. Chase," Mueller said. "Be sure to make an appointment to see me when you're back in the office."

"Thank you, I will," Kit replied, thankful to Owen for the rescue. "He wants to bribe me with Eva's job," she whispered to him as they retreated.

"Figures," Owen said. "So even if you suspect something about their double dealing, he's got you under control."

Before they went further, Kit checked the message that had arrived on her mobile phone. It was from Tom Baumgarten. "The statement shows hallmarks of payoffs or money laundering—unusual large deposits, and repetitive small amounts. This person could be involved in the scheme we're investigating. Try to get more evidence and take care!"

Kit sent a quick acknowledgement and whispered to Owen, "Looks like our celebrity therapist might be involved in the money-laundering scam."

"Only the best people are here," Owen said with irony, glancing back towards Maria.

Silver was still trying to attract Kit's attention from the corner of the room. "Look, my CI wants to talk. Can you cover for me?" Kit asked.

"Sure. I think the ladies' room is in that direction," he said in a louder voice. Kit nodded in gratitude and headed towards a vestibule where Silver was waiting.

"Where's the ladies' room?" Kit asked Silver.

Silver replied with a nod of her head towards an interior wall with an elevator guarded by a man preoccupied with his phone. She then motioned that they should take the staircase to the left, and they quickly moved away from view on the lower floor. At the top there was a small landing with a locked door. Silver extracted an implement from her pocket and swiftly inserted it into the lock. There was a satisfying click, and she opened the door. By now Kit was getting nervous. If they were discovered, her pretext of looking for the ladies' bathroom was unlikely to convince anyone. But behind the door, the coast was clear. Silver led her briskly along the hallway and picked the lock on the central room to the left. It was the US ambassador's study.

Chapter Thirty

They entered through the door, and Kit surveyed the room within. There was an enormous desk with a leather surface and a lamp. Bookshelves covered the walls on one side, while on the other, French doors opened out onto a terrace. Two upholstered chairs sat on either side of an antique occasional table. The room smelt of good taste and money. And power. Silver moved swiftly and pulled the curtains shut at the French windows that led out onto a small balcony. She switched on a lamp with a green shade. Kit remembered the study lights in the National Library reading room she had visited with Sergei in Ljubljana. Sitting on the desk was an active laptop computer, but the screen was locked.

"What's all this about?" Kit said.

Silver came close to her and said in a low voice, "They're doing the money transfers from this laptop, using secure, encrypted lines. They've got diplomatic immunity in these premises, so it's safe from the police."

"How do you know?"

"I've got my own contacts in the household. Plus the GRU Russian intelligence service is monitoring all telecommunications—much like the Americans do."

"So, what are you suggesting?"

"I hacked into the laptop and located the link to the bank account from which the money will be transferred.

But before I could change the transaction, I ran into a problem. There's a very long password that I couldn't crack in a short time. You said the funds transfer was happening soon."

"I believe so, yes. But what are we going to do about this password?"

"I don't know. But Sergei seemed to think that you might have a clue."

"I don't think I do, but… Go ahead, let's get on with it and hope no one catches us. They already spotted me downstairs. It's only a matter of time before someone comes looking. Owen can only cover for so long."

"Is he your young man?"

"Just a colleague. But we're on the same side," Kit said.

Silver nodded, slipped on a pair of surgical gloves, and sat down at the desk. Quickly she was through the basic password covering the locked screen and into the encrypted network. She could search the history of transactions from that computer and open a window to an account with the Austro–European bank.

"So, the American ambassador is in on this. He's probably taking a cut as well."

Silver nodded but didn't comment. The window to the bank account login sat open before them with the cursor pulsing. "I suppose the account name is the name of the ambassador."

"I suppose so. Try it," Kit said.

"I studied the guy's habits for the last few days. I think he's probably going with his initials and last name."

A trickle of cold sweat ran down Kit's back until the bandages still protecting her ribs absorbed it. She suddenly felt sick with nerves. Silver had obviously done this kind of thing before. She appeared unruffled and was prepared with her surgical gloves to avoid leaving fingerprints. "I don't suppose you've got a second pair of gloves, do you?" Kit asked.

"Sorry," Silver said. "I usually work alone."

"Okay, I better not touch anything then."

"Right, this is as far as I can get. See this thirty-two-character password. Given enough time, I could crack it, but we just don't have that time now. Got any suggestions?"

"I have no idea. Have you tried consecutive numbers one to three etcetera, or ABC?"

"Yes, but it didn't work."

"It could be a line of poetry or anything that's hard to guess, but easy to remember. Words from 'The Star-Spangled Banner'?"

"Well, make a suggestion and I'll try it."

Kit moved away from the desk. She suddenly needed fresh air, but she didn't dare open the blinds that screened the light from any observer outside.

"Just let me think for a moment."

Kit backed away and tried to think what Sergei would advise in the situation. He'd probably say to visualize her best outcome, and then it would somehow miraculously happen. That seemed unlikely now. But maybe it was herself saying that she had no chance of guessing the password. She tried to shift her consciousness, to breathe deeply and slow down her heart rate, which was racing in her throat. Her mouth felt dry, and she was jittery. She remembered being back on that bridge in Ljubljana, confronting the dragon of her fear—

the dragon that seemed to represent all that challenged her. As she stared at a spot on the wall, the shadows in the room seemed to close in towards her. She remembered that uncanny sensation in her lucid dream following the episode with Sergei where she had made a jump of consciousness, finding herself in a completely different setting, confronting the deceased architect. Plečnik had worked a lot with numerical codes in his architecture; she felt sure he had embedded some codes in his work. Then a seemingly random thought occurred to her, unconnected to anything else. He had said the word pi and told her to remember it.

"Do you know the value of pi?" Kit asked in a small, soft voice.

"Yes, of course," Silver replied. "They teach all children this in Russia. It's an irrational number that goes on forever. The ratio of the circumference of a circle to its diameter."

"Try it," Kit said, still looking blankly at the wall, her back to Silver, the shadows gathering around her.

Silver took a deep breath, and there was a brief clicking of the keyboard. Then she pressed enter and held her breath. Kit slowly turned around and moved back to her. She was already looking for the memory stick in her evening bag. Silver swore in Russian under her breath. "It works!" she exclaimed. "I'm in." Silver's fingers moved like true quicksilver over the keyboard.

"The transaction—650 million euros—is going to bank accounts in Malta, Austria, and ends up in Switzerland. I'm in time to cancel that transfer. I'm going to reroute it to a confidential account that I've used before."

Now Kit was bending down to inspect the screen. "Will they be able to trace it?"

"No, it's going on the dark web. It'll go through several transfers, end up as cryptocurrency, and then disappear."

"Remember, that money has to be returned to Kosovo."

"Yes, I know. How long do you think before they notice it's missing?"

"Well, if I lay a false trail, maybe a couple of weeks. I have to ask the banks for help, although they'll probably resist, claiming confidentiality."

"Don't worry, I'll respect our deal. This is my reputation as a hacker on the line. Much more important than any amount of cash. Besides, Sergei would kill me if I double-cross you. You think I'm joking?" She looked up sharply at Kit.

"No, I believe you. I really hope that you can recover those funds; otherwise I'll end up behind bars myself."

"Don't worry. I'll get it back, with interest."

"Can you download the financial information?" Kit asked and handed Silver the thumb drive. "I need to transfer this info as quickly as possible to a judge who's waiting to issue orders."

"Okay, the best thing is if I upload the info via Bluetooth to my mobile and then send it to you. I'll also take a copy on the memory stick."

"Do it," Kit said. She took a ragged breath. Relief coursed through her. They had accessed the account, but they had committed a crime on a scale that she had never thought possible. If they lost the funds on the dark web, she wasn't sure what she'd do. Silver was working quickly now, transferring data to her mobile phone and more slowly to the memory stick. But before Kit could relax further, there was a sound at the door. The two women both froze and looked up.

"Damn," Kit muttered. "We should have locked it."

To her horror, the door swung open, and Maria Montenegro stepped into the room. Now her face looked feline above her black, velvet dress and gleaming, silver necklace.

"I'm sorry. I can't let you do that," Maria said, gently closing the door behind her with a click. She flicked the lock behind her.

"What are you doing here?" Kit asked, signaling to Silver to hurry and complete what she was doing. Silver glanced up, but without missing a beat, she quickly finished the transfer and logged out of the account.

"I think you know the answer to that," Maria answered. "Did you think I wouldn't notice your interest in my photos and bank statements?"

"I don't know what you mean," Kit said.

"It's a pity. I had you flagged as a woman who is really going places, but your naïve, childish pursuit of justice is futile. I tried to explain the importance of working with your shadow, not against it."

"I am working with my shadow," Kit said. "We make a fine team."

Silver had closed the computer programs and smartly deleted the memory files of the laptop. She softly closed the cover and indicated towards the French doors and the balcony.

"Tell her to undo what she just did," Maria said.

"Sorry, no can do," Kit answered. "I have no idea what she just did."

"Kit, don't you know how transparent your lies are? I think I'd better call the ambassador right now. He's a good friend of my husband, as you know."

"Do what you like. We've got enough evidence to have his diplomatic immunity waved. He'll be going away for a long time. If I were you, I'd walk away and pretend this never happened. What does the ambassador have on you? Is he blackmailing you or your husband?"

"It's not like that," Maria said. "We have compromising information on each other. I have recorded analysis sessions with both his and Tirol's wives. They have details of our social weekends away in Albania. No one wants things to become public, so we work together."

"This psychobabble is crap," Silver cut in with a hiss, her hand already on a switchblade hidden inside her waitress's sleeves. "Do you want me to take her out? We gotta go. Now."

"That could be a neat way to tie up loose ends. Celebrity therapist discovered a heist in progress in the ambassador's residence and was killed by the thief," Kit said as if she was reading imaginary headlines. "Is that what you want?"

Maria looked from one woman to the other, assessing her chances of escaping to raise the alarm against Silver's likely speed using the knife. She thought she detected a hint of hesitation in Kit's expression and seized her chance.

"I'm leaving," she announced, stepping away from them. "I don't want any part of what you're doing." But as she turned around, she felt a hand on her wrist, preventing her escape.

It was Silver. "We need to finish this," she said firmly. "You know too much now and can't be allowed to tell anyone else."

Just then, they heard voices coming closer. It was Ambassador Stanton and Jacob Mueller, who had finished their conversation with the guests below and were coming to the study, probably to check on the money transfer.

Kit stepped forward then, placing herself between Silver and Maria. "Enough," Kit declared firmly as she turned around to face Silver with an unyielding gaze. "This isn't what we came here for tonight. We're here for information about money laundering, not murder." Taking a deep breath, she continued evenly, "What do you suggest we do instead?"

"We leave now," Silver said. "Let her take her chances with those two. They will blame her for the missing money, not some story about us."

Kit took the thumb drive and put it in her evening bag with her mask. There was a rattling at the door, and someone was trying to insert a key. Silver clicked off the light, and she and Kit quickly moved behind the curtains. Silver opened the door leading to the balcony and let Kit through first, following her. Glancing back, she saw Maria taking cover in an adjoining room before she closed the curtains behind them.

Kit found herself on a balcony overlooking the rear of the property. The back of the house was dark. They stood outside in the cold and dark. Silver flicked open her mobile phone and transmitted the file to Kit.

"We have to climb down," Silver said.

"You're kidding me," Kit said. "I can't climb dressed like this."

"We'll get you another outfit," Silver said. "We'll have to use the fire escape." Silver climbed over the terrace railing and edged along to the left until she could reach the fire escape ladder. It was pulled up, so she released it, and it fell with a shaking rattle.

"Sorry, about the noise," she said. "Are you okay?"

"I think so. I'll throw my walking stick down." With her bag secured across her shoulder, Kit hitched up her silk skirt. Grateful for the give in the garment, she got her leg over the railing and edged along the ledge until she reached the fire escape.

"Just one step at a time, remember your objectives," she breathed to herself. Taking a deep breath, she stabilized herself on the thin, metal ladder and climbed. Silver waited for her at the base, hidden in the shadows.

"I have to get back to the party before they realize I'm gone," Silver said.

"Me too," Kit said, smoothing down her skirt.

"We can't go in together. Wait a couple of minutes and then go through that side door. I'll be in touch. Don't worry about the money. You'll get it back, with interest."

Before Kit could draw another breath, she found herself in Silver's arms. Silver's body was strong and sinuous and unmistakably feminine. She planted a firm but gentle kiss on Kit's lips and ran her hand down Kit's back, caressing her hair before settling on the small of her back.

"That's a promise," she said, and in another instant, she had disappeared into the side door without looking back.

Kit had no problem waiting a few moments because she was utterly astonished. The beautiful and daring hacker, Kapitan Silver, had just kissed her. It was the first time a woman had kissed her romantically. Her body and mind were thrumming with adrenaline and spinning with confusion. The hack and their escape elated her. Was that the only reason she felt electrified?

A moment passed, and the cold pressing on her silk clothes brought her back to reality. She needed to be careful now, even more careful than before. She slipped back into the shadows and found the message from Silver with a copy of the incriminating bank transfers in it. With shaking hands, she forwarded the message to Eva first, and then to Judge Olga. Then she put her mobile phone in her evening bag and pulled out the fox mask. She felt protected behind the fox mask, and she turned her Egyptian ring on her finger. Time to return to the party.

She turned towards the door and was about to move towards it when a voice came chillingly close to her in the shadows of the overhanging eves.

"Too bad you stopped kissing. I was enjoying the show." It was a deep, heavily accented Albanian voice coming from a bulky shadow.

Fear and dread coursed through Kit, and she froze stock-still. Dasham Raco! The adrenaline that had been easing away after escaping from the ambassador's study spiked again, so that her every cell was trembling but unable to move.

"God help me!" she breathed.

"He won't help you escape this time," Raco said. "What were you two doing up there? Did you steal something? Let me see."

That was enough to make Kit overcome her initial shock. No way was he going to get her mobile phone, or anything else of hers.

"As you could see, we were just having a bit of fun. When did you get out of prison?" She tried to keep him talking while she slipped off her high heel shoes. Her feet were cold on the damp grass, but she could ground herself into the earth. She swayed slightly from side to side, feeling her weight moving, centering on her lower belly. He had the advantage of sheer bulk, but surely she could move faster, couldn't she? He had given up the element of surprise by alerting her to his presence. He wanted to play with her. With effort she tuned into her Krav Marga training, tucked her skirt up to allow more freedom of movement, and shrugged out of her jacket.

"You're doing a striptease for me. I like that," he said.

"Don't kid yourself," she said and took advantage of his ogling to leap forward, striking him full force with two blows to his nose and throat, following through with a kick to his lower body. He growled like a furious wolf and surged towards her. She turned and dodged lightly to the side, allowing him to crash into the topiary before the house. She kept moving, bouncing lightly on her feet. Her boxing training in the gym came back to her body memory. Owen had said to keep moving. She popped another sharp hook at a soft body part, this time sinking a punch into his belly.

"You think you're such a smart little bitch, don't you," he snarled. "Just wait until I pin you down. Then you won't be able to dance around."

"I'm still waiting, arsehole," she said, flashing teeth in his direction and landing another sharp upper cut on his jaw.

"I should have crushed you properly at the power station when I had the chance."

"Yeah, you should have," she said. Adrenaline was making her reckless. She needed to cool down and think more strategically. Her mobile phone vibrated under her arm. It could be Owen or Eva trying to reach her. It distracted her for a moment, and she took her eyes off Raco. He surged forward and caught her full-on, propelling her against the back of the house. His bulk pressed the air out of her lungs and painfully pushed against her dislocated ribs. A searing-hot pain lanced through her chest, and she couldn't breathe. His breath was foul on her cheek. He was a mountain of a man, and she grappled with a sense of her own powerlessness. A dark shadow of doubt winged across her mind. Was it even worth resisting?

But that sense of hopelessness only lasted for a dark moment. He eased away from her and fumbled with the fly on his pants. Now he was only pinning her with one hand. She dropped suddenly straight down, which he wasn't expecting. It was her intention to grab a handful of earth and throw it into his face. But when she felt for the earth, instead her hand found her grandfather's walking cane. She had forgotten about it after she had thrown it off the balcony. She gripped the top of the cane firmly with both hands and brought it up sharply at a forty-five-degree angle hard into Raco's body. It found a soft core, and where she had expected to feel hard muscle, there was only a momentary resistance, and then it kept gliding through.

He clutched his stomach and stumbled backwards, spluttering. It horrified Kit to see the cane extending out of Raco's torso. She hadn't even realized that it was a sword cane. The top must have become dislodged when it fell. She had impaled Raco on a sword.

Chapter Thirty-One

She ran for it, towards the nearest light. Abandoning the plan of entering quietly through the back door, she was yelling for help. A dangerous escaped prisoner had attacked her. Within a short time, she was giving a statement to police while they took Raco away on a stretcher to the ambulance. His face was grey, and he had lost a lot of blood. His medical condition wasn't immediately clear, but it wasn't good. Owen was hovering around her with concern.

"I was just taking some air, and he grabbed me. I had my grandfather's cane as part of my costume. I didn't even know it was a sword cane. I was just trying to push him away. He was going to rape me."

"He's an escaped felon," Owen said. "Wanted for multiple counts of murder and rape. A very dangerous individual." Owen put Kit's jacket around her shoulders and recovered her shoes. He held her bag and mask while she gave a statement to the Kosovo police. Kit was pale and shaking. She allowed herself to shrink down into acting a terrified woman. But she was not only that. The police disbursed the small crowd of partygoers who had congregated around them. Many of the guests were leaving early, not wanting to be associated with a violent incident. It had been an effective diversion from the hack in the ambassador's study, and no one seemed to have realized that she had been up there. No one except Maria, who seemed to be laying low now.

The policewoman taking the statement went away to consult a colleague, and Owen put his arm around Kit.

"Are you okay?" he asked, concern edged deeply on his face.

"I think so," she said. "We got what we wanted, but then Raco was waiting for me outside."

"Don't say more now. We'll discuss it later. I've been in touch with Matt and Eva."

"Good," she said.

Owen approached the small group of police officers who stood in a group a short distance away.

"If there are no further questions, I'd like to take Ms. Chase home. She's had a terrible shock, but luckily, she didn't sustain any serious physical injuries."

The policewoman nodded and informed Kit that she might need to come to the station to give a further statement in the coming days. The property was being scoured by police dogs, and they had picked up the scent of other members of the Podujevo Five gang down by the stream at the back of the section.

"Did it look like Raco was still alive when they took him away?"

"He wasn't in a body bag, but he didn't look good," Owen said.

"I hope I can get my grandfather's cane back." The sword cane was now evidence in the inquiry into Raco's attack on her and his serious injuries, so it wouldn't be returned anytime soon. This was the second time she had been forced to take extreme measures to defend herself.

The first time was to escape from Raco's nephew Enver that time they had kidnapped her. As much as she loathed Raco and all his brutality, she didn't want his death on her conscience. She hoped that no one would query why, if Kit was an innocent victim of the attacks, the other party ended up with the serious injuries?

Owen offered his arm, and they walked towards the parking lot. Kit was grateful for his steadying presence beside her. They were in time to see the OIDC vehicles containing Mueller and Burke and their close protection service leaving the premises, followed by Judge Tirol and his security detail.

"Let's take our time and let them leave first," Owen said as they walked toward the vehicle. "Did he hurt you?"

"Only my ribs again. He wanted to do more though."

Owen turned and gently tucked a lock of hair behind Kit's ear and kissed her softly on the cheek. "I don't think he'll be back again."

"We've thought that before," she said. Involuntarily, she leaned closer into Owen and his protective warmth. He opened the jeep door and stood by while she slid into the vehicle. He then went around, climbed into the driver's seat, and put the key in the ignition.

"The show isn't over tonight," he said.

"What do you mean?"

"Eva has all her ducks in a row. When she got evidence of the illegal bank transfers from you, she was ready to go. Judge Olga issued warrants right away. New York has already conditionally waived diplomatic immunity."

Kit gasped and turned to Owen. "Oh my God, does that mean they might get arrested?"

"Let's see. Matt said he had to wait until they leave the ambassador's residence."

Owen started the jeep and slowly drove out the driveway towards the road. Kit could see several police vehicles with flashing lights. Kit startled as they got closer. The OIDC vehicles sat at the shoulder of the road. Mueller and Burke stood nearby, and Judge Tirol was positioned a few meters away. Tirol was gesticulating angrily, while Mueller looked at the police, imperiously drawn up to his full height. Two police officers approached Tirol with handcuffs. Matt stood in front of them, reading aloud from several documents, no doubt the arrest warrants. Don flanked him with Max, the police dog. Kit saw a glimpse of Eva's pale face sitting in the back of their vehicle. Owen edged their vehicle close to Matt, who nodded to Kit as they drove past, a look of grim satisfaction on his face.

"We've got this," Owen said.

Chapter Thirty-Two

Epilogue

Ljubljana, Slovenia

Kit and Sergei sat together at the Ljubljana castle café, admiring the city below covered in a blanket of snow. Kit wore a russet puffer jacket with matching fleece boots and beanie hat. They enjoyed the commanding view of the city and drank their hot, spiced wine.

"So, how did the operation go?" Sergei asked her.

"Don't you already know that from your sources? Perhaps you can tell me," she replied.

He chuckled. "I want to hear it from you."

"Kapitan Silver accomplished the mission. She must have owed you a huge favor for such a complicated task."

"It's a matter of pride when she takes on a project. She wants to be known as someone who gets the work done, no matter the difficulty."

"She hacked into the bank accounts, but I was the one who figured out the password since we only had a limited time to access them before the money left Kosovo."

Sergei nodded in admiration. "I heard about your success. How did you come up with the password being pi?"

"I had a lucid dream about it when we were together last time and you opened up a new level of consciousness for me." She shivered slightly at the memory and added, "But I don't want to repeat that experience."

He continued to smile warmly at her.

"You've done an incredible job, Katarina. You're my white queen!"

"I had some help, Sergei, and I'm not anyone's queen," she replied.

"Tell me what happened then," he prompted her, ignoring her remark about not being his queen.

"There were a couple of snags. We were caught doing the hack in the ambassador's office."

When Sergei didn't comment, she continued. "It was Maria Montenegro, my therapist. I had only just learned of her connection to the scheme. Her husband works closely with the ambassador through a US aid agency in Kosovo. It seems they had compromising information on each other and had decided to work together. She tried to stop us, but we continued anyway. Apparently, she has been collecting recordings of the confessions of some of her high-level clients. I don't know where this leaves my therapy sessions."

"What did you tell her about me?" Sergei asked softly.

"Not much. I mean she knows about our connection but not the details."

Sergei sighed. "You shouldn't have told her anything."

"I know that now. I was taken in by her assurances of confidentiality."

"So, what did she do?"

"In the end, nothing as far as I know. Silver threatened her with a knife, and I threatened her with prosecution. We were interrupted by the ambassador and Mueller coming to the room. We left down the fire escape, and I think Maria hid. I suggested she should pretend she hadn't seen us. If she has any sense, she'll do just that."

"This is a loose end."

"You know, the funny thing was that Natalia gave me a tarot reading after you'd gone. She warned me about a deceptive blonde woman. I just didn't make the connection until now. That must have been Maria."

"Natalia is very good at what she does. You should have talked more to her rather than to Maria. And then there's Father Peter, who is available for spiritual guidance to our group."

"Well, I only just met Natalia recently, as you know. And I'm not sure about Father Peter. But back to what happened at the party, after Silver returned to continue her cover as a waitress, I had to defend myself against Raco again. He was waiting for me outside. This time I stabbed him with a sword cane that I was carrying as part of my costume. I didn't mean to; it just happened when I was defending myself. He was seriously injured, but his gang was waiting. They picked him up and escaped. But best of all, Mueller, Burke and Tirol were arrested. Ambassador Stanton is in CIA custody."

"That part of the operation was a great success," Sergei said. "You cut the head off the snake."

"Silver did an amazing job transferring all the funds into an anonymous, interest-bearing account on the dark web. At the end of the month, she moved six hundred and fifty million back to the Bank in Kosovo while retaining all the interest it had earned on deposit. I did the legal paperwork to get the official records from the banks. By the time that came through, the full amount of the funds, minus interest, was back in Pristina. Then, Silver invested that interest into cryptocurrency. She had the timing right. The value of the cryptocurrency surged over night. She moved the money generated from that interest into a private account that I have access to. We converted most of it back to euros, but some is still in cryptocurrency."

"And how much was that?"

"No one else knows about this. I'm going to tell you, only because you probably know already."

He took a sip of his hot, spiced wine, a seasonal speciality. He relaxed into the chair, savoring the moment.

Kit seemed to wrestle with indecision before telling him. "It's about fifteen million euros, give or take a few hundred thousand," she said at last.

"Brilliant. *Brava!*" he said. "And she handed it all to you?"

"There was a catch. Silver wants to help me manage the account, at least until I understand stock and crypto markets better. She's got her own cryptocurrency account, although she still likes to work as a waitress."

"She's got the right skills to do what she likes," Sergei said.

"I think she likes me," Kit said, glancing down at her mulled wine in an effort to hide the flush on her face.

"Do you feel the same?"

"My love life has changed a lot over recent months. I won a trip for two to Ljubljana at the party tombola and asked Owen to join me. He should be here in about fifteen minutes. He's the one I'm dating now."

"That's a pity. I was hoping we could explore the New Year holiday together here. But amuse yourself with the police officer for now. When you're ready to talk some more, I'll still be here."

"Sergei, I'm so thankful for everything you've taught me. All this success is because of you. I would never have been brave enough without your tutelage."

"I know," he said. "But I like to hear you acknowledge that fact."

"So, Mueller, Burke and Tirol are all in jail awaiting trial and at work we've got new managers from New York and Berlin. Silver said she'd see what other compromising information she can discover about them."

"This story keeps getting better," Sergei said. "Apart from these loose ends."

"The ambulance was taking Raco away with his injuries, but his gang hijacked it before they reached the hospital. They might have switched cars and fled to Albania, so he may not have made it out alive. I didn't even know my grandpa's walking stick was actually a sword cane before that night. There are already multiple warrants out for Raco's arrest, so this is one more."

"Darling, your policeman cannot appreciate all your amazing qualities like I do," Sergei said.

"Oh, I think he does," Kit said. "And he's there for me when I need him." *Unlike you*, she thought.

"I understand you're going through a transition, so this relationship with him can't be permanent. Did you tell Owen about your cryptocurrency account?"

"Uh . . . no."

"Good choice," Sergei said approvingly. "The fewer people who know about it the better. What are you planning on doing with the money?"

"Maybe I'll set up a crime-fighting organization or an environmental NGO. Silver wants to open a vegan restaurant in New Zealand so she can work as a waitress there. Plus, I get to go on vacation without thinking about the cost. It's such a relief to know I'll never have to worry about money again."

"You dumped your fiancé in New Zealand, then?"

"Yep. It turns out he was seeing someone else while I was away. He didn't put up any resistance when I suggested we take a break. I think we've just grown apart."

"Good move. If he'd found out about your new fortune, you'd never get rid of him."

"In other news, my father contacted my mom after two decades of being apart. I'm curious to see what comes from that."

"Just be careful: he probably wants something from you. Do you want me to do a background check on him?"

"Why are you so cynical? Maybe he just missed us and wants to reconnect." She paused to think for a moment. "But yes, maybe a background check might be a good idea."

Sergei stood and embraced Kit in his thick shearling jacket before kissing her on both cheeks, drinking in the expression on her face. The cable car was making its way up the hill, and Kit could make out Owen inside, waiting by the exit.

"Owen's here ahead of time. Make yourself scarce if you want to avoid being arrested."

Sergei paused for a moment and frowned. "One last thing. What happened about that Interpol wanted notice against me?"

"My organization decided it wasn't worth provoking the Russians over one of their diplomats, so I had the request for your arrest cancelled while I was in charge. Now Eva has been reinstated as the chief prosecutor again. She's delighted that she was proven right about the corruption. It restored her reputation. So she's not worried about your Red Notice being pulled. That doesn't mean that Owen won't try to arrest you though." She laughed.

Sergei nodded with satisfaction. As he had asked, she had used her position to cancel the Interpol Red Notice for his arrest for organizing the Staro Dorbi killings. He pulled Kit close and kissed her forehead, then walked away.

"Until we meet again," he said, joining the tail of an organized tour group at cable car returning to the town. Owen passed Sergei as he left the platform without paying him a second glance. His eyes were only for Kit. She lit up with joy as they embraced.

-The End-

The Crime Scene Kosovo series continues in *Explosive Reprisals*.

In *Explosive Reprisals: Crime Scene Kosovo Book 3*, Kit Chase, an international prosecutor in Pristina, takes on her most dangerous case yet. When an organized crime group sets off a series of explosive attacks in Kosovo, Kit finds herself caught in the crossfire. As she works to unravel a web of corruption and violence, she becomes a witness and a target.

But that's not all. Kit's personal life is just as complicated as her professional one. With a new boyfriend and an old flame still in the picture, she must navigate the dangerous waters of love while fighting for justice. And when her long-lost father makes an appearance, she'll have to confront a whole new set of challenges. *Explosive Reprisals* is a gripping legal thriller that will leave you breathless. Don't miss out on this must-read book!

Coming soon in ebook and print formats.

More Books by Tasmin Turner

Thanks for joining Kit in this adventure. If you enjoyed the book, please rate and review it on your favourite platform! It's always much appreciated.

The Crime Scene Kosovo books will include the following:

The Missing Diary #1
The Price of Justice #2
Explosive Reprisals #3

A fourth possible book tentatively titled *In Plain View* is under consideration. Join my newsletter to be notified of new releases, giveaways, and pre-release specials at www.wish-books.com or email joann@dreamlifenz.com

About Tasmin Turner

Tasmin Turner is the author of the Crime Scene Kosovo Series, which is based in the early 2000s in post-conflict Balkans. Tasmin lives in the heartland of New Zealand, after two decades living in Europe and the US. She's passionate about writing and enjoys frequenting cafes.

Author's Note

Information about Kosovo

The Crime Scene Kosovo series is set in a fictional post-conflict Kosovo, with fictitious characters, organizations, and events. The information below is a brief account of Kosovo's real historical background.

Kosovo is a self-declared independent country in Europe's Balkan region. Although many nations—including the United States and several members of the European Union—acknowledge its 2008 declaration of freedom from Serbia, Russia and some other countries, including some EU states, do not recognize Kosovo's independence. Most inhabitants are Albanian, and the minority are Serbs, together with other ethnic minority groups. The official languages are Albanian and Serbian.

The name Kosovo is derived from a Serbian term meaning "field of blackbirds." After serving as the heart of a medieval kingdom of Serbia, Kosovo was governed by the Ottoman Empire from the mid-fifteenth century to the early twentieth century. This was an era when Islam grew in importance and the number of Albanian speakers in the region grew. Then in the early twentieth century, Kosovo was incorporated into Serbia (later part of Yugoslavia). By the second half of that century, Muslims of Albanian origin outnumbered Eastern Orthodox Serbs in Kosovo, leading to frequent interethnic tensions in the province.

In 1998, an ethnic, Albanian-led secessionist rebellion escalated into a global crisis, resulting in NATO's 1999 air bombardment of Yugoslavia, which at that time was a remnant state comprised of Serbia and Montenegro. Peace was restored afterwards, and Kosovo was administered by the United Nations and supported by several other international and regional organizations during post-conflict times.

A landlocked country, Kosovo is flanked by Serbia to the north and east, North Macedonia to the south, Albania to the west, and Montenegro to the northwest. About the same geographic size as Jamaica or Lebanon, it is one of the smallest countries in the Balkans, with a population of less than two million people in 2021, predominantly of Albanian descent. The capital, Pristina, is also the largest urban area. Albanian and Serbian are spoken languages, with most Kosovars adhering to Sunni Islam.

The information in this description is drawn from the following source: Allcock, John B. , Young, Antonia and

Lampe, John R.. "Kosovo". Encyclopedia Britannica, 8 Nov. 2022. https://www.britannica.com/place/Kosovo. Accessed 16 January 2023.

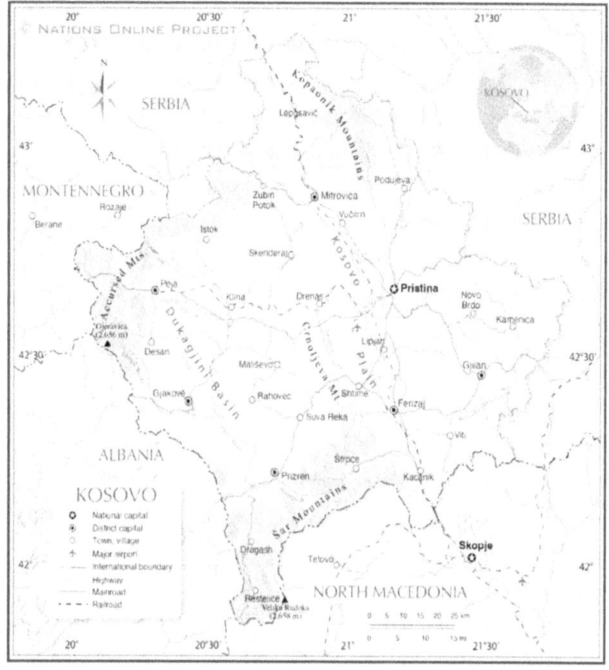

Map of Kosovo

The source of the map is Nations Online Project accessed 10 January 2023 https://www.nationsonline.org/oneworld/map/Kosovo-map.htm

Map of Slovenia

The source of the map is Nations Online Project
accessed 2 May 2023
https://www.nationsonline.org/oneworld/map/slovenia-
map.htm

* 9 7 8 1 9 9 1 1 9 2 4 4 8 *